Polarized Love

LISA RENÉE

REVIEWS

This contemporary romance will take you across the world and back—elicit laughter, tears, and probably every emotion in between. It's a beautiful story of love, faith, and trust. Lachlan stole my heart from the moment I met him. I couldn't get enough. I needed him and Beth to be a thing. He was—is—such a swoony hero. I fell hard. But of course, there wouldn't be a story without obstacles. The journey that Beth and Lachlan had to endure in order to come back together left me riveted. I couldn't put it down. Renee paints a heartbreaking story with tact, grace, and a unique voice and style. I haven't read a book that forced so many different emotions through me in a long time.

Sara Beth Williams, Selah Finalist

A tale of second chances, sweeping romance, and learning to follow God's path, Polarized Love will take you on a romantic adventure that you must not miss.

Tabitha Bouldin, Author of Mishaps off the Mainland

DEDICATION

Dear Margaret,

May my readers receive insight by sharing some of your story. God has worked all things for good for those that love him.

CHAPTER ONE

BETHANY MICHAELS STARED at chunks of beige vomit splattered across the Navy officer's polished shoes—her vomit. Had that really happened? She clung to the Rottnest ferry rail, willing her stomach to pipe down and stop its convulsions. Thank goodness, she'd only fed it coffee that morning. Minimal damage to report.

Slowly, she raised her head to the smooth tone of an American voice.

"You all right, Miss?" Deep brown eyes found hers, offering consolation.

His Navy colleague, seated behind, grabbed a handful of napkins from his backpack and shoved them into the hand of the man she'd just puked on like passing a baton in a relay race. Onlookers stared, some with empathy, others with disgusted frowns. One Asian woman covered her mouth, cringed at the mess, and slunk to the back of the cabin.

It's seasickness, not a virus, lady.

Bethany blinked in slow motion. If only she could lie down somewhere soft. The man before her came into focus again. He steadied her other arm. Aftershave mingled with whispers of salted air swirled around her.

Must sit.

He handed her the napkins. As she wiped her lips, she mumbled, "Thank you—and I'm so sorry." She pulled from his hold, kneeled to the fiberglass floor, and swiped the brown saliva concoction from his black steel cap boots.

"Ma'am. I'm fine." He touched her shoulder. "Please, come sit down."

As he supported her arm, his gaze bounced from her eyes to her lips, and settled on her chest. Typical sleazebag. Like his Navy buddy behind him, who had checked her out earlier.

"That's a lovely cross you have there." The stranger's drawn-out words sang in her ears.

Bethany clutched at her necklace. "Oh, yes. This is very special to me."

He straightened to his full six-foot-frame. "For its spiritual significance or as a gift from someone special?"

Her brow furrowed. Asking questions usually fell to her as a struggling reporter. If this sailor wasn't turned off by her retching on his shoes, he must be desperate for female company. Bethany wouldn't be drawn in by his act of kindness—not from his type.

"Yes. I'm a Christian—one who believes in the whole Bible. Including abstinence until marriage." Her face heated. What had she said? Way too much information. He might genuinely want to help her and nothing more.

The man chuckled. "That's admirable. Not many women I meet at port confess such moral standards." His laugh lines relaxed. "I'm the Navy chaplain. And I hold the same beliefs."

The flush on her face must be tomato red by now. "Oh my—I do apologize, sir. I thought you were—" She eyed the sailor seated on the metal bench, tapping his phone screen.

"Unfortunately, our reputation in Fremantle isn't that . . . upstanding. The American Navy sure think Australian women are beautiful, but I do try to keep the boys in line." He shrugged.

A swish of waves from a passing speedboat revived her nausea. She grappled for the rail. He held her free arm. "Miss, you should sit. Let me get you some water." He led her to the bench, near the younger sailor, then strode away.

His friend glanced at her with a lop-sided grin. "Trouble with your sea legs, ma'am?"

She forced a smile. The acid in her throat still stung. Bethany faced the staircase. The chaplain's toned legs pounded the stairs and disappeared to the drink and snacks bar on level one. She didn't want to be left alone with his buddy too long.

"I'm Officer McKillip. But call me Wally."

Bethany turned toward the guy, and he offered a peppermint Tic Tac. She squinted at the offer. Did her breath stink? How embarrassing. She took two mints from the container and nodded. "Nice to meet you."

Crunching on the candy, she scanned the cabin, relieved most people were preoccupied and had stopped staring—all except an old Italian woman wearing dark sunglasses. The little lady probably thought the tint hid her eyes well enough. Or maybe she didn't care and found the scene before her entertaining.

"And you are?" Wally interrupted her thoughts with his distinct southern twang.

Why couldn't she bring herself to have a basic conversation with this guy? Her father, a pastor, had raised her with strict adherence to etiquette and made her greet congregation members at their little fellowship in Fremantle. Like fingerprints, the code of conduct had melded into her psyche.

High school memories flashed in her mind—the ones of sailors coming into port, taking over the streets, arms dangling from pub windows. They'd whistled and leered, finding something alluring about her school uniform. More bile rose to her throat. She wouldn't throw up on this sailor too—would she?

"I'm Beth." She slumped against the rigid seat, her spine grating against the cold aluminum. Bethany gazed at the view of the sparkling ocean and took slow, deep breaths. The saltwater sprayed like pins past the window as the ferry bounced at high speed. Land only minutes away. Why couldn't she handle a thirty-minute trip to Rottnest Island? Ridiculous. And she hoped to be a cutting-edge reporter? She shook her head. If she didn't get the scoop on the Quokka mystery, then perhaps the story of a woman throwing up on a Navy officer could be her back-up. A local story might get her boss's attention—although a tad boring, the *Fremantle Herald* might print it.

She peeked from the corner of her eye. Wally had given up for the moment and tapped away on his phone. Thuds from the stairs made her head turn and lock eyes with the well-built chaplain. His uniform contoured to firm muscles. She mentally rebuked herself—not the way a pastor's daughter should think—even for a single thirty-one-year-old.

With a broad smile that could melt icebergs in Antarctica, the handsome chaplain held out a bottle of spring water. "This should help." His smooth accent soothed like a healing balm.

"You're so kind—even after I ruined your shoe."

"And I took another hit." He pointed to his chest and winked as he sat beside her. His muscular thigh brushed hers.

She inched away and spotted two wet patches on his khaki uniform. Bethany ground her back teeth. That must be why he took so long, cleaning up her mess. Had she sprayed him when he'd bent to help her earlier? So gross.

"I'll buy you a new one when we get to the island." She rushed her words.

His eyebrow twitched as a grin formed. "They sell Navy uniforms there?"

"No. But there are souvenir t-shirts. It can remind you of when a nit-wit reporter couldn't keep it together on the Rottnest Ferry." She gave a sheepish grin, then took a sip of the water, letting the cold soothe her throat.

"A reporter, hey?" His brown eyes sparkled as he angled toward her. "What are you investigating?"

"There's been an unusual amount of deaths among the Quokka marsupials. They're already vulnerable to extinction. Rottnest Island has kept them safe from predators like foxes or cats, but scientists are trying to work out why an increased number has become sick recently."

His eyes widened. "So, I better not touch one? They might be diseased."

She leaned in and whispered, "No. They've ruled that out. Now the police are involved. Something suspicious is going on.

One corpse had traces of plastics, but they could've been poisoned on purpose."

He scrunched his brow. "Who'd want to hurt those cute mini-kangaroos?"

She let out a laugh. The Quokkas did look like baby roos, and they were adorable. "I know, right? It doesn't make sense. That's why I'm on a mission to find out. But I only have today to investigate."

"Can we help?" He glanced at his friend and back. "If you don't mind Wally coming along, that is?"

"You've noticed I'm not keen on your mate."

"Yes, I saw the warning *don't-you-dare-go-there* look. You can see through his façade." He lowered his voice. "I understand. I'm assigned to keep an eye on him. He got into a brawl last night at the Sail and Anchor pub with some lady's boyfriend."

Wally's face had a slight mauve-gray mark below one eye. That'd teach him. Why did sailors annoy her? Not all should be judged by the bunch of meatheads she came across at sixteen.

"What do you say?" The chaplain raised a brow.

She straightened her back and tilted her chin. "What's your name anyway?"

He offered his hand. "Chaplain Peters, they call me in the Navy. Lachlan is my preferred name."

She gave him a firm handshake. "They call me Private-eye Detective Michaels."

He sniggered. "Nice."

"Most people know me as Bethany or Beth." She grinned. "It may be to my advantage to have you both on my investigation team for the day. No one would expect American tourists to be snooping up a scoop."

"This could be a lot of fun. I'm up for an undercover adventure." He gave a ridiculously attractive smile.

"To be honest, I'm a part-time copy editor for a local newspaper. They paid me for two articles, but the rest were free submissions. I want to become a full-time journalist, not the sub-editor. I'm at the bottom rung of the ladder." She shrugged. "But I've got to start somewhere."

"True."

"If this ends up a bigger story than imagined, I'll submit the article to the *West Australian*. That would be a dream come true—published in the state's newspaper."

"I hope I can help those dreams come true." He lowered his voice. "And, hey, if Wally acts out as usual, maybe it'll make national news." He chuckled, then shook his head. "No, that would be bad on my part. I'm assigned to him, so we keep our reputation intact. And save his butt from being discharged and sent back to the U.S."

She angled toward him. Her pulse tripled in speed when his kind eyes connected with hers. "It'd be my pleasure to have you assist me, Chaplain Peters—free of charge, mind you." She offered a cheeky smile and a handshake.

"Lachlan will do." He shook her hand in agreement. So warm and inviting. Tingles flew up her arm.

Bethany reclaimed her hand. Chaplain or not, this guy lived elsewhere. He didn't belong in Australia, but she did. No point in getting all light and fuzzy from his charms. But she could enjoy his company and friendship for today—no harm in that.

Wally called to Lachlan, "I see the island."

Bethany's tummy turned again. How would she manage to join the crowded lines of people without feeling claustrophobic?

Lachlan rubbed her shoulder. "You look a little green. Are you going to be okay? Shall I find a sick bag?"

She must look like a weak female. But she'd rectify that impression once on land. Bethany Michaels was no damsel in distress—as the eldest of six siblings, a born leader, she showed initiative and managed her life as an independent, more than capable, woman.

"I'm fine."

He raised a brow. "You sure about that?" Lachlan lowered his hand to the middle of her back, heat seeping through the cotton. "I can stay close, just in case you have a spell again."

Bethany didn't want to come under any spell, but with his closeness, she became weaker. The bumpy ride wasn't the only thing making her feel dizzy.

"Thanks, Lachlan. I appreciate your concern." She gazed into his eyes. He suited the role of chaplain. His genuine kindness relaxed her shoulders, and the knots in her stomach dissipated. She could do this.

The ferry slowed as it approached the jetty. A steady hum from the motors underneath sent vibrations up her legs. But as the boat swung in a ninety-degree turn, she swayed into Lachlan. The engine growled as the boat paralleled to a stop, and her face plunged into his neck, intoxicating her with his woodsy scent.

He placed his arm firmly around her shoulder. "Steady breaths." His voice became slow and comforting. "You'll be okay."

She put a hand to his chest and pushed herself upright. "Sorry."

His muscles flexed under her palm, and she retracted her hand, heat scorching her earlobes.

"Don't be sorry." His gaze made her insides flutter. "Stay close and lean on me if you need to. I'll help you to the rail. We'll take our time." He pointed. "And I'll grab your backpack."

Bethany turned, grateful that her camera bag had remained safe near the spot where Lachlan had first tried to help her. Little had he known, it would cost him to come to her rescue. He didn't seem to regret it. Still here. Still holding her.

People rushed past them and lined up at the exit signs. The crew on deck looped thick ropes over the hook stumps in a criss-cross pattern. An announcement over the PA system thanked the passengers for choosing Rottnest Express and wished them a pleasant day on the island. A crew member in a red polo shirt slid a small metal bridge across the gap, connecting to the jetty. He stepped back and waved the passengers through, offering a nod and "thank you" to each person.

Wally passed them. "See you on the other side." He winked at Bethany.

Lachlan squeezed her shoulder. "Ready?"

How silly did she look? A grown woman incapacitated by a brief ferry ride. The boat had stilled mostly, and she didn't need a man to help her. Bethany gently shook off his hold and stood.

A swirl rushed inside her head, and she blinked, regretting standing so quickly. But she'd show Lachlan what she was made of—one hundred percent pure Australian stubbornness. One step in front of the other, she sensed his body heat behind her, following like a shadow. She reached below the rail to collect her camera bag, but Lachlan brushed his arm down hers and grabbed the handle first. Now, her hand on top of his, she let go like she'd touched a dangerous flame. This guy seemed too much of a gentleman.

"I've got it." His breath tickled the top of her hair.

"Thanks." She dared not turn into that captivating gaze again. Bethany marched stiffly to the metal bridge, then stepped into the glorious West Australian sunshine. She might've kissed the ground if tourists didn't swarm about the jetty. The wind whipped her ash-blonde ponytail into her face. She gulped in the fresh, pure air. Ah, better already. Calmness washed over her.

"Aren't you glad that's over?"

She turned around.

The tall and handsome chaplain half-grinned and held out her bag. "Let's go on that Quokka investigation, Private Eye Michaels."

CHAPTER TWO

LACHLAN SQUINTED AGAINST the bright sun reflecting off the scattered clouds above as he held out Beth's backpack. The color had returned to her face. She must feel better already.

The wind tousled her bangs, and from where he stood, he could now appreciate the full effect of this firecracker of a lady. Cute, khaki shorts stopped just above her knee, matching his Navy colors. But not one of his female colleagues had Beth's figure. The Navy women were usually stocky, tall, and broad-shouldered. Beth had slender legs and a feminine frame. He averted his gaze from her attractive features and focused on the zip dangling from her bag. He wouldn't repeat the mistake of an overseas attachment. It just didn't work. No point starting something he couldn't finish. His contract had another two years before he could consider settling down.

When Beth took the backpack, her smile reached her eyes for the first time. "Thanks." She swung it over her shoulder and glanced around them, the crowds moving on. "Where's Waldo?"

He grinned at the phrase. His sidekick may not be wearing a striped red and white shirt like the cartoon character, but with his height and uniform, they wouldn't have trouble finding Wally. Asian tourists mingled nearby, adjusting hats, and one held an umbrella despite the blue sky and bright sunshine. Perhaps their skin darkened easily.

Farther down the jetty's wooden planks, Wally positioned for a selfie with two female tourists. Lachlan shook his head. Not even five minutes had passed. Wally sure had a way with the ladies and used his uniform to full advantage. A day on the island may not be as relaxing as Lachlan had hoped. He strode toward the scene, leaving Beth to follow.

A giant Quokka cut-out, the size of a person, stood at the end of the jetty. Wally and a blonde huddled around the fake Quokka while the other woman snapped photos.

"Hey, buddy. We gotta go." Lachlan called a few feet away.

The lady with the camera turned and gawked at him. She puckered her red-painted lips, said something in Swedish, and took some snaps of him. He froze, not sure if he should smile or protest. Someone ploughed into his back. A soft yelp behind him. Beth.

He turned. Beth rubbed her button nose, her thin eyebrows angled inward.

"Sorry about that." He offered a puppy-eyed apology.

She tilted her head, peeked past him, and scowled with a huff. Wally lived up to her first impressions. Hopefully, Beth saw that Lachlan wasn't cut from the same cloth.

Wally spoke in broken English. "My friend. Lachlan. He found woman on boat already." He pointed to Beth then to his chest. "Me not taken. Me single."

Lachlan cringed as Beth's eyes went wide. Red flashed across her face, and the lines on her forehead deepened.

"What?" She growled under her breath.

"Don't listen to him," he whispered. Lachlan turned to Wally and glared. "Cut it out, Wally. You're with me today. Let's make a move."

"I am." He grinned at the Swedish blondes. "Can they come with us?"

"No." Lachlan and Beth spoke at the same time. A double "no." Beth might help with keeping Wally in line today.

"Double standards." Wally's accent drawled.

"You know why. Do I have to spell it out for you? Embarrass you in front of your new friends?"

"The ladies don't understand English well, anyway." He smirked, then frowned. "Okay, I'll go with you." He had no choice.

Wally's shoulders slumped as he faced the women. "Mean boss. Say I must go. No fun."

The blondes sighed. "Ohhh." They stared at Lachlan with a scowl and muttered gibberish. Next, the ladies threw their arms around Wally and kissed his cheeks. Boy—women all over the guy. Didn't they see right through him? At least Beth had. He dared not look at her expression about now. She'd be ticked.

Wally sauntered over like a sulky overgrown toddler sent to the naughty mat. How had he gotten into the Navy? Everything seemed like a game to him. For Lachlan, serving his country gripped his focus and gave him purpose. Yes, he needed a break now and then, and he would enjoy the time at port. But they certainly had different ideas on how to go about that.

He patted Wally on the back. "Cheer up, buddy. We'll have some safe fun that won't get you deeper in trouble with the Sergeant. I'll give an accurate report when we get back regarding your behavior. I won't lie to save your butt. You need to get back in favor with your team captain, or Simmons will make things harder for you back on the ship."

The twenty-three-year-old sailor gave a half-grin, half-frown. "He'll have a long list of jobs for me as it is. Can't a guy have fun for once?"

"Getting into brawls isn't the kind of entertainment the sergeant approves. The Aussie men don't like us sailors. They think we're just after their women."

"Darn right, we are."

"Not this sailor." He moved his backpack from his left to his right hand. *Shut up, Wally. Beth already despises you.*

Wally huffed. "And you promise you're not—"

"I'm not. Just because I have morals and respect women, doesn't mean I don't like them—" He lowered his voice, aware Beth stood beside him now. "In that way." He cleared his throat. "Now, our guide here—" He gestured to Beth. "—has a mission for us today." He turned to face her. "What're our orders?"

Her smile returned but didn't light up her aqua blue eyes this time. "There's a Dome café on the island. Let's grab a coffee, and I'll go over my plan."

"You have a plan?" He raised a brow.

"I will by the time we sit. I didn't know I'd have two assistants." She glanced at Wally with a twitch to her lips. "I'll split our follow-up leads."

Lachlan's stomach dropped. "Aren't you staying with us for the day?"

"Some of it. I figured we'd be more effective covering different parts of the island. Plus, you'd want to do some touristy things too. I'll get to work while you have a look around."

"We did bring our swim gear and rented a snorkel." He gave a cautious smile. "Maybe you could join us. Have a break."

She bit her bottom lip—a plump, kissable lip. He mentally slapped himself. *Rein it in, Lachlan Peters. You're thinking like Wally. Get a grip.*

"I did bring my bathers. If it gets too hot, I may go in for a quick dip at one of the bays."

"Great." Or maybe not. Depending on what bathing suit she wore. Maybe a stupid idea, especially with Wally Walnut cracking his moves.

"Let's grab that coffee." She flicked her ponytail as she turned. He and Wally followed. Lachlan kept his gaze above Beth's head, resisting the temptation to watch the sway of her hips. Being single at thirty had its setbacks. His past relationships only broke his heart. No point in dating until it could lead to marriage. That stage of life bobbed too far in the distant future.

* * *

Huddled in the café's emerald green, leather booth with their lattes, Beth sprawled the Rottnest map across the table before her recruited assistants. A corner flapped, stirred by the swirling ceiling fans.

"Right-e-o." Beth pointed with her index finger. "We are here."

She glanced at Wally, who leaned into his palm with a glazed look about him.

At least Lachlan studied the map with interest. "Seems the first bus stop is only around the corner. The ferry's video said there's a ride every fifteen minutes."

Beth wriggled forward, and the leather seat squeaked. "Yes. But I want to talk to the Fish 'n Chip manager before we leave the central area. He posted about the Quokka situation on Facebook, and he may have some leads." The chaplain's warm, brown eyes focused on her. She ignored the flutter in her belly. "Lachlan, can you go with Wally to have a casual chat with the general store staff? See if they'll speculate about the reason for the decline in Quokkas."

"Sure."

Wally's eyes lit up for a brief moment. "And we'll stock up on snacks for the bus tour."

"Oh, and I nearly forgot. The souvenir shop is next-door." She smiled sheepishly at Lachlan and retrieved a twenty dollar note from her bag. "You can buy yourself a shirt. Are you allowed out of uniform?"

"Our commanding officer said while we're in Fremantle, he prefers us to wear the NWU. But on the island, we can change into casual clothes."

Wally gave a sly grin. "Lachlan can't kiss a woman if he's in uniform. So, you better send him to get that shirt, so you both have something to remember each other by."

Lachlan gave a nervous laugh. "Quit the jokes, Wally. She doesn't find it funny."

"I wasn't joking."

Beth crossed her arms and squinted at Wally. "I won't be kissing any sailors, that's for sure." She handed the note to Lachlan. "But I owe you this money."

Lachlan held up a hand, but she insisted. "Please, take it."

"All right." His words stretched, emphasizing his accent, and he took the cash.

Was that a shade of pink over his tanned cheeks?

Beth stood with her takeaway cup in hand. "I'll get a head start and meet you at the bus stop in thirty minutes."

* * *

Bethany paced the pathway near the bus stop. The guys were taking their time. Hopefully, that meant they'd had more success than her. Wally's annoying company might be worth a lead. She shook her head. Without him, she might feel strange hanging around Lachlan alone, a man she knew little about. The chaplain title didn't mean he'd become a glorified saint. Her ex-boyfriend had proved that.

A small Catholic church sat on the hill opposite her. She strolled over, scuffing leaves from the shady pavement. Ravens squawked from the pine trees that towered around her. A light aircraft rumbled in the distance.

Beth kneeled, extracted her Nikon from her bag, and zoomed in on the bells above the white cross. Focusing through the lens, she took several shots. The Tuscany-colored building must be at least a hundred years old. The stained-glass windows still glowed a kaleidoscope of color.

"There you are!" Lachlan's voice came from across the way.

She swiveled, found him framed in the circle of her lens. An aqua shirt stretched across his muscled chest. Irrationally, she held the shutter button, taking a burst of photos as he strode toward her. What had come over her? She lowered the camera, flicked to view mode, and admired the model shots. A sigh escaped her lips. He looked even better out of uniform in shorts and a shirt.

She tilted her head. "Didn't they have your size?"

"Only one large left in my favorite color." He tugged at the cotton near the Rottnest logo. "The rest were medium or small." Lachlan stood before her now.

She flicked her gaze away from his chest. "You look . . . good. Blue suits you." She cleared her throat as Wally joined them. "So, any luck?"

Wally held out a business card. "Tim, the general store manager, believes littering is killing the Quokkas. Tourists' toxic food scraps. The animals can't cope with all the additives."

Beth twisted her lips to one side and frowned. "But the Islanders have increased the clean-up efforts, and there's no change in the number of sick Quokkas reported each week."

Wally shrugged. "Call him. He's happy to speak with you."

"Did you tell him about me?" She placed a hand on her hip. "What I'm reporting for the newspaper?"

He blinked like a teen in trouble with the teacher. "Wasn't I allowed to say that?"

She huffed. "It doesn't help for the word to get out. My colleague has already traveled here, and she suspects there's more going on." She slowed her speech. "That's why we are undercover, Wally." Beth crossed her arms. "How did you get into the Navy, anyhow?"

He tapped his nose. "It's not what you know. It's who you know."

Lachlan smirked. "That about explains it." He met Beth's glance. An apology graced his features.

She breathed in deeply and released the built-up tension from her shoulders. "Have any of you seen a Quokka yet? They are nocturnal, but when I came here years ago, they were all over the place, scabbing food from the visitors."

"Nope. Not one," Wally said.

"The sign says not to feed the Quokkas." Lachlan scrunched his forehead.

"True. But people pretend to offer them food so they can get close and take a selfie with one."

"I have some crisps in my bag." This from Wally. The name suited him so well. Didn't he take note of what the local said—additives?

"I've brought something more appealing for the little creatures." She swung her camera behind her back. "First, we need to find one. Keep a lookout among the shrubbery. They sleep in the shade." She marched toward the bus stop, and the men followed.

CHAPTER THREE

LACHLAN LOOKED FORWARD to seeing a Quokka for the first time, but rather enjoyed getting to know the Australian woman sitting next to him on the bus, Beth Michaels.

They passed several yellow shacks with tin roofs. The bus driver made an occasional commentary when they passed something noteworthy. "This is where the cruise ship guests resided for quarantine during the breakout of Covid-19."

Mostly bush scrub and native trees dominated the view. A lake popped up to his right, and now and then, the coast peeked from the left.

Wally sat on the back seat. But Lachlan chose to sit with Beth and ask questions. He took more than half of the double seat. A good thing she was tiny in comparison. "Other than working for the paper, what do you do with your spare time?"

Beth scrunched her too-cute freckled nose and paused for a moment. "My father pastors a congregation of about two hundred. I fill the role my mother would have—if she were still alive.

Admin, event co-ordinator, pastoral care—anything that needs doing."

He blinked, not expecting that response. "Sounds like you're a busy woman. Sorry to hear about your mother."

"She'd been unwell for a long time. I'm the eldest of six. When I was fifteen, Mum first became ill with chronic fatigue, which led to other illnesses later. I took on the mother's role with a toddler still in the home. I've only gotten my life back these last few years."

"Incredible." This woman lived the gospel, laying her life down for others. "That's very admirable of you."

She adjusted her position and faced him. "What about you? How did you end up as a chaplain on a Navy ship?"

He cleared his throat. "After I finished school, I trained in hospitality and worked in the industry for a few years. In my twenties, I started to take my faith walk seriously and wanted to help people. I wasn't sure where to start, so I went to Bible college. Studied counseling. After I graduated, my pastor told me about the chaplain position he saw advertised in his network." He smiled as he lifted his palm. "Three years later, I'm still here."

She returned his smile. "How long will you continue?"

"I signed a new contract not long ago and have two years left."

Beth's posture slumped. "Right. You must love it. That's a long time."

"There are many challenges, and it's often lonely. But God is using me. I know that much. Bible studies are growing in number, and I've seen a gradual transformation in the men I minister to." The bus rounded a corner and their shoulders brushed.

"That's wonderful, Lachlan. Good for you. I know I couldn't do something like that. Certainly not on a ship."

He laughed softly. "I can't see you on that ship either. Land suits you much better."

The bus came to a slow stop. Outside, a few tourists with bikes gathered around, taking photos of something to the side of the road.

"Quokka!" Wally called out. Then a whack sounded from the ceiling.

Lachlan turned. Wally rubbed his head as he ambled down the aisle. "Let's get off here."

Beth had already collected her things and joined the line. They followed and got off the bus after her.

Outside, a stocky lady wearing a bike helmet squealed with delight as a large, rat-like-creature hobbled around her red bicycle. Then there were two more. Wally and Beth crept up slowly. Beth kneeled and retrieved a container from her bag and offered the Quokkas a snack.

The large woman with wind-blown tufts poking from her helmet scolded Beth with a tsk. "You're not allowed to feed them, dear," she said in a robust Irish accent.

"I won't. Just tricking this one so I can get a close-up." Beth slowly angled her camera with the other hand, and with the skill of a pro, circled her lens and took the shots.

The Quokka fussed around Beth, sniffing the ground.

"Aww. Isn't it adorable, Lachlan?" She rubbed her thumb to her forefinger, clicking her tongue, enticing the creature to approach. "Come here, you cutie." Her voice changed like a mother cooing for a baby.

Beth became the adorable one. She must love animals. He pulled out his cell and took a few photos of her with the Quokka.

Wally moved to the other two animals a few feet away, taking several shots too. One straightened on its hind legs, and wiped its front paws several times. The Quokka smiled at the camera. Lachlan blinked and looked again. It was smiling or that was how its mouth appeared. Amazing little critters. No wonder people came from all over the world to see them.

Beth angled her head and squinted up at Lachlan. "Come down here. Get a selfie with a Quokka."

He hitched up his shorts and squatted next to Beth. Holding out his phone, he tried to angle it so he could get her and the Quokka in the frame with him. Beth adjusted and slapped on a big smile and snuggled next to him. Where had the Quokka disappeared to? There. He angled again, but it just wouldn't work.

"Beth, can you move your head under my chin. Then I can fit all of us."

Without hesitation, she placed her head on his chest. He half laid on the asphalt, leaning on his forearm with one knee bent. The Quokka popped its head up in the background, raising its nose in the air as if to say, "What the heck are these people doing, and where's the food the lady promised?"

"Cheese!" Beth gritted out a smile.

Lachlan laughed, his chest making her head bounce.

"Stay still, you." She patted his chest. "Take another one. I blinked that time."

Beth's hair smelled like coconut and sunshine. His arm went limp, totally distracted by her closeness.

She grabbed his phone. "Let me." The screen whirled in her hand until she found the perfect frame. At a forty-five-degree angle, she snapped away, changing her expression with each shot. He kept on grinning. Nothing could rub the smile off his face. Except—

"Don't you two look cute together." Wally towered over them, blocking the sun. "Nice and cozy, Chaplain Peters. Good thing you're out of uniform."

Beth scrambled upright and placed her hand on her hip. "Waldo, you dork." She glanced over her shoulder. "You scared the Quokka away."

"Stop calling me Waldo." His tone had a whine to it.

"Well, stop acting like a cartoon character—popping up everywhere, unexpectedly."

Lachlan bellowed a laugh. "Come on, you two. Knock it off." He stood and dusted the sand from his shorts.

"She started it." Wally played the annoying teen well.

Beth gave him a sisterly whack on the shoulder. "No, he did." She giggled in the most endearing way.

The Quokkas had scattered under a nearby bush. The other tourists huddled around, taking over the scene.

"That, my dear fellows, is the famous Australian Quokka," Beth said with pride.

"The one I filmed had a joey in its pouch." Wally held out his phone screen.

"Did not!" Beth tippy-toed, and her eyes widened. "Oh, so cute."

Lachlan smiled. "You've turned into mush over these animals."

"Now you can see why I want to help them."

As the next bus approached, Beth rushed her words. "Delay the bus if you can. I'll be one sec. I wanna zoom in and get a shot of the baby Quokka." Her ponytail flicked as she ran to the bushes.

Wally shook his head. "She's something else."

Lachlan smiled, agreeing. Unique. Sweet. A delight to be around.

They took their time boarding the bus, and sure enough, Beth dashed over just before the doors closed, and jumped onto the metal steps with a thud, huffing away. "Thank you," she gasped to the driver. He grunted and rolled his eyes.

Back upon the cushioned seats, Beth unfolded her map to a chorus of crinkles. Wally peered over from behind her.

She pointed to stop ten. "Let's get off at Little Salmon Bay. You guys can go for a snorkel."

Wally squeezed Beth's shoulder. "You need to have some fun too. You said you brought your gear."

Lachlan eyed Wally's hand, lasering holes in it.

"I am a bit hot after flustering over the Quokkas in the sun." She folded the map. "There's an ice cream truck too. That should cool me down."

Beth stood causing Wally's hand to drop. "I'm going to chat with the driver. Back soon."

* * *

Once at the front of the bus, Beth cleared her throat. "It's a terrible thing about the sick Quokkas. You must be devastated as a local."

The weathered faced driver glanced over his shoulder. "A shame, all right. Not enough effort has gone into solving the problem." His voice croaked, sounding like he'd smoked all his life. He veered the bus around a windy road. "They're cute and all, but if the Quokkas go, there'd be hardly any tourists. The island's welfare depends on them."

Beth shifted her weight on her feet, bracing the pole. "So, who'd want to ruin the livelihood of the Islanders?"

The man's head snapped back, and he scrunched his forehead. "You think someone is killing them on purpose?"

Her throat dried. Could it be true that she'd missed the mark? "Um. It's a possibility. The pollution excuse doesn't make sense."

"Mmmm." He remained silent as he lowered gears to climb a hill. "Developers wanted to lease from the government. There were hot debates a few months ago. Then it fizzled. But that isn't an excuse to pay out on the innocent Quokkas. I can't believe that for a moment."

Beth bit her bottom lip. How to dig for more information? "Developers? They'd make a lot of money transforming the island with fancy hotels and whatnot. Those yellow shacks are outdated."

He huffed in response. "Adds character, I reckon. The original buildings hold history. Visit the museum. The island once ran as a boys' reformatory in the eighteen-eighties. A thirteen-year-old who stole cake would get three months confinement." He shook his head. "Imagine the faces of kids today when the school groups visit. They don't know how good they've got it."

The view had changed to turquoise patches of water with several fishing boats anchored. Foaming waves crashed against large rocks covered in coral. Seagulls and shags perched on a reef. The island embraced wildlife and tourists alike.

"What if rumors leaked that the Quokkas were diseased? Would the lack of tourism give the government reason to sign the lease to gain returns?"

He gave a strange look of disbelief. "You must watch too many investigator movies. Who'd be so heartless to drive the Quokkas into extinction all for a quick buck?"

"Greedy developers, that's who."

The driver shrugged. "I hope you're wrong."

Beth whispered. "I hope so too."

She left the driver to focus on his job and made her way to a spare seat in front of Lachlan. Wally had moved to the back row of seats. Good.

"You were talking to the driver for a while." Lachlan swung his arm over the steel rail between them. "Any leads?"

She tucked her leg under the other and leaned against the window. "Maybe." Beth gazed into his amber-brown eyes, needing encouragement. "I suggested the developers who were refused leasing rights may be inciting trouble to affect tourism. The government would change their minds and sign contracts. The driver thinks I'm crazy."

Lachlan touched her arm. "You're not. You're a smart woman. A determined one." He retracted his hand. "I think you're onto something."

"How am I going to find out more?"

"First, you need to ask the locals if they know the names of the developers. And if any of their representatives are still on the island."

She nodded. "Mmm."

CHAPTER FOUR

THE BUS SLOWED at the next stop. A bronze-painted caravan converted into an ice cream truck had set up shop on the side of the road. "A local. I can ask questions while you and Wally visit the lookout." She ducked her head as she pointed to massive binoculars at the cliff's edge.

Lachlan called to his colleague, and they got off the bus.

The wind blew fierce at a higher point of the island, and the afternoon sun caused the temperature to rise. Beth lined up behind other tourists, two Japanese ladies, and a middle-aged couple. Lachlan's faint scent drifted from behind. Her senses forever homed in on his presence or location.

"Can I buy you an ice cream?" he whispered into her ear.

Tingles ran over her. He made it hard to concentrate on her mission. Her body started to lean back into him. The word 'yes' sat on the tip of her tongue.

She straightened and focused ahead. "Let me buy you and Wally one, for helping me today."

"We haven't helped much. I should pay you for being our tour guide." He squeezed in next to her, smiled down with those attractive lips, and playfully bumped her hip with his. "What flavor do you want?"

She twitched her mouth and took in a breath to steady her heart. *Lachlan Peters, you're slaying me with your charm and good looks.*

"I haven't tried pistachio before. I'll have one scoop, please."

"Great. Ice cream coming up. Wally and I can go to the lookout while you ask questions, then join us for snorkeling. It can't be all work and no play."

She wobbled her head. "I've barely worked."

"You're making progress. Patience." He squeezed her in a side-hug. "Go have a seat and relax." He stepped to the counter to order.

Wally had already received his waffle cone and strolled over to the binoculars positioned on a black stand.

Five minutes later, sitting under a striped umbrella at a picnic table, Beth bit into her green pistachio ice cream. "Mmm." She licked her lips. "This may not look appealing, but it's delicious."

Lachlan remained silent for a moment and just stared at her mouth. "It looks delicious to me." He brushed his thumb over her bottom lip. "You missed a spot."

Heat flushed through her cheeks, and she quickly offered her cone to take the attention away from herself. "Do you want a bite? It's so good."

"I'd love some." He held out his cone to her too. "Try mine. Butterscotch."

With their arms crossed, she first took a bite of his. Lachlan took a chunk of hers, but before he pulled away, Beth gave a small push and squashed some ice cream over his chin.

She laughed. "It's juvenile, I know. But I couldn't resist."

He chuckled, grabbed a paper napkin from the dispenser on the wooden table, and proceeded to wipe his face. Next, he rubbed the paper onto her forearm. "Take that."

"I deserve it." She couldn't hold back the bubbles of laughter. Lachlan had a way of releasing her to be free and have fun. She did slip into serious mode way too often. Beth needed today as a lesson on how to live again. Life wasn't meant to be all work and ministry. God had made this beautiful island for His people to enjoy.

"I like you, Beth." He leaned back, holding his ice cream. "I hope we can catch up again before I leave. I plan to go to a church this Sunday. Can I come to yours?"

Her lashes fluttered in surprise, along with her stomach. What did he mean by *like*?

"Sure. You're more than welcome." Now her dad would find out that she'd been hanging around sailors. Great. "It's called New Life. In Fremantle. Starts 10 a.m." But to see that beaming smile of Lachlan's would be worth the interrogation from Dad.

"Awesome. I'll bring some buddies with me."

She tucked some hair behind her ear. "How long are you in town?"

"We leave on Monday."

Her heart sank. Why—she didn't know.

He reached out and touched her hand. "Hey. We can keep in touch. Send emails."

She mustn't be good at hiding her disappointment. Beth pushed out a laugh and flittered her gaze to the napkin dispenser, reluctant to reveal any more of her thoughts to him. "That'd be nice. To remain friends." She bravely connected with his eyes. "You're a refreshment to my soul, Lachlan. I could do with more friends like you."

He squeezed her hand, then removed his. "I feel the same way."

They finished their ice creams in comfortable silence. Her teeth crunched into the last piece of the cone. Would they stay friends via email? Would that be a good thing or not?

Lachlan arched his back and rubbed his belly. "That hit the spot." Then he leaned forward and threaded his fingers, elbows on the table. "I took it upon myself to do my part of the investigating." He grinned. "I asked the ice cream lady a few questions and if she remembered the name of the interested developers."

She straightened. "And?"

"Pacific Master Builders. National company. They're loaded with cash. The gossip is that someone offered the counselor representative a bribe but he refused. After that, the developers laid low to avoid potential infringements. The counselor didn't report it, just gave them the warning to back off."

Beth widened her eyes. "Now that's a reason for the developers to get nasty. It sounds like they're the corrupt type to offer bribes in the first place."

"We should find more answers back in town. But let's go for that swim." He stood and waved for her to join him.

* * *

Beth exited the change rooms at Little Salmon Bay. With snorkel around her neck, but no flippers, she easily made her way to the shore. She squinted across the glaring beach sand to Lachlan, waving her over from the water. He had no shirt. Fantastic. Just the torture she needed—to be close to Lachlan's muscled torso.

She tugged at the ends of her bather shorts as she walked, making them longer, even though they were well beyond modest. Lachlan didn't seem reserved. Guys could get away with showing extra skin. Her brothers didn't wear surf shirts either. She simply needed to relax. With a shake, she stepped into the cool water. The wet sand crunched between her toes. The gentle waves lapped against her knees.

Disappointment plagued her mind. She didn't know any married men who'd kept Lachlan's fit physique. By the time she finally married, she'd be forty and never get to run her hands over—*Bethany Michaels, stop it*. She winced. Oh, if her father could see her now, she'd get thirty-one minutes of timeout. She laughed on the inside. But the wave of truth hit her. Her future Aussie hubby would have a beer belly. Or more appropriately, a food baby. Gee. So unfair that most women made a considerable effort to stay attractive for their man, but rarely the other way around.

"You're frowning, Beth. Is it too cold for you?"

She shook her head.

Lachlan lifted his brows. "What are you thinking about then?"

She waved her hand in the air. "The travesties of life, but there's no point worrying about things I can't change."

He crab-crawled over to her, staying low in the water. "On a small scale, we can make a difference." He stood, and water cascaded over his sculpted body. "In our little worlds, we can do our part." He circled his finger between them, stepping closer. Too close. "What's something I can do to help change that travesty in your mind?" He pretended to drill her temple. "You worry too much."

Where was Wally when she needed an interruption? The gulls and ocean filled her silence instead.

"You need to unwind. Have fun." He took her hand in his. "Come spend time with me. I'm only here for a little while, and I want to enjoy this beautiful place with my new Australian friend."

Friend. Right. Ignore the electric waves traveling up her arm by his simple hold. She sank into the water and let him lead her to the deeper part of the bay.

"There's a cave over here. It's amazing. Let me show you." He pulled his mask over his eyes, and she did the same. He held her hand as they swam underwater together. The floating sensation helped loosen her tension. She didn't need to worry. Lachlan wouldn't struggle with the same attraction.

* * *

Thankfully, Beth wore shorts and a swim shirt. Lachlan could relax, be comfortable around her, and enjoy the friendship forming between them.

He had considered keeping his shirt on and letting it dry later. Usually, he wouldn't care, but he could tell Beth had high morals, and he wanted to respect that. Wally would make a big deal of it and ask why he let his shirt get wet. A whole slew of unwanted questions would follow. Better not to complicate matters.

They snorkeled, floating on the bay's surface. A school of tiny, gray-silver fish scattered ahead. He looked over his shoulder, his arm connected to Beth's, and both had air bubbles over their skin.

He pointed with his other hand, directing her to come down with him. He duck-dived, holding his breath. He gently led her as he powered his feet like a propeller. When he turned back again, her lengthy hair flowered about her. The highlights captured sun rays, creating a dreamy effect. So beautiful.

They arrived at the cave, and he pulled her upward, coming out of the water. They stood, both breathing heavily after removing their snorkel and mask.

The salty air had chilled from the cavity. Light shimmered off the crystal waters onto the cave wall and created the most romantic atmosphere. Beth's skin reflected an angelic glow. In this open cave, he'd found a rare jewel. Unlike anyone he'd met before, Beth seemed free-spirited, transparent, and naturally beautiful. Their eyes locked as they gained their breath. The drum of his heart thumped against his rib cage. He couldn't resist staring at her, droplets falling from her hair. She didn't seem to mind the intimacy and the quiet lapping of waves swirling about their knees. Alone.

At that moment, he imagined Beth as his girlfriend, and how he might kiss her. Her gaze fluttered to his lips. Hang on. Was that desire in her eyes too? All common sense had left him now, and he stepped toward her. He would kiss Beth, capture this special moment with her that he may not have again. He inched closer, and she leaned in. She wanted him. This was going to happen. He would let it happen. Nature drawing them together, it seemed so right.

A wave crashed against their waists, knocking them from their footing. Beth went under and came up laughing. Oh, he deserved that splash of cold water that had hit his face. To wake him up, slap him into reality.

"It's slippery here." She wobbled to her feet, then glanced around. "You're right. It's amazing. I should go snorkeling more often. This is fun." But her eyes never met his. The moment lost. And so it should be. He swallowed back the disappointment. It would only cause trouble, anyway.

"I better check on Wally." He needed some space. The third wheel came in handy. Wally didn't know it, but he made a good chaperone.

* * *

Two hours later, back in the main hub of the island, it came time for the ferry to leave. Lachlan glanced at his phone. Twenty minutes before departure. Where had Bethany gone? Wally sat at the bakery's outdoor table, stuffing his face with a Quokka-shaped custard tart.

All three of them had asked questions of the locals willing to discuss the problem. Nothing. No further insight.

The conversational hum of groups and pairs of tourists blended with a raven's cry in the trees above. Children climbed a central steel-roped playground surrounded by white beach sand. Lachlan stood and swung his bag over his shoulder. "Stay here a minute. I'll see if I can find her."

Wally's cheeks bulged with pie, and he mumbled through the crumbs, "Okay."

Lachlan strode around to the back of the main buildings to find Beth crouched next to a patch of shrubbery. She'd found another Quokka.

"Hello," he called.

Beth flinched and turned. In her surgical gloved hand, she held some kind of medical device.

"What're you doing?" He lowered his voice and sneaked across the sandy pathways.

She'd already turned back to the Quokka and didn't answer him. He squatted next to her, careful not to scare the creature away.

"I'm taking a saliva swab," she whispered.

"Are you allowed to do that?" He glanced around to find this back part clear of people.

Beth shuffled closer to the animal. "Probably not. As long as this little guy doesn't mind, it should be fine. I'll be gentle."

"What if he bites you?" The concern in his voice matched the panic inside him.

She gave him a side glance. "I'm willing to take the risk. They've been clinically checked and cleared of diseases."

"Every single one of them?"

"I doubt all ten thousand."

"Beth!" he whisper-shouted.

Before he could stop her, she swiped the large cotton tip inside the Quokka's mouth while it nibbled on its food. Treats probably from Beth. She slipped the swab back into its plastic tube. "Done." She slipped off the disposable gloves, packed her things, and stood.

He joined her, releasing his breath. "Bethany Michaels." He shook his head. He could scold her, but no point in trying to tame the Australian female specimen. They were in a class of their own. Feisty when they wanted to be.

Beth looked up at him with sadness in her expression. "I've got no more leads. I don't have enough details for a solid story. I want to help the Quokkas, I really do. I also need this break to make something of myself in the industry." She dropped her gaze to the ground and scuffed her shoe into the dirt. "I don't have the time to keep coming back here. Today is my only chance. Someone else will probably work it out. Get the news-breaking story."

He lifted her chin and looked into eyes that glazed with unshed tears. He cupped her cheek, her skin soft and supple. How long had it been since he'd held a woman? He blinked the distraction away and dropped his hand to his side.

"I'm concerned about your safety. If the developers are corrupt, it's better to report your suspicions, and let a team of investigators take over from here. You can ask for exclusive rights to the story, once it's safe to expose them."

She gazed at him like a sad puppy. His heart ached for her.

"The way you want to help these animals and serve your church and family shows your heart of gold. There's a scripture in Deuteronomy which declares His chosen people are His treasured possession, out of all the peoples on the face of the earth. I have been to many places these last three years, and you, Bethany, are a treasure. Don't sell yourself short."

He didn't know why, but the words kept spilling from his mouth. "You're unique. Precious."

He angled his neck and rested his forehead against hers, drilling the message home. "Do you know this?"

Her breath caressed his lips, and her gaze changed. Did she want him to kiss her? He inched his face slightly back. He would like to, but not when she was upset. Not a time to take advantage of her emotions. Plus, he wasn't sticking around. The cave was a weak moment. He had his wits about him now, and he wouldn't just kiss any girl. A kiss must lead to a trusting relationship. One that could last. His career didn't allow for that.

Beth whispered, "Have you been eating chocolate?"

"Yes, do you want me to share?"

She nodded slowly, and her eyes drifted closed.

He pulled out a Snickers bar from his back pocket and stood back. "I had a two-pack. Here's one half."

Her eyes flashed open, and pink flushed her cheeks. "Thanks." But she didn't take it, instead dived into his arms for a bear hug. "Thanks for your kind words, Lachlan. I needed that." Her words muffled against his chest. "You're a true friend."

"Guys! What's going on here?" Wally's words echoed from afar.

Beth jumped, and her head knocked into Lachlan.

"Ouch. You've got a hard skull, missy." He rubbed his chin.

She turned and pointed at Wally, "You again."

Wally held up his palms in surrender, grinning. "Hey, I'm not the guilty one this time."

"Lachlan is built with strong arms, perfect for comforting a woman in distress. I feel safe and secure with him. He can be trusted, unlike some sailors I know."

"Whatever." Wally scoffed. "Sorry to interrupt, but the ferry is boarding. We need to go."

CHAPTER FIVE

BETHANY SAT NEXT to Lachlan and his four Navy buddies on the front pew. Her father stood tall behind the pulpit, glancing above his spectacles to the crowd between Scripture verses.

"The apostle Paul reminds us here . . ."

Beth peered from the corner of her eye at Lachlan's strong hands clasped together on his lap. His erect spine might be from habit, or perhaps the wary expressions Dad sent their way made him tense. Lachlan's thigh against hers broke the six-inch rule. He just had bulky legs, likely from all the Navy exercise regimes he took part in. Dad would always see her as his little girl. But she'd grown and needed to break free eventually.

When mum had passed, she'd obliged her dad by returning to live with him in the family home. Beth had moved out two years ago and could finally breathe again. Although, living with Melissa and her toddler wasn't precisely freedom. Occasional tantrums echoed from Melissa's side of the house. Something Beth found all too familiar, having grown up in a large family.

What did Lachlan think of Dad's preaching? She'd heard a version of the message before, so Beth had zoned out after ten minutes. Were Lachlan's buddies believers too? His disciples? She smiled and let out a small sigh of admiration.

Lachlan nudged her and angled his neck to the side without taking his eyes off the pulpit. "Are you paying attention, missy?"

"Mmm." She smirked.

"I'll be asking questions afterward," he whispered.

Dad glanced their way, raised his brows, and continued. Gee. He didn't miss a beat. After all the years of her filling the role of a co-parent, Dad still treated her like a kid. The fact became more evident when others were around. Like now. Total embarrassment. Thankfully, Lachlan remained respectful but not intimidated by her father's stiffness. Her fast introduction had avoided interrogation, with little time before the opening song. Dad was likely happy to have five extra seats filled. If Lachlan had come alone, he'd be more suspicious of the Navy chaplain's intentions with his daughter. Beth bit back a smile.

Lachlan smoothed his hands over his long khaki slacks, then returned his hands in a tight clasp. The tiniest spots of perspiration on his forehead glistened from the dangling industrial lights above. What were his intentions? Friends via email to help him combat loneliness? A Christian friend to confide in? Or something more? Her insides flipped at the possibility of a developing relationship.

"Can the band return to the stage?" Dad's words interrupted her musings.

Sally, Ben, and Anthony stepped up the carpeted stairs, picked up their instruments, and soon, a slow worship song flowed through the overhead speakers. The congregation rose, and

Lachlan's steady baritone warmed her soul. A strange urge to thread her fingers with his surprised her. She hoped that one day, she would worship the Lord beside her husband. Lachlan was the type of guy she could see herself with, but reality told her that he wouldn't be the one. Gone tomorrow, occupied for another two years, a citizen of America. Too many obstacles prevented Lachlan from joining her in her corner of the world. Why did she even entertain the idea? Fairy tales.

A soft touch to her lower back startled her.

"Are you all right?" Lachlan whispered. "You aren't singing."

She glanced at her father on the opposite side of the church, who had his eyes closed. Beth tippy-toed and leaned into Lachlan's shoulder. "I'm enjoying yours. You've got a nice voice."

Soft creases formed at the corners of his eyes. "You're easily distracted today?"

"Yes." Only natural when a gorgeous man stood too close to a single female.

He turned to the screen and continued to sing the words. This time, she joined in, singing the melody that blended perfectly with his low tones. They sounded good together.

When the song ended, Sally dismissed the congregation to enjoy beverages in the break-out area. Within seconds, several members swarmed around the uniformed sailors and greeted them. Wally hadn't come. She had mixed feelings about that, relieved but also disappointed. Lachlan would continue to reach out to him, no doubt.

Dad approached Lachlan and shook his hand again. "I hope my message encouraged all you, young men."

"Yes, sir. Very much so." Lachlan swung his hands behind his back and stood with his legs apart like he was reporting to a sergeant. "Your exegesis on the book of Timothy made me see it in a new light. I'll make it a plan to study those passages in our chapel services."

Dad's chest puffed out as he nodded. "Wonderful." He glanced at her, then back to Lachlan. "How did you meet my daughter again?"

"She threw up on me, sir." He chuckled at Dad's shocked expression. "So, I repaid her by assisting her to—"

"Dad, I told you." She nudged in front of Lachlan and patted her dad's arm. "The chaplain helped me with my sea legs. I had a spell on the ferry. He asked me about my necklace cross and found out I was a Christian. Long story short, he's here to join us for church." She eyed Lachlan to leave out the finer details and turned back to her father. "I'll take him out to lunch to thank him for his kindness."

"Will you now?" Dad's eyebrows scrunched inward.

Beth turned to Lachlan. "Are you free this afternoon? There's a great restaurant nearby. I know the owner, and he's American. You can bring your friends, of course."

Lachlan hesitated as he looked at her dad's frowning face. "I'll see what the others want to do."

"Great." Beth grabbed his arm and steered him away from her father and headed to the rest of the group. She mumbled under her breath, "Now you can see why I'm still single at thirty-one."

A glint sparkled in Lachlan's eyes. "Over-protective daddy?"

"Yep."

He gave a reassuring smile. "He loves you. Wants the best for his girl."

"Well, he doesn't need to worry about you then." Oops. Please, don't read into that.

Beth wriggled into the circle of young adults, making room for Lachlan. Isabell seemed entranced by one of the sailor's stories. Watch it, Issy. Don't get sucked in as she had. Who would've thought Bethany Michaels would fall for a sailor? Huh? She wasn't falling for anyone. Gone tomorrow. Gone.

Lachlan had asked the men what their plans were. Clive spoke on behalf of the others, "Going to Pot Black to play Snooker. You comin'?"

Lachlan shook his head. "Beth has an American friend she wants me to meet. I'll see you guys back on the ship."

"All right." Clive, Ted, and two others—she'd forgotten their names, headed to the back doors. Isabell and Clarissa followed— no surprises there.

* * *

Seated together before the floor-to-ceiling windows at Bayside Manna, Beth sat back with satisfaction, enjoying the view of the foreshore and The Fremantle Yacht Club in the distance.

Lachlan browsed the menu. "This all looks amazing. They feed us reasonably well on the ship, but this is five-star."

"Wait 'til you taste the food." Beth kissed her fingers for effect. "Magnifico."

Lachlan smiled. "Call me a traditionalist, but I'd like to pay. Plus, we don't get to spend our money on deck, so I'm happy to splurge. Order what you'd like."

She sat upright and collected her menu. "Okay. A lady doesn't need asking twice." Beth ran her fingers down the plastic-covered

LISA RENÉE

menu. Where was that dish she had last time? There. "I'll have the King Ora Salmon, thank you, Lachlan."

"A woman who knows what she wants." He adjusted in his seat and studied the menu with further concentration.

"I've eaten here many a time. I have my favorites. The first time I ate free. The newspaper sent me to do a sponsored feature article for the owner. They received a lot of bookings straight away, so my boss asked me to look after Bayside as a client and run their coupon specials."

Lachlan nodded, seemingly impressed.

"I've become good friends with the staff here, and the owner introduced me to his wife, who runs a Christian mentor program. I volunteer once a week at Youth Connect, teaching teens English and journalism. They've had more articles published than me. Not paid, of course."

Lachlan placed his menu on the table. "Wow. That's great, Beth. You're really making use of your talents to help others. God will bless you for that."

"He does. Better to give than receive. I love helping the kids. It's the highlight of my week."

A waitress approached and took their order. Lachlan finalized his choice for a lamb shank.

Beth touched the young woman's arm. "Emily, can you tell the chef that I'm here? I want to introduce him to my friend."

"Will do." Emily topped up their water glasses and headed to the kitchen.

A few minutes later, Chris strode over, dressed in his chef's uniform and a matching black beret. "Beth, how are—" Chris froze and stared at Lachlan. "Lockster! Is that you? Bro!" Chris rushed forward.

Lachlan pushed his chair back with wide eyes and stood. "Chris, you old man!" They slammed into each other in a brotherly hug.

Chris stood back, holding Lachlan at arm's length, looking him up and down. "Bro, you filled out." He scuffed Lachlan's bristle top hair. "Not the skinny teenager anymore. What are you doing in Australia? What's this?" He pulled on Lachlan's khaki shirt. "Soldier—Navy? Dude, who'd have thought, Mark's annoying younger brother, becoming a marine."

"Navy Chaplain, actually." He beamed a smile. "I didn't know you moved to Australia." He glanced at Beth. "And what's this about a wife Beth mentioned?"

Chris smoothed his hands over his striped apron. "And a baby. I'm an Australian citizen too. Love it here." He splayed his palm, showing the room. "Started my own restaurant. I'd traveled the globe, but this just felt like coming home. Perth is a little like San Diego, only quieter."

"Man, I can't believe it. You look great, despite the grays on the side." He winked. "Have you heard from my brother?"

Beth cleared her throat, and they stepped apart to acknowledge her presence. "You two go way back, hey?"

Lachlan straightened his shirt. "Yes. We grew up together in San Diego. Chris is good friends with my older brother." He glanced at Chris and smiled. "This guy loved to wrestle me. Hold me down. I think I could give him a run for his money now."

Chris flexed his biceps. "I still have my guns. I admit the gut is growing. Family life does that to a man."

Beth scoffed. "It's always the way."

Lachlan laughed at her. "You'll keep."

What was that supposed to mean?

The men continued to chat, catching up on what had happened the last five years, while Beth quietly sipped her water. When Emily reappeared with their meals, Chris returned to the kitchen.

Lachlan pulled his chair in closer as he took the first bite of his mashed potato and lamb. He gulped as if he hadn't chewed it first and looked up at her. "I still can't believe, on the other side of the world, I'd bump into Chris. He looks happy."

"I'd say he is. Always got a smile on his face. He mentors youth as well. Trains them in the kitchen, but starts each shift in prayer and has the guys share an online Bible plan. That's how he met his wife, Cassie. She's the CEO of Youth Connect." She forked a piece of her salmon.

"That's great that he can mix ministry with his work."

"And it's a beautiful story, how he got together with Cassie. She thought she couldn't have children, but now they have adorable Johannah. I get to play with her on Fridays. Cassie has a playpen set up when she works in the office."

Lachlan swallowed more food. "Cute. How old?"

"Two."

"Wow. Time goes fast. My brother hadn't mentioned anything about Chris. I don't get to chat with him too much these days, so I guess we stick to only family news."

"Tell me more about life back in San Diego." She dug into her lunch while she listened.

"Mom and Dad run a real estate business together. Mark is seven years older than me. He's a bathroom renovator. Married. Three kids." He scratched his chin. "Um, Kayce's divorced. She has two girls. And I'm the baby of the family. Thirty years old."

Beth blinked. "Oh, I'm older than you. Only by one year, but the maturity difference is obvious." She feigned a straight face, took a sip of water, but nearly dribbled, trying not to laugh.

"Ha. You'll get gray hairs and wrinkles before me. That's all." Lachlan placed the last scoop of his meal into his mouth.

Chris approached the table again. "How was the lamb, Lachie? Soft and tender?"

"Amazing." Lachlan leaned back and tapped his belly. "The best food I've had in three years."

"Whoa. I've had rave reviews, but that'd be the best." He crossed one arm and pointed to Lachlan. "Put that on Google Places for me, bud."

"I will."

"And, Beth, you can put yours in the paper." Chris winked. "Can I get you dessert? On the house. In fact, the whole meal on the house for my long-lost friend." He slapped Lachlan on the shoulder. "Hey, didn't you do hospitality after you finished high school?"

"I did."

Chris flicked a cotton napkin over his shoulder. "Didn't like it?"

"I enjoyed working in hotel restaurants. Smorgasbords were less pressure to keep up with. I ended up at Bible College. I worked dinner shifts to pay the tuition. Then I got this job in the Navy."

Chris nodded, then his eyes lit up. "Hey, if you ever want a working vacation, I'd love to have you here. You can travel around the South West, lots of great fishing spots, camping, surfing. You used to like all that. Scouts, I remember. All those badges you had."

Lachlan laughed. "You have a good memory, old man."

Chris flicked his gaze to Beth and pretended to whisper, "And if you're as lucky as me, to meet a beautiful Aussie girl, I'll sponsor you toward Australian citizenship."

Lachlan covered his mouth with his fist, coughed, but a smile curved his lips. "You're a piece of work, Chris. I'll keep that in mind. Thanks, man."

Chris smacked his hands together. "Now, what would the lovely couple like for dessert?" His smile reached his eyes. Chris must be having so much fun, teasing Lachlan.

"Crème' Brulee, for me." Beth patted the corners of her mouth with her serviette, hoping to cover any flush on her cheeks.

Lachlan flicked the menu to the back page. "I'll have Coconut Tapioca, please."

"Good choice." He flashed his teeth. "I'll have Emily bring them out for you." Chris strode away.

Beth smoothed out the tablecloth, and let Lachlan speak first.

He sipped his water.

She fiddled with the crystal base on the vase.

Lachlan looked out the windows.

A sigh escaped her lips as she leaned on her elbow and watched the boat masts bob on the water in the distance. Wasn't he going to say anything? Comment on the food? Small talk, at least? The silence between them continued, but soft saxophone music played in the background. Maybe he was feeling full after his lunch. He ate so fast.

Emily came to their table. "Who ordered the Crème Brulee?"

"Me." She raised her hand.

"I should've known." Emily placed a ceramic dish before her.

"Your Coconut Tapioca, sir."

"Thank you." Lachlan straightened in his chair and picked up his spoon.

Emily cleared away their used plates and cutlery, then returned to the kitchen.

"Mmm. This tastes good." Lachlan took a second scoop.

"Yes, that's number two on my list of favorite desserts from here. But I'm a sucker for Brulee."

Lachlan gestured to the windows. "I have a couple of hours before I need to return to the ship. After this, do you want to go for a walk on the beach?"

Her shoulders relaxed. "I'd love to."

CHAPTER SIX

AFTER A WALK down the beach, Lachlan and Beth sat below the sandbank. Speckles of light sparkled like diamonds on gentle ripples lapping onto the shoreline. Gulls flew against the bright blue sky, searching for a fish below.

Lachlan picked up a spotted shell next to him and flung it toward the water. Missed.

Would he miss an opportunity for something more with Beth? Since the cave encounter forty-eight hours ago, all he could think about was how he nearly kissed her. Where would an actual kiss have left them now? He was already craving her—imagine what two years of distance would be like? Misery.

"Have you ever wanted something you know isn't good for you, and it hurts to choose the right thing?"

She nodded quietly.

"In Corinthians, it talks about how we may be allowed to do anything—but not everything is beneficial." He threw another shell. "We have free will, but we get to choose wisdom or not." He turned and studied her expression.

A tear formed in her ocean blue eyes. Man, he hated to hurt her. But he couldn't lead her on.

"Remember I said that you're a treasure? A rare find." He swallowed. "I hope you hold onto that. Don't let anyone steal that truth away from you. You're valuable, Beth. A woman of great worth."

"Thank you. And you're going to make me cry now." She swiped under her eye. "Why am I feeling so sad?"

Tears stung the back of his eyes too. What was going on with his heart? It was compassion. He'd caused her pain by giving her false hope that they could be more. The other day, he'd blubbered they could email because she looked miserable. She'd grown attached in a short time. What had she said in the church? Her dad didn't need to worry about him. No way was Lachlan Peters the best thing for Bethany Michaels. She'd be waiting for years, and he had no plans to live in Australia. His home was in San Diego. Friends and family he missed, waited for his return.

He'd been in a long-distance relationship before, pining over someone he couldn't have while overseas—a waste of emotional energy.

"So, this is goodbye, huh?" She said softly, barely audible.

"Beth . . ." He drew out a pause. ". . . about the cave."

"Don't." She held up a palm and averted her gaze. "It's okay, I understand."

His stomach sank. "I'm sorry."

Her wide eyes found him and she gave a tiny smile. "Hey, I want our last memories together to be good ones, not sad. I'm glad I met you. I've learned something about myself. You've helped me." Another weak grin. "Brothers and sisters in Christ. We're family. All over the world, we connect. That's what this is about." She pointed between them. "We've connected because we have our faith in common, and you've encouraged me in mine."

"And by your example, you've been the same to me, Bethany Michaels." He brushed her chin with his thumb. Darn, he shouldn't have touched her soft skin. The pull between them was not brotherly-sisterly. Who were they kidding?

"Man." He ran his fingers over his short hair as he slumped onto his back, hitting the sand hard. Looking at the blue sky with scattered clouds, he prayed from his heart, *Help me, God. Why is this so difficult?*

Beth stood, and he listened to her steps crunch into the sand as she moved toward the water.

How long did he have left? An hour? He could go back to the ship earlier. He didn't need to spend the whole time with Beth. But he wanted to savor every minute. He liked her company. He liked her . . . a lot. But not like this, seeing her disappointed. Maybe they could email now and then. Feelings would phase out as they moved on with their busy lives. Then it wouldn't be hard. They didn't have to say goodbye now. Not forever.

Right, he would enjoy these last moments, relax, be himself, and kick awkwardness to the curb.

He got up, swiped off the granules of sand, and rolled up the ends of his pants to join Beth by the water's edge.

"Hey." He gently nudged her.

"Hey." She gave a somber smile.

He placed his arm over her shoulder and pulled her in for a side-hug. They both looked out to the horizon, and he tilted his head, leaning gently on hers.

"I look forward to reading your emails when I'm on those rocky seas." His voice became husky. "They'll make my day, I bet."

She smiled for real this time and looked up at him through thick lashes. Man, she was gorgeous. As natural as can be with little make-up. Her face—so close to his. He willed her to look away before he did something stupid.

But she didn't. Instead, she turned into him, and the open trust and longing in her gaze compelled him to face her too. His hand swept into her sun-kissed hair, combing it away from her neck. His throat pulsed as his heart kicked into overdrive. She kept her gaze on him, willing for him to lead wherever this might go.

"Beth," he whispered. He couldn't say anymore with his suddenly parched mouth. He licked his lips, and her lashes fluttered. Was she waiting for him to finish what he'd just started?

He placed his hands on her shoulders and leaned his forehead against hers. He released a breath and closed his eyes. Then he slid his hands across her back and ever so slowly drew Beth into his embrace. His cheek rested against hers. She fit perfectly, molding into his body. *Lord God, I don't want to let go of such a treasure.* Why had he signed another two years of his life away? He had no choice. He couldn't shake loose of his commitments. He had a duty to his country. He was American. He didn't belong here. But Beth felt so right, like she belonged with him.

Her palms left his waist and smoothed over his back, sending sweet sensations through him.

The intensity of her touch was too much. His hands mimicked hers, and he let himself follow the curve of her back, enjoying her delicate frame. How to come back to friendship from this? How could he look her in the eye and pretend the electricity between them was never there?

Seconds had passed, and he blinked from the trance, enraptured by Beth's floral scent and her soft body pressing against his. He released his hold, she did the same, and he slid his hands down her arms as he took a step back.

"You're something else, all right." He tapped her button nose and smiled. "Thank you for the hug. I . . ." He gulped air. "It was nice." Too nice.

She laughed softly. "Yes, it was." Beth flicked hair over her shoulder, turned to the view the water, and hugged herself.

Beth's wavy hair swayed in the warm breeze. "Will you be in danger, Lachlan? How safe are your missions?"

"Fairly safe." He stepped closer to her side, looking out to the ocean. "I'm assigned to a training ship. Guys like Wally are only starting their careers. But we occasionally get called into Emergency Relief situations with other countries. I'm a qualified counselor—that's what I studied at Bible College—so I'm on the ground helping people deal with grief and loss, sometimes with an interpreter."

She glanced across to him. "I didn't know that. You must find a lot of satisfaction in your job."

"I do."

A seagull circled near them, squawking as if asking for food. Beth flicked her hand, and it flew away.

"I'm glad to hear you're not on a battleship or whatever you call it—war-related missions."

"My mom and sister are too." He smiled. "I try to keep them updated, but sometimes work gets hectic."

"Do you still want to stay in touch with me?" Her eyes were wide with anticipation.

Had he led her to believe he didn't? He touched the tips of her fingers. "Yes. I would like to."

She faced him and collected his hand and placed it onto her cheek. "Lachlan, it's okay if you want to kiss me. It's not a marriage proposal."

He laughed nervously. If Beth only knew how much he wanted to. If not for his desperate hold on self-control, he'd scoop her up, carry her to the sandbank, and kiss the woman senseless. But he would return to the ship within the hour, and he needed to stay focused and disciplined. Kissing Beth now would be amazing, but he'd suffer later. Dreaming about her and missing her touch. Unnecessary torture.

He cupped her other cheek and gazed directly into her eyes. "Beth, if we meet again, I promise you, I'll kiss you like there's no tomorrow." He smiled. "But today is not the day for that. I'll be away for two years. I don't want to do that to you, or me. Let's stay friends. We can be good friends. And if God has a plan for us, then somehow He will make it happen."

Beth smiled sweetly. "I respect you, Lachlan. You're a true man of honor."

He agreed, but why did he hurt so bad?

CHAPTER SEVEN

BETH SWIVELED THE black office chair to face Chelsea. "This is brilliant." She tapped the draft article. "You're learning so fast. A catchy title. Great hook for the first line. Main points in the first paragraph. The rest flows so well, and it's within the word count for the youth column."

Chelsea beamed a smile, causing her lip piercing to rise. "I have a good teacher."

"The best." Beth nudged her. "You guys are getting more articles printed than me. I'm working myself out of the job."

"Do you want royalties on our zero commission?" Chelsea raised her thin brows.

Beth laughed. "Welcome to my world. You can do copy-editing like me—at least that pays the bills. Maybe you can get an internship at the *Fremantle Herald* once you finish the program at Youth Connect. How long do you have left before you graduate?"

Chelsea's green eyes, surrounded by thick black liner, lit up. "Two months. I'd love to work for the paper. Will your boss take on someone like me?"

Beth glanced at the colored tattoo on Chelsea's neck, then back to her eyes. "If you have the talent, I can't see why not."

Timothy tapped on the glass door. Beth waved him in. Conversations from the other workstations flooded the room as he entered.

"Cassie wants to know when you'll be ready for the English lesson?" Timothy leaned his skinny frame against the doorway. He nodded to Chelsea.

Beth looked at her. "We've gone overtime. Go get a quick bite to eat in the lunchroom, and I'll see you in ten minutes for class." Beth smiled at Timothy. "I'll skip my lunch and start right on time. Where is Cassie? I'll tell her myself."

"She's with her daughter in the nursery games room."

"Great." Beth clapped her hands. "I'll say hello to Johannah as well."

Beth stood, and they all exited the room. Her small heels clicked against the polished concrete floor as she walked down the corridor to the colorful games room.

Cassie had a messy bun on top of her head, with a pen wedged down the side. Nice working-mum look.

Leaning over the red and blue playpen, Cassie handed two-year-old Johannah a plastic pony. "Keep it in here, bubba. Stop throwing it out, you cheeky girl."

Johannah's brown eyes widened and pointed to Beth. "Bef, Bef."

Cassie turned. "Hey. How are you? All set for class?"

"Yep. All ready to go. I wanted to say a quick hello to Jo Jo." She waved at the little girl.

Johannah, a mini version of Cassie, opened and shut her palm in slow motion. Oh, she melted Beth's heart.

Cassie stood and smoothed her palms down her black skinny jeans. She could pass as a teen at her size and didn't look like a forty-something-year-old. A sly grin slid up Cassie's cheeks. "Chris told me about Lachie. But he didn't tell me what you were doing hanging around a sailor." She crossed her arms and tapped her Nike shoe to the ground. "Fill me in."

Beth wobbled her head as if she had nothing to tell. "We met on the Rottnest Ferry, spent the day together on the island." She sighed wistfully. "Had a good time. He came to church. Went to lunch. Now he's gone."

Cassie's forehead creased. "That's all?"

"No." She crossed her arms to match Cassie's. "I'm so attracted to him, it's ridiculous. A lust demon must've taken over my body."

Cassie burst out laughing. "Beth. You're being silly now. That's normal chemistry. You know that right? You're so sweet and innocent."

"Cassie, I've had boyfriends before, kissed them, and gone further than I would've liked with the ex-worship leader. But I didn't even kiss Lachlan, and oh, how he made me feel . . ." she shivered. "It's a good thing he's gone, or I would've fallen into sin."

Cassie tilted her head. "He might not have let you—if he's the real deal and respects you enough to wait."

"We can't do anything now, anyway. Lachlan's with the Navy for another two years, at least. He didn't make any commitments to me. We're just friends." Beth frowned. "He said he'd email, though."

Cassie picked up the toy pony again that Jo Jo had thrown on the floor. "Maybe the distance will help with the crazy hormones, and you can get to know him better over time."

"He hasn't promised to wait for me. He might meet other girls at another port, and I didn't realize it, but there are women in the Navy too."

Cassie laughed. "Maybe not as feminine as you. And you share the same faith."

"Why are you trying to get my hopes up?"

She shrugged and dropped the toy in the playpen. "Just saying, don't wipe the possibility away. Love doesn't come around every day."

"Who's saying it's love? It's a crush. He's absolutely gorgeous and charming. I'm acting like a teenager, not a mature rationale woman."

"I looked him up on Facebook, he's nice looking, but not drop-dead gorgeous. You're probably super attracted to him for other reasons."

Beth huffed. "Wait 'til you see the photos I have. She whipped out her cell from her back pocket and clicked on her favorites album. She'd transferred the zoomed-in images from her Nikon, and Lachlan had air-dropped their Quokka selfies on the ferry ride back to Fremantle.

Cassie came closer and peered over Beth's shoulder. "Yeah. He's okay. Built like a brick, I admit, but not unusually attractive." Cassie touched the screen and enlarged a group photo. "Who's this guy next to him? I'd say he's better looking."

"Ugh. Wally?" Reflux rose to her throat. "He's so sleazy. Desperate."

"See, I told you. It's the way a man treats a woman, which makes them more attractive. Is Lachlan kind and thoughtful? His faith, admirable?"

She nodded. "From the moment we met."

"When Chris and I were teammates working together at Youth Connect, I didn't notice his good looks. Then we started spending more time together, shared fun moments, and he showed how he cared about me. His kindness became personal. That's when I fell for him."

"We did have fun. And Lachlan helped me relax for once."

"See, it's personality too. You're attracted to who he is, not just physical attributes."

"I see your point." She slipped her phone away. "Anyway, the long-distance thing won't work. I'll get over him, soon enough."

Cassie lifted her palms. "All right. If you say so."

Beth shook her head. "I better get to class." She turned and strode away, her heels thudding the floor. A quiet giggle from Cassie followed. She might find it amusing since Cassie had won her American's heart and had him move to Australia. Or, perhaps Chris had decided that before they got together. She'd forgotten the details.

What if Chris could offer Lachlan a job to qualify for a working visa? Beth quickened her pace. The teens would be waiting. Despite his absence, Lachlan remained a big distraction. And when would he email her? Had it only been five days? She growled under her breath. How could she handle two years?

* * *

After teaching in her English class, Beth rushed across town to keep her appointment with the Police Investigator. Once she'd rattled off the conversations she'd had on the island and concluded with her suspicions, the uniformed man froze with his mouth agape.

"So, do you think we have a case?" Clutching the folder containing her so-called records and lab test results, she sat in anticipation for Sergeant Andrews to respond.

The stocky fifty-something-year-old closed his mouth for a moment. "We?"

Beth straightened. "The Navy officer who'd assisted in the investigation strongly suggested I hand the details over to you and avoid putting myself in any danger. Still, I respectfully request for exclusive rights to the story."

Sergeant Andrews' eyes widened. "Navy officer?"

"From the United States." If he refused this last hook, she'd lost him.

The man's peppered brows rose. "Why is the American Navy involved in this?"

"Lachlan Peters happened to be visiting the island off-duty and spoke to some of the locals. He agreed that the situation seemed suspicious." She placed the blue folder on his mahogany desk. "His conversation with the ice cream server and others has been documented, and his email address is here if you'd like to contact him. His ship has left port."

"I agree there's a need for further investigation." He cleared his throat. "Now, about your request for exclusive rights to the story, I'm not sure if I can promise such a thing."

Beth placed her palm over the folder and spoke in a firm, low voice. "Sir, I could sensationalize this story across news headlines tomorrow. But . . . " She paused for effect. "The developers will back off, cover their tracks, and get away with . . . Quokka murder."

The man smirked.

"Sir, I'm serious. These terrible, terrible, money-hungry swindlers, need to be brought to justice." Beth slapped the file. "And, your team can bring that victory."

Sergeant Andrews rocked back into his chair and gave her a golf-clap. "Nice speech, Miss Michaels." He chuckled. "Look, if we find some solid evidence and arrest someone, we will let you know so you'll have first dibs on the story. Have a press release drafted and ready to go. That's all I can offer you."

Beth's insides bubbled with excitement as she rose from her seat. "Sir, that's wonderful. I appreciate your co-operation."

He shook his head. She must appear like the try-hard-reporter nitwit she wanted to avoid.

Sergeant Andrews stood and leaned across his desk, offering his hand. "Thank you for coming forward with this information."

Beth gripped his hand in a firm, manly handshake. His large leathery hold dominated and swallowed her smaller one. Oh, well.

"Thank you, sir. Please, keep me informed. My card is in the folder."

He gave her an amused smile. "Will do."

CHAPTER EIGHT

LACHLAN SAT HUNCHED over on his bed, staring at the photo of Beth snuggled against his chest for the Quokka selfie. Her magnificent smile, magnetic eyes, and natural beauty caused a defeated sigh. She had him.

He studied his face in the picture too. He looked happy. That day on Rottnest Island was the best day he'd had in three years. Beth seemed uninhibited, free to speak her mind, funny, and although she wore modest clothing, the woman drove him crazy. How had he resisted kissing her with all the opportunity she'd given him? And to the point of Beth asking him to on their last day together. Gee. Talk about making it difficult for a guy.

Seven days had passed, and he'd willed himself not to contact her yet. He didn't want to stir up love before its time. If they communicated too much, it could make his stay on the ship unproductive. He'd be wanting another life—one he couldn't have right now.

Lachlan switched off his phone, stood, and stretched side to side. The gym would help work off the extra energy that Beth Michaels had created. An hour of exercise, followed by a shower, would have him collapse into bed, and sound asleep in no time.

* * *

Fourteen days and no word from Lachlan. Should she simply email the guy? Maybe tell him about the investigation, keep it formal, and start a conversation.

Beth crossed her legs at the ankles with her feet propped on the ottoman. The laptop grew hot, and its fan whirled in protest. She opened her email app and drafted a message to Lachlan.

Hello from down under,

I've been waiting for your email. You must be busy.

Delete, delete, delete. She corrected her posture and raised her chin.

Hi Lachlan,

Just letting you know, I saw the police investigator last week. I gave him your email address in case he needed more information from you. Have they been in contact?

Hope you're doing okay.

Beth.

Send.

Shuffled footsteps grew louder behind the sofa. Beth shut the laptop, placed it to the side, and looked over her shoulder.

"Hi, Melissa. You still up?"

Melissa scratched at her messy blonde hair and yawned. "I am now. Hannah wet the bed. She hasn't done that in a year. I hope it's a one-off."

"Do you need a hand with the sheets?"

"No, I've sorted everything. They're in the washing machine soaking." Melissa walked to the adjacent sofa and plonked herself down. "Why are you still up? Midnight's late, even for you."

Beth rubbed the back of her neck. "Couldn't sleep."

"Thinking about that Navy guy?" Melissa smirked.

She hesitated and glanced at the coffee table between them. "A little." More like twenty-four-seven.

"I'm surprised you fell for a sailor." Melissa tucked a leg under her knee. "You always seemed the sensible type. No-nonsense. And sailors have a bad reputation here. I remember my nightclubbing days and when they were in port. So sleazy."

Melissa didn't hold back. She always said what she thought, no filter.

"I surprised myself, Melissa." She wrapped her dressing gown tighter. "I didn't want to fall for an American sailor. But I'll get over it soon and return to my serious self."

"I'm glad I have a little girl to look after that keeps me out of trouble." Melissa pushed some loose strands away from her eyes. "Not many men want to take on someone else's kid. I'll be single for the next decade." She smiled wistfully. "I'm okay with that. Hannah is the best thing that's happened to me. Other than Jesus."

"You might meet a nice guy in church one day."

"You have a better chance at that, Beth. Forget about the sailor. Pray for God to bring someone to you. Someone available and ready to commit."

Beth sat straighter. "Melissa, that's the best advice I've heard about this situation. You're absolutely right." She placed her hands on the armrest and pushed herself up with determination. "I'll forget about Lachlan, starting now. I'm going to bed and will not give him another thought. Good night."

Melissa's blue eyes widened, then creases formed at the corners.

Beth strode to her room with her mind made up. Too bad that she'd sent the email already.

* * *

Lachlan's phone beeped at five-thirty a.m. Time to get up. He stretched to his bedside table and collected his cell. The bright light pierced his vision. Two more years of these early mornings. His eyes focused on an email notification—Beth Michaels. He bolted upright and clicked on the screen. Two weeks and she'd finally emailed him.

As he devoured each sentence, his posture deflated. Where was the "I miss you" line? Just a business email. Did nothing else matter to her? Only making it big by getting this news story?

He tapped the screen with rapid punches.

Hi Beth,

No, I haven't heard from them. I'll let you know if I do.

Yes, I'm doing good, thanks. I hope you are too.

Lachlan.

Take that, Bethany Michaels. He fell back on his bed and let his phone slip from his hand. It thudded the floor. That would teach him to avoid overseas attachments. Stupid, stupid, stupid. He needed coffee.

He rolled off his bed, changed into shorts and a t-shirt, and sprayed some deodorant under his arms. Room locked, he headed down the corridor.

Ten other guys were scattered throughout the gym. Lachlan gritted his teeth as he pushed hard against the chest press machine. Three years of vigorous workouts had packed on muscle. What would he look like in another two years? His folks wouldn't recognize him.

Mike hopped on the exercise bike next to him. "Hey, Chaplain. You've been here at least twice a day since we left Australia. Becomin' a gym junkie like me?"

Lachlan grunted as he pushed the extra weights he stacked on the machine. "Gotta keep busy. I have more time on my hands than the rest of you. And I'm not going to sit in my room, stuck on Facebook, like some." What had put him in such a foul mood?

"Wally told me about the pretty Aussie girl you met." The ginger-headed twenty-one-year-old pressed the start button on his machine. "Said every time he turned around, she was in your arms. You finally succumbed to our ways, Chaplain Peters?"

"Not likely." Lachlan held back a bark. Wally spreading rumors about him—he'd have words with him soon. "Beth's a church girl. She's not like that. And neither am I."

Mike shook his head. "I don't know how you do it. So much self-control."

"Working out helps. Lots of focus and determination. And good old-fashioned morals." Lachlan grunted as he pushed past a count of thirty. He let the weights smash back into place.

He got up and moved to the rowing machine, far away from Mike. He needed to snap out of his mood. A chaplain shouldn't act like this. When he'd been in a long-distance relationship with Laura, the first six months of phone calls and emails had only wasted his time. She met someone else back home. That'd probably happen with Beth. He'd continue to be polite and email her on occasion, but keep them strictly friends. No emotional talk, just surface conversation, and let Beth fade out of the picture.

CHAPTER NINE

Twenty-One Months Later

THE FREMANTLE HERALD office buzzed with activity. The scuttle of tapping keyboards mixed with the hum of multiple phone conversations as the editorial team raced to make the deadline. Beth peered over the cubicle divider. "I've finished my jobs. Do you need me to help with anything? I can hear you huffing and puffing from here."

Melanie smiled through the loose strands dangling over her shiny forehead, the rest of her hair in a tight ponytail. "Yes, please. I'm not going to make it otherwise."

"What do you need?"

"We have a small space left on page sixteen. Can you do a quick article for me?"

Beth blinked. "An article? In thirty minutes? You've really left things to the last minute. Why didn't you ask for help?"

"I had plans on what to write, and it's only two hundred words." She blew the wispy ringlets away from her face. "Time got away from me."

"Okay. What do I write about?" Any chance for an article was an opportunity Beth would take. Sub-copying had long fallen into drudgery.

"Just an announcement about the U.S Navy ship coming into port this weekend." Melanie handed over a yellow post-it sticky note. "Here's the name of the ship, and the basic schedule."

Beth took the paper between her forefinger and thumb, holding it out like it was covered in contagious germs. Melanie angled her screen and got back to work.

What was Beth's problem? Lachlan wouldn't be on board. She'd received one of his newsletter emails a few months ago. The one where she'd been blind carbon copied like the rest of his family and friends.

Beth lowered herself into the cushioned chair. Oh, Lachlan had proved to be such a disappointment. Just the thought of him stirred anger within her. She'd poured out her soul about losing the Quokka story, and his cold response had infuriated her. Some chaplain. No validation, no empathy for her. She ground her teeth.

She had explained in detail how the suspect developers diverted their interest into upgrading Christmas Island instead. The health of the Quokkas had improved dramatically since the investigation started. The link seemed obvious to her. Pacific Master Builders must've realized they were being observed and focused on other developments.

Lachlan had responded with one line. One. Line. *At least the Quokkas are okay.*

She growled under her breath as she tapped her keyboard to wake her computer.

Of course, she wanted the Quokkas safe. What did he take her for? Did he think she was just about getting a big story? Becoming a famous journalist? Ridiculous. Readers hardly glanced at the author's name. She had only wanted to report important news that exposed the truth. Those developers should have been brought to justice. Over four hundred Quokkas had died. The possibility that Sergeant Andrews had taken a bribe still irked her. Why else would he drop the case so easily? No evidence, he'd said. Unlikely.

She pounded Lachlan's name into her email search bar. Where was he now? Nowhere near Australia, but she wanted to double-check.

For a year, she received an occasional email from him. Usually monthly, with a few questions pertaining to how she was, how the church was doing. Chris's family. Her work. He had nothing much to say. Maybe his job didn't allow for much detail. As a chaplain, he wouldn't share counseling information, and the Navy might require him to keep things vague as far as their location and projects.

Beth scrolled through the list of emails from Lachlan. The second year of their communication, he'd converted to a general newsletter. She had still replied with some chit-chat of what was happening in her part of the world, but usually, he responded with no more than two sentences. The last email was dated several months ago. It didn't state his whereabouts. Anyway, what did she care? Her heart had kept Lachlan Peters at bay, far away, so he couldn't disappoint her.

Beth read the sticky note. *USS Independence II arriving Saturday. Two weeks in Fremantle. Four weeks at Exmouth Naval Base for training.*

She googled for more information and gave the article her best effort. Once it left her workstation, it would go to press.

* * *

On Sunday, Beth placed a visitor information card on every third seat while the musicians shuffled around the stage. The guitarist tuned his strings, the singers warmed their voices, and the drummer fooled around with some beats. It sounded like a secular song she'd heard on the radio. A good thing Dad was upstairs in the prayer room. If he knew Asha was playing a heathen song in the house of the Lord, oh, there would be hell to pay.

By nine forty-five members filled half the seats. Beth greeted familiar faces at the entrance to the sanctuary.

"Hello, Mrs. Morrison. Those colors look great on you. I like your necklace. Nice match." Beth shook the older woman's frail hand. White pigeon wings fluffed at her temples, softening her crowning tight perm. The dear lady had made a great effort to appear in her Sunday's best.

"And so do you, dear. It's nice to see a young woman still wearing dresses these days. A rare sight, indeed." Her pink, painted lips lifted in a smile.

"Thank you." Beth rubbed her shoulder. Such a sweet old lady. And the children loved how she handed out lollipops after service each week.

Nigel and Issy came in next, holding hands as newlyweds. Issabel's face glowed. Was she pregnant already? She said at thirty-six, she didn't want to wait long.

"Hey, you two." Beth shook Nigel's hand and gave Issy a gentle hug.

Next came three newcomers. All of the men had the same haircut, short back and sides, one-inch wedge at the front. Sailors. Ugh.

Beth pasted on a smile, cringing on the inside. She shouldn't be quick to judge. They were here to worship, not pick up a woman. The pubs would be better for that.

The first man nodded and shook her hand in both of his palms. "Good morning, ma'am." He had a strong American accent, and although they weren't in uniform, she had no doubt they were from the *USS Independence II*.

"Welcome."

The second sailor, likely in his early twenties, flashed straight teeth and bounced on his toes.

"G'day, sheila," he winked.

Beth's eyes widened, and she nearly choked. Seriously? "Hi."

He laughed. "Just wanted to say that, pretend I'm one of the locals. Sorry, ma'am."

"We don't talk like that in the cities. Maybe some do in the outback, but not here. Have a good service, sir."

His face turned pink.

Lastly, a tall man with a medium build, perhaps a little older than her, stepped through the double doorway. "Good morning, ma'am. Don't mind him, it's his first time out of the States." He took Beth's hand and shook it slowly. "I'm Nick. Thank you for having us today." His smile seemed genuine.

"You're welcome. There's a visitor's lounge in the back foyer. We'd love to host you after the service with some cakes and coffee."

"Sounds great. Thank you." He squeezed her hand and made his way to the left section, the second row from the front.

Beth continued to greet congregation members, but her mind had drifted to the sailors. She would avoid the visitor's lounge if she could. Dad could do the socializing today. She'd find some excuse to keep busy or get Mrs. Morrison talking.

* * *

After the service, Beth managed to float around the room, chatting with the people she'd known since she was a little girl. Her people. She kept herself from Dad's line of sight to avoid having to entertain the sailors. She shivered.

With car keys in her hand, she lingered at the front foyer, packing away the brochures about upcoming events and Bible study groups.

"There you are." Dad strode over.

"Dad." She feigned a smile.

"The Americans are coming to my place for lunch. Can you grab four barbeque chickens and roast meals from Chicken Treat on the way over? Salad bowls too. They probably eat a lot."

"Really? I wanted to have the afternoon to relax. Can you order home delivery?"

Dad's brows furrowed. "Bethany Michaels, you're the Assistant Pastor. We always fellowship with newcomers after service if they're open to it."

"They'd be better off sightseeing in Fremantle. Did you invite them over? They may feel obliged."

Dad adjusted his tie. "The one called Nick suggested lunch. He wants to have prayer time with us after."

"Okay. But I'll leave straight after that." Beth switched off the photocopier behind her and collected her phone. "Who else is coming?"

"I've had little time to organize anything, so it's just the five of us."

"All right. I'll get the food and see you soon."

* * *

Beth stood behind the black granite counter and plated the chicken pieces onto five plates. The crispy skin smelled delicious. Still, she peeled it back from her drumstick. Extra fat she didn't need. But she couldn't resist the chips and popped one into her mouth. Nick flashed a grin her way. Caught.

In the dining room, Dad, Nick, and two younger sailors chatted with enthusiasm around the table. Nick seemed to dominate the conversation with his animated stories of the God encounters they'd had in the last few months.

"I woke up from the dream, dripping with sweat. I wrote all the vivid details." He opened his palms. "A map of the world rolled out before me. Next, a golden jug appeared, and a transparent liquid poured over Jerusalem first, then spread to cover the whole surface of the map. Then, from the four corners, the scroll rolled onto itself until it disappeared, and I woke."

"Wow," Dad said. "And that happened in the early church, Acts chapter two. An outpouring of the Holy Spirit started in Jerusalem and spread with the Good News across the globe."

"Yes." Nick clapped his hands. "But it's also a prophecy for today. I believe a great move of the Spirit will start in Jerusalem. Soon. And it will be the beginning of the end times."

Beth spooned portions of coleslaw and chips as she listened to the men discuss Scripture relating to the end times. Dad was in his element, and it seemed he'd found a kindred spirit in Nick.

She moved around the counter and placed two plates at a time on the Tasmanian Oak table. Each person acknowledged her with thanks, but when she gave one to Nick, he paused and met her eyes. "Thank you, Beth. You're a blessing. Thanks for hosting us today."

"You're welcome." Her earlobes heated from the attention he gave her.

She sat in the empty chair opposite Nick and next to Dad.

"Lord, thank You for this food and fellowship. Lead us in our conversations this day. Amen." Dad opened his eyes and then tucked into his food.

"Beth." Nick smiled in her direction. "Have you ever wanted to go to Jerusalem? To see where Jesus once walked?"

Shredded carrot lodged in her throat. She took a sip of water as all eyes directed to her. "I haven't traveled out of Australia yet. It would be amazing to visit another culture. Exploring the Holy Land could deepen my perspective of the Scriptures."

Dad lifted his brow. "I didn't know you had the desire to visit Israel, Beth."

"I haven't given it much thought. Our lifestyle hasn't allowed for such plans."

Dad placed his hands in his lap. "But now all the children are grown, the church has a stable team structure, you'd be free to travel."

Wow, this was the first time she'd heard Dad say anything of the sort. To have his blessing and encouragement to leave the nest entirely? Her belly fluttered. The possibilities.

Nick swallowed his food and patted the corners of his mouth with a serviette. "I've sought the Lord for when He will release me to go to Israel. I've decided to leave the Navy and pursue ministry. This will be my last voyage. After a total of six weeks in Australia, we head home. I'll settle my things in Los Angeles, visit my pastor there, and ask for his blessing and support as I go."

Nick turned to Dad. "I would appreciate it, if you would ask for God's favor upon me in our prayer time. That doors will be open to minister in Jerusalem."

"Gladly." Dad nodded.

After lunch, they moved to the family room. Dad turned on the worship music, and all five of them stood in a circle.

Nick positioned himself next to Beth, which didn't surprise her at all. He'd seemed drawn to her and often directed questions her way during lunch.

Each person prayed, one at a time. Nick began and seemed to lead the way. At the end, he asked everyone to hold hands in agreement with a final prayer. This didn't surprise her, either. His warm, steady hand engulfed hers. She didn't feel tingles or any attraction, but it was nice to hold hands with Nick. Perhaps the peace filling her came from connecting with a person who appreciated her spirituality. She didn't feel any connection with the other guy next to her.

Nick closed in prayer, then they all opened their eyes. He held onto her hand a little longer than necessary. She bit back a smile. Beth couldn't deny the ego boost of having a man like Nick appreciate her.

They all meandered to the door, and just before they left, Nick turned to her. "Would you do us the pleasure of showing us around town tomorrow? It would be nice to have a local take us to the popular spots. Are you free at noon or after work tomorrow?"

She gave a shy smile. "I can take the morning off. My work's flexible, and I have some hours owed to me."

Dad looked at her with an inquisitive eye and grinned. Usually, he became overprotective of her when it came to men. But obviously, Nick had gained his favor.

"Even better. Can you meet me at the coffee stand opposite the port? It's in the parking lot there."

Had he said, "me"? Weren't the others coming?

Beth fiddled with her necklace. "Sure. Nine o'clock."

His grin reached his captivating green eyes. "Perfect."

CHAPTER TEN

THE WIND WHIPPED around Beth's face as she squinted from the bright morning sun. Her aqua floral top flapped as gusts of air swirled around her. She held down the wrap-around skirt so as not to expose her legs. Where was Nick?

The green industrial shed converted into a café stand had several tourists milling about. Most of them wore comfortable shorts and t-shirts. One middle-aged lady had a money purse strapped around her waist. Beth strolled toward the line, drawn by the scent of Italian brewed coffee.

Hands slipped around her eyes. "Guess who?"

She flinched and turned into Nick. Hot flushes zoomed from her toes to her cheeks. "Hi." Beth blinked repetitively. This guy was bold.

He laughed. "I couldn't resist sneaking up on you. I'm in a silly mood today. It's so great to get off that ship." He spun, scanned his surroundings, and took a deep breath. "Australia is a beautiful country." Nick turned toward Beth, and his pupils enlarged as he focused on her. "And what a pleasure it is to have a sweet young lady as my tour guide. I'm a blessed man."

She smothered a giggle. His enthusiasm was contagious. "I'm not that young, you know."

"Thirty-three years old. Your dad told me all about you at church. Gave me a long list of your accomplishments and talents. Is he trying to marry you off or something?"

Heat flushed her cheeks. "Usually, he beats the men off with a stick." She laughed. "Not many, but any that dare approach me. I'm surprised by his behavior lately. But, don't worry, I'm a woman with my own mind." Beth smoothed her hair back from her face. "Where are your Navy buddies?"

"They had other commitments. Anyway, I'd much prefer spending time getting to know you and this gorgeous city you live in."

"Are all sailors smooth talkers?" She placed a hand on her hip.

He chuckled. "I'm barely a sailor. I've only been with the Navy for six months. It's not the lifestyle for me. I see it as an extended mission trip, sharing the gospel with any men willing to listen. I'm ready to move onto greater things." Nick winked. "Starting today, where are you taking me, lovely Beth?"

She shook her head and grinned. "The Maritime Museum is on the way to the café strip." Beth pointed to the artistic-shaped building in the distance. From where they stood, it appeared similar in style to the Sydney Opera House. "How about we have a look through, get a bite to eat in town, then head to the Fremantle Markets? Then, if you're keen, we can catch a train to Perth City and visit Kings Park."

"I'm keen." He rubbed his hands together.

It was evident he was keen as beans.

Once inside the museum, Beth strolled, gazing toward the high ceiling where the *Australia II* yacht hung above. "Agh. There's the secret keel underneath that helped us win the America's Cup in 1983."

"Oh, so long ago, dear Beth. Who really remembers these things?" He smiled.

"The Aussies do." She tsk-tsked.

They moved across to another display with a giant copper whale, showing the size comparison to a dingy.

Nick handed her his phone. "Can you take a photo of me next to the whale?"

"Sure." She took the cell and moved back to frame as much as she could of the whale. Although he must be around six-foot, Nick seemed small in comparison. He froze in a funny pose, with his mouth and eyes wide open, scared of the creature coming for him.

Beth held back a giggle. This guy loved to clown around, and she didn't mind. His lack of inhibitions was refreshing, and she enjoyed his company.

Later, when they walked down South Terrace, they spoke loud over the traffic and noise about them. Nick kept asking questions, wanting to know her dreams and future plans.

"I once wanted to make it in journalism, but I've had no breaks in the industry. I work for a small paper, and the other reporters get assigned the exciting stories. I'm mainly an editor." She swished a fly from her face. "I nearly got a big story, but in the end, the facts didn't line up, and I wasted a lot of my time." Lachlan's image flashed in her mind. "And emotional energy." She flicked the irritation away like she had the fly. She'd enjoy Nick's company. Uncommitted to the Navy, unlike Lachlan had,

Nick held a different appeal. By his questions, she could tell he wanted to know if their direction in life could align. Nick's outlook promised adventure, and she tried not to get ahead of herself, but the possibility of traveling the world, serving in ministry, excited her.

At Pizza Bella Roma, they shared Bruschetta and a Caesar Salad. With full stomachs, they continued to the markets. When they passed the Sail and Anchor, a wolf whistle came from the top balcony. Nick waved at his Navy colleagues. Then touched Beth's elbow and urged her to quicken her pace.

"Sorry about that," he whispered into her ear.

"Don't be. I'm used to the sailors coming into town. I just ignore it."

"I'm not like them. I promise." This was the first time she'd seen him somber.

On the corner stood the Markets' historic red-bricked building. Emerald lamp posts graced the entrance on either side. Inside, the scent of incense mixed with musk wafted in the air as they passed the first stall.

Compact mini shops crowded the lane. In the middle, the gray painted concrete floor had red footprints showing the way to go. Industrial fans whirled above on posts, with fluorescent beams hanging from the raked ceilings lined with aluminum insulation.

An acoustic guitar played in the distance along with a Gaelic melody—buskers, no doubt. Sale signs boasted of bargains on natural products, souvenirs, jewelry, bakery goods, and down the other end, fruit and vegetables.

Nick approached the tarot card reader and stood before him. "I can tell the future too, and I won't charge you any money."

The stallholder scrunched his brows.

Nick sat on the chair opposite him. "When you become very unwell, you will go to a man of God in this city. He will pray over you, and you'll be delivered and healed. But you will not go back to this magic. Realize how your soul was overcome and evil penetrated into your physical ailments."

Nick stood. "Know this, there are no good spirits, and you don't get to choose which ones to listen to. They are all evil. Accept Christ and trust the only true one, God's Holy Spirit. He will lead you into all truth."

The man stared with his mouth ajar. Nick nodded goodbye and moved on. Beth scurried after him, and when she caught up, linked her arm with his. "You were amazing back there. Bold."

"I had to say something. I feel sorry for the man. So deceived."

She admired Nick's expression, lined with concern. "You have a good heart."

Their eyes met, and he smiled. "As do you. That's why we get along so well." He patted her arm.

He led her to a Pandora store. With his hand on her lower back, he bent over the glass cabinet before them, displaying tiny trinkets. "Do you have a Pandora bracelet?"

"No." She studied the selection.

"They're nice for collecting charms around the world as a memento of where you've been. Can I buy you one?"

Aware of the price, the reason she didn't have Pandora in the first place, she hesitated. "That's okay. You don't need to do that."

"I want to, Beth. As a thank you for taking me out today." He collected her wrist. "Silver would suit your skin." His thumb brushed her hand as he placed it onto the glass. "And lookie here." He pointed. "An anchor charm. I'll buy that as our first memory together."

Her heart pounded in her chest. Did she hear that correctly?

A saleswoman in a blue pencil skirt approached and offered her assistance. Nick ordered the items while Beth remained erect like a stunned emu. Then her knees became weak, unable to believe this confident man beside her wanted a future together. Had God spoken to him already? The way he'd shared revelations to her father, it seemed he had a close relationship with the Lord. She wished she could hear God's voice as easily as Nick did.

"No need for the packaging." Nick tucked the receipt into his back pocket, then took the bracelet from the woman. He turned to Beth with a satisfied grin, holding the unclasped bangle for her to thread her hand through.

"Thank you, Nick. You're so thoughtful." She inserted her hand, and he fixed the clamp into place around her wrist.

He collected her hand and placed a kiss on top. "You're welcome."

Nick placed his warm palm on her lower back and kept it there as they continued to walk around the markets. Were they a couple now? They sure acted like one, laughing, eye gazing, walking hip to hip as if they were in love.

After a long time in the markets, Beth glanced at her phone when they stepped into the sunshine outside. One o'clock.

"I need to get back to work." She shrugged. "Sorry."

"That's okay. Let's go to Kings Park on the weekend."

"Sounds good."

"And how about dinner tonight? Are you free?"

She blinked. "It's my niece's birthday. The family is getting together for cake."

He gave a playful frown.

"Why don't you come and meet the rest of my family? Did Dad introduce you to any of them at church? Not all of them go to New Life."

"No, I haven't met them. I'd love to come. Can you meet me up at the port again?"

"Sure. Six-thirty?"

"I look forward to it." He leaned down and kissed her cheek. "I'll call Carl and hang out with him until then. You have a great day at the office."

She floated away and headed toward *The Fremantle Herald*. A contented sigh left her lips. Wow. She hadn't dated anyone in years and started to doubt she'd meet someone with the same standards—and one who pursued her. Most of the single guys she knew weren't interested in serving in ministry or compromised their faith in some way. She wanted to be with someone who shared the same convictions. Were her single days nearly behind her?

* * *

On the way to her sister's house, Beth gave Nick the rundown of the family dynamics. "Amy's married to Brett with one child, Talicia. It's her fifth birthday." She maneuvered through a roundabout, as the streetlamps flickered into the car's cabin. "Trudy's engaged to Michael. And Shanae is dating Phil, a Baptist guy. He won't be coming, as Dad hasn't warmed to the idea yet. She goes to Phil's church. Dad hasn't said so, but it irks him."

"Sheep stealing?" Nick laughed.

"That's part of it, I'm sure." She flicked the indicator on and turned into Amy's street. "My two younger brothers, Simon and Jacob, are single. They may or may not be there tonight."

"That's a big family. I'm not sure if I'll remember all the names." He sat upright. "I'm an only child. My mom was probably turned off having any more kids after she had a demanding toddler. Apparently, I was a handful."

"That's not hard to imagine." Beth gave a cheeky smile. "You love to muck around. Are you sure you're thirty-eight?"

"When I wanna be."

They parked in the dim driveway. "Well, brace yourself. Our family is loud."

Standing on the doormat, Beth tightened her hold on Talicia's present. Nick's hand touched her elbow as they waited for someone to greet them.

"Um, Nick. For tonight, it's best if we don't . . . touch each other." She offered a small smile. "Let Dad get to know you a little more first."

He chuckled and jumped back with his hands raised in surrender. "Yes, ma'am." He swung his hands behind his back. "Six-inch rule."

"Is that a thing in America too? It's a bit of a joke in our church circles, but Dad agrees with it."

"The rule goes way back, but no one follows it these days. I'll be on my best behavior tonight. Your Dad loves me, practically offered me dowry money."

She slapped his shoulder. "He did not." She playfully scolded Nick. "You'll keep." Where had she heard that saying before?

The door opened with a gush of sibling love. "Beth!" Amy hugged her tight. "Talicia has been waiting for you. Thinks you've bought her a unicorn. You haven't, have you? Dad would have a fit." Amy glanced at Nick. "And who's this? I didn't know you had a date?"

"Nick, this is Amy. See. My family is loud, and they speak whatever comes to their mind. No filter."

Nick laughed and shook Amy's hand.

Amy pulled him into a hug. "We're huggers in this family. Welcome. Come in."

As they entered, a waft of cinnamon and chocolate floated about them making Beth's mouth water.

Squeals of delight came from the living room. "I always wanted a Peppa Pig house. Thanks, Uncle Simon. You're the best."

"Aye." This from Jacob. "You haven't opened my gift yet."

Her sisters all laughed. When Beth poked her head around the corner with Nick on her tail, the room fell silent for a moment.

"Aunty Beth. You're finally here." Talicia stared at the present and put her hand out.

Everyone laughed again.

Dad stood. "Nick, how are you, son?" He walked over and offered a hand.

Son? Nick was right. Dad was trying to marry her off.

Trudy and Michael looked at each other with question in their eyes. Simon and Jacob stood as Dad did the introductions around the room.

Beth kneeled and gave Talicia a hug. "Happy Birthday, sweetheart. Let's sit on the rug so you can open your present." Beth led her to the center of the room, placed the gift on the floor, and sat in a single seated sofa chair. Nick sat in the one next to hers.

All eyes toward little Talicia, as the precious girl picked at the paper and peeled it back slowly. Her eyes lit up, and her mouth formed an O. "Aunty Beth! You're the best."

More chuckles filled the room as Talicia lifted the lifelike doll in the air.

"She looks like me!" Talicia swung the doll in front of her grandfather's face.

Beth smiled, glad her niece could notice the resemblance in the blonde hair and green-eyed doll. Talicia ran to her and jumped in her arms, then wriggled onto her lap with her gift in hand. She peeked over to Nick and whispered in Beth's ear. "Who's he? Is that my new uncle?"

Beth flushed, hoping no one heard, but even Talicia's whispers were loud. She'd asked the question that seemed to be on everyone's faces.

Beth tucked some hair behind Talicia's ear and whispered, "He's a friend."

Her niece sat upright, her eyes big. "Ohh."

Nick placed his hand on Beth's chair, and looked at Talicia with a smile. "Maybe one day, I'll become her very special friend."

"Good. Because I want a cousin."

Beth smothered a laugh into Talicia's neck, the heat in Beth's cheeks intense. She dared not look around the room, but the giggles told her that everyone was having a good time at her expense. Nick! She'd throttle him after.

Soon, the family settled into easy conversation. Talicia sat on the rug playing with her new toys. Dad, her brothers, and Nick chatted away. Nick had them laughing on several occasions.

Beth joined Amy in the kitchen to help her make teas and coffees. The cappuccino machine gurgled as it heated.

"Beth, I like your new *friend*. How come you didn't tell me?" One brow rose.

"Tell you what? I've only been out with him twice."

"He's keen. You look like you've been dating for a while. Comfortable with each other."

"Okay. I admit it. It's all happening pretty fast." Beth bounced on her runners and held out her wrist. "Nick bought me this bangle today. He's so sweet."

"It's gorgeous." Amy played with the hanging anchor charm. "How long is he in town?"

"Two weeks, then he'll be a twelve-hour drive away. Exmouth. Four weeks."

"Are you going to follow him and stay up there?"

Beth gasped. "What would Dad say?"

"It's your life, Beth. You won't do the wrong thing, anyway. I know you."

"He's staying at the Navy barracks there. I could take holidays and rent a caravan." She touched her neck. "I can't believe I'm considering this. I'll see if he asks me first. If he does, I'll take it as a sign."

Amy jiggled a tea bag in a floral cup. "Oh, he'll ask you, all right. Nick's besotted by you."

Beth nodded. "He is."

CHAPTER ELEVEN

LACHLAN HAULED HIS heavy duffle bag onto his shoulder and shut the Uber car's trunk.

"Thanks, man," he called to the driver, who waved from his driver's window. The Toyota zoomed away, leaving him in gasoline fumes.

He faced his parents' house. The living room's light glowed through the lace curtains. Home. He adjusted his strap. Well, for tonight, it would be. He wanted to see family on his first day back, not arrive at his empty bachelor pad.

Sprinkles of rain touched his cheek. He clamped his jacket collar closed as he strode toward the front door. He hoped Mom had heated the spare room.

He pressed the doorbell, then ran his fingers over the familiar wooden door, well-worn over the years. He stood back and faced the peephole, waiting to hear Mom's squeal.

"It's Lachie." Muffled words from the other side.

Yes. Open the door. Freezing out here.

The door flung wide. "My baby. Come in, come in." Mom grabbed his sleeve and yanked him inside.

As the door closed behind him, his bag fell with a thud as he wrapped his arms around his little mother. "Missed you." His voice rattled with emotion.

"Son." Dad embraced him next. The human contact refreshed his soul like drinking a gallon of water after months in a lonely desert.

Dad squeezed his bicep. "Your guns are loaded. Man, you got big."

Lachlan chuckled, wiping away an escaped tear.

"Let's sit in the dining room." Mom pointed down the hallway. "I have some of your favorite chicken noodle soup warming on the stove. Have you eaten?"

"Not yet." He tapped his belly. "Saving room for my mamma's cooking. The ship's food isn't bad, but nothing compares to your recipes."

She pinched his cheek and grinned. "You'll keep." Mom always said that.

Once they settled around the ten-seater walnut table, Lachlan dug into the soup as his parents told him the latest family news. The warm liquid soothed his throat, along with the familiar voices that relaxed him.

"Mark's flooded with work. So, if you need a job in the interim, he could do with a laborer."

"I'll keep that in mind." He didn't want to do bathroom renovations, but if he didn't find work in the first week with his qualifications, he could help his brother for a while.

Mom placed her hand on the table and leaned forward. "And Kayce's dating again. She's met a nice fellow. A young widower with two children."

"Wow. Instant Brady Bunch. That's big news." He took another sip of his soup.

Dad gave a wry grin. "Sorry to say, Lachlan. Not many singles at our church now. Everyone's engaged or married off since you left." He peered over his thin-framed spectacles. "Did you meet anyone overseas?"

Lachlan gulped hard and glanced from his bowl, the condensation warming his chin. "No." A pair of blue vivid eyes flashed in his mind. He sat straighter. "I wanted to wait until I finished with the Navy. Less complicated that way."

"Well, there's always online dating. That's how Kayce met Daniel."

"Really? That's good for her." He'd prefer God to bring his Eve. Hopefully, he wouldn't need internet dating. Sounded scary.

Dad continued to chat about Kayce and Daniel, but Lachlan's mind wandered back to Beth. How did life pan out for her? The image of Beth looking up at him with innocent eyes, almost vulnerable at times, remained in his head. If she'd met someone, he hoped the guy would treat her well, love her like she deserved.

An upstanding woman like Beth would be his benchmark. If he could meet an American version of Bethany Michaels, he'd be a happy man.

That night, as Lachlan stared toward the ceiling in the dark, he contemplated the conversations he'd had. Life in San Diego seemed to move on well enough without him here. He adjusted his position on the memory foam mattress. The bed was super comfortable compared to what he'd been used to in the last few years. Why couldn't he just fall asleep? Many sailors found civilian life strange for a while. He'd need to keep himself busy and establish a new routine. He'd get up early and exercise first thing. That seemed to clear his mind and help him focus for the day. That and morning prayer.

"God, what's my life about?" he whispered into the chilly night. "Am I meant to stay in San Diego? I've been gone for so long. I don't know if I belong here anymore."

He closed his eyes and waited for an answer. But he knew one wouldn't come. He didn't hear God that easily. Usually, it was a knowing within that guided him—a peace when making decisions. There were no decisions to make right now. He'd take one day at a time and wait to see what doors opened.

* * *

The next day, back at his own place, Lachlan crouched low, and pulled the weeds from his garden bed. It was a monotonous job, but he needed to keep occupied, and the front lawn and hedges needed trimming next. Mark must've been too busy. The tenant moved out four weeks ago, and the house smelled stale from being locked up for a month. The people before must've liked curry or something. There was an unusual smell, and it wasn't his. He smiled at himself.

The next-door neighbor's garage squeaked as it opened. Lachlan stood with a crack from his back and brushed the dirt from his hands. A blue Lexus reversed over the brick-paved driveway, then the car braked when Arnold noticed Lachlan. His neighbor switched off the engine, got out, and strode across his lawn. Lachlan greeted him over the half-fence.

"Buddy, you're back." Arnold gripped his hand in some kind of cool handshake, then they bumped shoulders.

"Returned last night. It's good to be home." Was that a lie? It was great to be off the ship, that was true.

"Thought you had a couple more months left?"

"When the ship needed to dock on the West Coast for supplies, my team captain suggested I skip the last few months since the last bit of training didn't involve me." He shrugged. "So we started the discharge process." Lachlan had joined in extra, non-required training to build friendships with the men, but felt at peace that he'd reached out enough over the years. It was time for a new season.

Lachlan rubbed his hand over his two-day stubble. "How's Marnie and the kids?"

Arnold's eyes lit up. "Great. Really good."

Lachlan looked Arnold up and down. "You've lost weight. A lot. Have you been taking your meds?"

Arnold chuckled. "Yes. Don't worry. There's no way I'd risk losing everything I've recovered these eight years. I changed prescriptions last year. A new drug, slow-release. No food cravings or slow metabolism. I lost forty pounds in the first three months."

"Whoa. Dude, that's awesome." He was so happy for Arnold. The guy deserved a normal life. Eight years ago, his manic episode had him in the hospital for two months and unable to work for the rest of that year. Lachlan had awoken when he'd heard all the commotion from next-door. Then Marnie had rushed over, at one in the morning, and asked for assistance to get Arnold to the mental health unit. Not much made sense to Arnold at the time, but thankfully he'd trusted Lachlan enough to get in the car.

"Yep, work is good. Promoted to senior manager. The pay is enough that Marnie's cut her hours to part-time."

"Your girls must've grown. What level are they in now?"

"Nineth and tenth grade."

"I can't believe Annie is a Sophomore student. Man, the time has gone fast."

Arnold crossed his arms. "What about you? You must have some stories to tell."

"I do. The emergency relief projects were life changing. Such a privilege to be a part of rebuilding communities. I'll never be the same. It's hard to come back here and settle. I'm ruined for normal."

"That's what it was like when I had the manic episode. My brain got so high that it was hard to return to normal. My doctor says that's why a lot of patients don't stay on their meds. But the low isn't worth the high." He shook his head. "Or wrecking the family life. I just had to get used to a new way of life."

"Well, I'm glad you've stuck to your regime and the check-ups." He stood back and lifted his palms. "Look at you now, no one would ever know you have Bipolar. You're a walking testimony."

"Thanks, man. It hasn't been easy, but it's as good as it's gonna get, and I'm a happy husband and dad. Life's good."

"It is. Even I need a reminder now and then."

CHAPTER TWELVE

BETH WAITED AT Pizza Bella Roma for Nick to join her for dinner. She scrolled through their recent messages and reread the beautiful words he'd sent yesterday. *I'm adrift in the ocean of new love. You are my God-given gift from above.*

They spent every spare hour they could together—a morning stroll, her lunch break, dinner, and the weekend. Tomorrow was his last day in Fremantle. She'd miss him—unless?

Nick waved through the window before slipping inside. Before he sat, he kissed her on the top of her head. "How's my girl?"

"I'm well. Not much has changed since lunchtime." She smiled.

"Maybe you need some more excitement in your life." Nick winked and picked up the menu. "Have you ordered for us yet?"

"Garlic bread for starters."

"Good. And I feel like some greasy pizza."

Beth scrunched her face. "Ew. Sounds gross. I'll have the grilled field mushrooms with a Greek salad."

"Mmm. That almost sounds yummy—if you're a vegetarian."

A waitress placed a large pizza between a couple on the next table, then came over and served garlic bread to them. The mix of garlic and herbs rose to her nostrils.

"You look hungry, Beth. I'll pray, and you can go for it." He held her hand and closed his eyes. "Bless this food to our bodies and be with us this evening. We commit our future into your hands, Lord. Amen."

Her lashes fluttered open to meet Nick's intense gaze. Something significant would happen tonight. "Amen."

Beth tore a piece of crispy bread and let the flavors ignite her taste buds. "Mmm."

"I'll go to the counter and order our mains."

She covered her mouth and nodded.

When he returned, she offered him the remaining garlic bread.

"No, I'm good. The ground meat pizza will fill me up to overflowing." He reached over and brushed some crumbs from the corner of her mouth.

They hadn't kissed yet, would tonight be the night?

Nick placed his hands under the table and leaned his chest against the edge. "I've made some contacts in Israel. Messianic Jews. I've booked a video conference call for next week."

"That's wonderful, Nick. It's all starting to unfold for you."

He returned his hands to the table and held hers. "What about you? Do you want to come to Jerusalem with me one day?"

Beth tried to suppress the shock. Nick had missed a couple of steps that needed to happen before they go on overseas trips together. Like courting and a proposal. A wedding ceremony and honeymoon.

"What do you mean by 'one day,' exactly?" Her voice remained soft.

"I've got four weeks in Exmouth, and then I'm free. Whenever the Lord says go, I'll go."

The waitress approached with their meals, and for the next ten minutes, they ate in near silence. But Beth's mind wasn't quiet—it whirled with questions. Unanswered ones.

Nick touched her hand. "Are you feeling okay?"

She blinked. "Oh. Sure. I'm fine."

"Good." He grinned and patted her hand. "Beth, I've had an amazing two weeks here. Every minute has been fun, and I love spending time with you. Are you able to visit me in Exmouth? I know it's a long drive, so I'm happy to pay for your flights." He held both of her hands and gave his puppy-eyed plea that he was so good at. "Can you get time off work or come for a weekend?" He tilted his head. "I'll pay for your accommodation and visit you between training schedules. We'll do touristy things. Have a blast."

A slow grin tickled her cheeks. "I thought you'd never ask. I hoped you would."

He kissed her hand. "You've made me a happy man."

"You're always happy."

"That's because I have the Lord, and now you in my life." Nick leaned back and circled his belly with his palm. "Shall we go for a walk around town? I need to walk this off." He patted his stomach. "Full as a bull."

"Sure." She smiled, tidied up her side of the table, and dropped a crumpled napkin on her plate.

Outside, the warm breeze fingered her long hair. Nick wrapped his arm around Beth's waist as they walked through the Esplanade park. The tips of the pine trees swayed side to side, and beyond the full moon, the stars shaped into the Southern Cross.

They passed a colorful playground, and to the left, there was a well-lit skatepark, empty of people. To the back of the oval, a massive Ferris wheel towered with blinking lights.

Nick pointed. "Hon, let's go on the Ferris wheel."

The ticket lady offered to take photos first. Beth wasn't keen, but Nick insisted. He kissed her cheek as the camera flashed.

He helped her into the steel carriage. Nick hopped in and sat opposite her, then the ride operator shut their gate, and secured the bolts. The man pulled down a lever, and their carriage swung to the next level so that another couple could join the ride. Five minutes later, they were two-thirds to the top.

Nick gave a cheeky grin and used his weight to rock the carriage.

"Stop it, you." She slapped his knee.

He feigned a pout but stopped his child's play. The wind was enough to add movement.

Next, circus music increased in volume, and the Ferris wheel moved at a steady pace. Beth's belly fluttered as the carriage climbed the peak, and she gazed at the miniature playground below. Nick touched her leg, and she flinched.

She placed her hand on his and met his gaze. "It's higher than I realized."

"You look beautiful tonight." He moved across and sat next to her, still holding her right hand. He tucked the floating strands of hair behind her ear. Then stroked her cheek with a finger. "I'm sorry if I surprised you at the restaurant by asking you to come with me to Jerusalem."

"That's okay," she whispered into the night air.

"I just got ahead of myself." He shook his head.

Their carriage passed the base, and Nick nodded a hello to the operator. They began their climb again, but as they approached the top, the machine slowed until they stopped at the peak. Beth peered out the side. Perhaps they give each couple a turn at staying on the top. When she turned back to Nick, he was on one knee. Her eyes widened.

He gave an adorable smile, his eyes sparkling from the lights surrounding them.

"Bethany Michaels, you have stolen my heart. I believe my coming to Australia was no accident. We were destined to meet and meant for each other." He held one of her hands, and in his other was a huge diamond rock.

She gasped, "Nick." She covered her mouth with her free hand. Tears formed at the corners of her eyes.

"Will you do me the honor of becoming my wife?"

"Oh, my goodness." She touched her throat. "Yes! I'd love to be your wife." Trickles ran down one cheek.

He slipped on the ring, and in one swish move, sat next to her, brushed her tears away, cupped her cheek, and kissed her tender and slow.

When Nick pulled back, he smiled the widest smile she'd seen on him. He leaned to the edge of the carriage and gave the thumbs up to the man below.

"You planned all this?"

"Of course. I wrecked the mood at Pizza Bella Roma, but you forgave me."

She tilted her head back with a laugh. "I did have a moment of disappointment, but I should've known better." Beth held out the ring and let the light catch all the fine angles. "Nick, this is beautiful." It must've cost a small fortune.

"By the way, we have your dad's blessing."

She startled. "You asked Dad first?"

"We're old enough to decide ourselves, but I knew he would appreciate the respect. I can tell he's big on tradition."

"Oh, Nick, that's so sweet of you to honor him like that. Thank you." She snuggled into his side and breathed in his delicious scent. With the security of his arm around her shoulder, the view from here just got a whole lot better.

CHAPTER THIRTEEN

NICK EXITED THE carriage first, then turned to his fiancée, and offered his hand. Wow. She looked beautiful and soon she would be all his. His heart thumped in his chest when she placed her hand in his and gazed at him with loving eyes.

He helped her to the ground, and put his hand around her waist, resting on her hip. With his other hand, he dug into his pocket for the fifty-dollar tip he had ready and handed it to the operator. "If she said no, it would be a ten." He winked.

Beth giggled beside him. Oh, how he loved to make her laugh. One of the many reasons he found her attractive. The main one being the God factor. The Lord had guided his steps. He glanced at Beth. And now he'd been rewarded by his obedience to His voice.

Nick collected their photo at the booth and tucked it into his inside jacket pocket. With barely a soul around, they walked back through the Esplanade—the park theirs to enjoy alone.

"I feel like a kid at Christmastime." He swung her around in a dance, her hair gliding through the night. "Let's go to the swings. Who can reach the highest?"

She laughed. "I'll race you there."

That a girl. Nick bolted and, of course, arrived at the playground first. He offered her a swing. "I'll give you a push for a head start."

She wriggled onto the rubber strap-like seat and gripped the metal chains. He stood behind and held onto the side loops, pulled back as far as he could, then rushed forward, letting go.

"You can do better than that," Beth called back.

"Right. I'm going to send you to the moon next." He stepped backward, and when she swung close, he rushed her forward, and repeated the action until the swing went nearly as high as the top beam. Her laughter echoed throughout the Esplanade.

He hopped on the next swing. "Now, you have an advantage." He hoisted his weight back and forth, swinging his legs to gain momentum.

Beth's hair covered her face as she went backward, but her wide smile still showed through.

Soon, at equal heights and timing, he pushed one last time, and at the peak, pointed his feet. "I beat you by a shoe!"

"Not fair!" Her laugh was contagious.

They eventually slowed and gently swayed, swirling their shoes in the white sand.

Beth breathed hard. "I'm not as fit as you. That was a good workout."

"I'm too competitive. I should've let you win like a true gentleman."

"No, I don't like to win unfairly. I'm sure we'll find things I can beat you in."

"We have a lot to learn about each other. And a lifetime to do so."

"That we do." She angled her head in his direction, with the sweetest smile. Beth was in love with him. How he gained favor with her so quickly must've been God. The Lord had been good to him and forgiven him for all his past mistakes. Still, there were things he should tell Beth about himself before their wedding day. He didn't need to go into details, but a mention would be better than her finding out later. Nick would wait on the Lord for the right timing. So far, their conversations didn't go in that direction.

"What are you thinking about, Nick?" She gave a small smile, but it didn't reach her eyes.

"Thinking about God's timing. His perfect will." He dug his shoes into the sand and stopped the movement on his swing.

He switched from his serious expression and burst into a grin. "So, while I was organizing tonight's proposal, I came up with another grand plan." He stretched the last two words. "How about, the last day before I leave Australia, we get married so your family and friends can be there? Then you can fly over to meet me in Los Angeles a month later."

Beth's blue eyes widened. "You want to get married in four weeks?"

"Why not? It makes sense—saves money with all the travel. We can put that toward a honeymoon or our trip to Israel. Both."

"Um, I suppose it would be hard to have a long-distance relationship." She swallowed. "Well, we are mature enough to know we're right for each other."

"Exactly." He got out of his swing and quickly scooped her up into his arms like a bride. She flung her head back and laughed as he twirled around.

"I love you, Bethany Michaels."

She angled her head to meet his eyes. "And I love you, Nicholas DeHann." Beth touched his cheek, and he responded with a kiss to her lips.

He placed her feet to the ground and rested his arms around her waist.

"I've already done my research." He smiled. "We'll need to register for a marriage license tomorrow in Perth. Then it will arrive in time to have the ceremony in Australia. The ship's coming back to Fremantle for two days before leaving for the States, so it will work perfectly."

"You do have it all planned." She raised her brows. "What if I said no."

"I would have to return the dowry money to your dad."

She feigned a whack to his chest. "Nicholas. You're terrible."

He flung his head back and laughed to the heavens.

Pulling her into his embrace, he whispered into her ear. "You're so easy to stir."

They cuddled for a few minutes, then he pulled back. "I need to get back to the ship. I'll walk you to your car, and if you could drop me off at the port, that'd be great."

"Okay. We can video call later, before you go to sleep."

"I'll talk on deck and use my headphones. It's not private in my shared room, so I can't talk all gushy with my fiancée."

"I look forward to our gushy conversation then." She slipped her hands over his shoulders, claimed his lips, and weakened his knees. It was a good thing their wedding was soon.

* * *

Beth jiggled the Lipton teabag, staring into space, dreaming of Nick. The stereo in the Youth Connect kitchen crackled out some tunes, but the words seemed to fade as Beth lost concentration on what she should be doing.

The squeak of a cupboard door jolted her to the present. "Oh, Cassie. You scared me." Her hand flew to her throat.

"Scared you?" Cassie's scrunched her forehead, then her eyes bulged as they focused on Beth's hand. "It is true!" She rushed over and took Beth's wrist. "Melissa texted me this morning. Said I should talk to you."

She wilted her hand like a posh lady. "Isn't the ring spectacular? Nick didn't hold back in spoiling me."

Cassie dropped her hand, mouth ajar. "Beth. It's been two weeks. How can you say yes to a proposal this soon?"

"I know it sounds crazy, but he leaves Australia in four weeks." She shrugged. "We want to get married here so my family can come."

Cassie placed her palms to her cheeks. Chris had bought her a solid rock too. Maybe not as big as hers. "What did your dad say?"

"He's all for it. Dad believes it's God's timing."

Cassie rolled her eyes and muttered something under her breath as she went to the fridge and grabbed the milk. She slapped the carton on the counter, and the white liquid spluttered from the cardboard spout. "I'm in shock." Cassie continued to fuss around the kitchen, making herself an instant coffee.

Beth squeezed the excess tea from its bag, then popped it in the bin below the counter. "I'm getting older. Time is running out. I need to get on with life, family, and ministry."

Cassie shot daggers with her eyes. "What have you been doing here then?" She flapped her hand in the direction of the offices down the hall. "Wasting your time? You minister at Youth Connect and your church. You have a large family and a busy life." Cassie raked her fingers through her nutmeg, wavy hair. "I'm sorry." She closed her eyes for two beats. "I'm concerned for you, that's all. I've been divorced, so I see through a filter. Not all marriages go well. How can you know enough about him in such a short time?"

Cassie walked to the white melamine table and gestured for Beth to join her.

Beth added a teaspoon of sugar, stirred, then sat at the table with the cup in hand.

"Have you had an opportunity to see Nick mad? Frustrated? Under pressure?"

Beth lifted the corner of her mouth. "No."

"How is he with money, responsibility, or commitments?" Cassie raised a brow.

Beth huffed out a sigh and stared into her tea. The cup's warmth offered no comfort, while Cassie gave her a lecture.

Cassie crossed her arms. "What's his past, family background, future ideals?"

"Okay, okay. I get your point. I know hardly anything about him." She shook her head. "I was just trusting God with this. It seems like a divine connection. Nick and Dad think so."

"You thought the worship leader was God's choice too."

Beth felt a stab to her pride. Why did Cassie have to mention Braydon? "I may have been happily married with children if I'd forgiven him at the time."

Cassie straightened. "Huh?"

"Well, he did the right thing when he got Nina pregnant. He married her. If I hadn't rejected him in the first place, he might not have ended up with her."

Cassie placed a reassuring hand on hers. "Beth, he shouldn't have pressured you and tried to make you compromise. You told Braydon 'no' more than once, and you did the right thing in telling the pastor."

"My Dad, you mean. Who made him step down from ministry."

"If Braydon took the reprimand, he would've been given another chance. But he left the church. That's on him. And getting Nina pregnant was his mistake to fix. Good on him for marrying her, but you don't know if they have a good marriage. You just see the Facebook pictures. Fakebook. Anyone can pose for a selfie."

"True." Beth took a sip of her tea, somehow bitter more than sweet.

Cassie tugged at her necklace. "Is it only me that's concerned? What about your sisters?"

Timothy entered the kitchen. "Hi, ladies." He looked between them, raised a brow, darted his gaze elsewhere, took a soda from the fridge, and fled.

The ceiling's fluorescent globe irritated Beth's vision. Cassie had her under the spotlight. Should she take the warning as seriously as Cassie's expression—pretty scary.

"And your brothers? Has your family met Nick?" She leaned forward.

"All my family love him." She gave a small smile. "Dad especially."

Cassie lifted her hands. "Okay. I gave my opinion. I don't know Nick. Haven't met him. I could be blowing this out of proportion." She lowered her voice and connected her gaze with Beth. "But I encourage you to seek God's heart. The answer won't be clear if every spare moment you're with Nick or on the phone to him. You need quality alone time with the Lord to quiet your soul and hear from His spirit."

Beth nodded. "I am, and I will continue to do so. You're right. It's hard to hear from God when my emotions want this so much."

Beth's phone buzzed with her English class reminder. "Gotta go." She placed her hand on Cassie's. "Thanks for the motherly chat."

Cassie grinned. "Anytime. And sorry for freaking out so much."

Beth pinched her forefinger to her thumb. "Just a little."

They both laughed, and the tension eased.

Beth poured her leftover tea into the sink, rinsed her cup, and headed down the echoey hallway. How would she concentrate in class?

She'd registered for the marriage license that morning with Nick. Plans were underway. Nick had booked the park home in Exmouth, and he left with the ship an hour ago. At least she had a few more weeks to get to know him better. He should understand her wanting details about his family background and past relationships. And if he was the offensive type, she better find that out now, so she knew what she was getting into.

Beth swung the door open to the studio room, where four students sat around an oval table. She pasted on a fake smile, which these teens would probably see through. Beth needed to focus on these precious people before her. Chelsea, with her piercings and humble heart. Luke, with his gothic style and goofy laugh. Ruth and her big mouth that always interrupted the lesson. And Nigel from Singapore who'd bring her sushi nearly every week. Her smile became genuine from the love she had for each, but a pang of sadness took residence in her heart. She'd miss them when she was gone. And how would she announce that she was leaving so soon—suddenly? Following Nick across the globe would cost the people dear to her. But she must dream of the bigger picture as Nick explained last night on the phone. The possibilities—endless.

CHAPTER FOURTEEN

AFTER THREE HECTIC days of organizing, Beth had broken free from most of her commitments to leave for Exmouth. A long thirteen-hour drive north. She'd stayed overnight in Geraldton to break up the trip. Maybe she should've taken up Nick's offer to fly. But the price was three hundred one-way. He'd already paid for her accommodation. How much money did he have, anyway?

As her tires crunched over the red gravel driveway, she sighed in relief at the sight of the corrugated blue cottages. A bed awaited her inside, where she could stretch out her tired body.

She scanned the unit numbers as her faithful Toyota Yaris rolled past. Unit eight. That was her. The caretaker said the key would be in the door. Off-peak season ensured there weren't many guests.

When the car door swung open, a flood of humidity assaulted her skin. Whoa. No wonder the tourists had left. It'd take some time to get used to this climate. Was that a kookaburra she could hear laughing nearby? As if on cue at her arrival? A lovely song of a magpie joined in, and soon peace filled her, content to be close to nature. The beach, only a walk away, and several bush trails were some of the features listed on the RAC Holiday website.

Beth ascended the mini two-level steps and unlocked the front door. Terracotta tiles, pine furniture, and a compact blue kitchen came into view. Thank goodness—an AC unit on the wall. She headed back to her car and used her remote to pop the trunk. She tried to pack light but still ended up with three luggage bags and her laptop pouch.

Her boss wanted her to continue editing work online as he preferred two weeks' notice. Fair enough. But he did cut her hours to fifteen, so she'd have plenty of free time to see Nick when he was available. She promised Cassie she'd do a zoom meeting for an hour on Fridays until they found another volunteer. Hopefully, they wouldn't need to cancel the English class altogether. That'd be a real shame.

A cramp in her calf muscle made her wince. She leaned down and rubbed her fist into the strained spot. After some relief, she hoisted her bags onto the paved driveway, stacked them together, and rolled the matching green set inside.

She fussed around, making herself at home, washed her face, and ate some of the complimentary fruit from the fridge. She headed to the bedroom and flopped onto the bed. Nick wanted to meet her in two hours. Enough time for a quick nap.

* * *

Nick steadied the Standup Paddle Board as Beth gingerly climbed on the deck pad. The gentle waves lapped around his knees, doing little to cool him as the water was still warm.

"That a girl. Crawl to the middle." Maybe she wasn't cut out for water sports. He hoped she enjoyed it once they got going. Turquoise Bay would have to be the most stunning beach he'd seen in his life. The pristine beach bare of seaweed or pollution and the crystal-clear waters made it a spectacular experience. Farther down the beach, a small number of his Navy buddies fished off the beach. The sun dipped toward the horizon. Sunset, not far away.

He laid the paddle adjacent to the board. "Now grip onto this."

Uncertainty filled her eyes as she searched his. He smiled and nodded. Then she wobbled as she let go of the sides and gripped the paddle with fierce determination.

"Great. Now, I'll hold the board steady while you stand up with the paddle."

"Okay. I guess I have nothing to lose. The water isn't cold if I fall in."

His toes curled into the sand when a more substantial wave pushed against him. Nick glanced to the horizon. No more large waves for a while. She should get a few minutes of grace while she worked out how to manage her balance.

"Okay. You're good to go. Keep your head up rather than chin down."

Beth pushed from the board and shuffled to her feet. He gritted his teeth as he held the board still. He smiled as he gazed up at his queen, standing high with her sceptre.

Nick trudged through the water to take her waist-deep. "You ready for me to let go?"

"If you have to."

He chuckled. "Yes, I do. I want to get on my board and join you. Look at the view."

Beth scanned her surroundings and nodded at him. "It's pretty amazing." She breathed in deeply and exhaled. "Okay. You can set me free."

He gave a gentle push, parallel to the beach line.

Beth gave a little squeal of delight. Too cute. And she looked great in her matching aqua swim shirt and shorts.

Nick glided through the water toward the shore, then stomped through the wet sand. He grabbed the t-grip handle of his rented board and turned back to the sea. Beth remained standing and gave small flicks with her paddle, barely gaining traction. He shook his head and grinned. He cupped one hand around his mouth and called, "Turn the paddle the other way."

She looked over her shoulder and squinted at him. He bent and picked up his paddle and demonstrated the action. It was an easy mistake. In canoeing, the ore angled in the opposite direction. Beth did as he said, then resumed paddling side to side.

To his right, Sonny and Michael strode toward the beach line with Standup Boards too. Argh. He tried to keep a distance from the other guys so he could have Beth all to himself. He'd spent all day with the sailors, and he needed a break. They'd soon realize she belonged to him. He dashed into the water, creating mini waves, splashing either side of his body. He whacked the paddle across the board and pushed off with his feet, then laid flat as he skimmed toward Beth.

She flinched but smiled as she spotted him coming. But one moment later, she wobbled, windmilled her arms to gain balance, and hollered. Her feet shuffled forward, then backward, forward, and oh, no—the board tipped to one side. *Splash.* He winced.

Beth came up spluttering and scratching at the board like a drowning cat. Her legs had curled under the board. She kicked but that helped little, causing the paddle board to flip and whack her head. Ouch, that would've hurt.

He let go of his board as it was strapped to his ankle anyway, swam to Beth, wrapped an arm around her waist, and hoisted her onto the deck.

"Are you okay?"

She huffed dramatically and wriggled her nose, then swiped it with the back of her hand. "No."

"Don't give up, honey. You can do this. Best to get back up before you think too much about it."

Beth feigned a growl, making him laugh.

"Sorry. I should be more sensitive." Strands of hair matted to her forehead. She looked a sight. But he couldn't hold back the smile within a smile.

"At least one of us is having fun." She wriggled like a caterpillar to the middle of the board.

Nick handed over his paddle and looked to find where hers floated. There. He swam to get it, then got on his deck to demonstrate how to do it correctly. But when he turned, she had paddled away. Ha. Miss Independence didn't need him anymore.

* * *

One hour later, Nick and Beth picked at the last remaining fries at Blue Lips. Beth had showered and changed, but he still wore his damp board shorts and a fresh t-shirt.

Bellows of laughter came from inside the fish and chip shop. The sailors were everywhere, taking over the quiet town. He hoped he didn't come across as anti-social, but his days with the Navy were numbered. He'd reached out to as many men as he could in the last few months. He'd have some extra time on the way back to the States. But right now, right here, his priority was his new fiancée.

"What do you say to scuba diving tomorrow morning?"

Her brows furrowed. "Don't I need a license for that?"

"You don't have one?" He shrugged. "Silly question?" He smiled. "There's snorkeling with the Whale Sharks. You up for that?"

She gasped. "Sharks!"

An elderly couple at the next picnic table glanced their way.

He leaned forward and lowered his voice. "Not the man-eating kind."

"Oh." She placed a hand to her chin. "And it's safe to swim near them?"

"They're big, so not too close. I'll send you the links to the website and videos. You can let me know tonight if you're up to it."

Her shoulders lowered, and she sank against the wooden bench. "All right."

He reached across the table and collected her hands. "You said earlier you wanted to talk about something. Is here okay, or do you want to go for a walk?"

Her gaze flickered around the table, everywhere but on him. Not a good sign. Knots formed in his stomach.

She took her hands back and started to clean up the table. "A walk sounds good." She rolled up the butcher paper around the leftover scraps. Then Beth inched sideways out of the bench seat and stood.

Two American sailors exited the shop with their packages of hot chips. Nick nodded in their direction. "This table is free now."

Beth walked on and headed to the footpath.

"How'd you manage to have that chick follow you up here?" The fool elbowed his friend. "Why didn't I think of that?"

"We're engaged." He turned and didn't wait for a response, but the sniggers of amusement drifted behind him.

Beth's face had a hue of pink. She must've heard the comments. He slipped his hand into hers. "Don't listen to them, hon." He pointed to the distance. "I believe there's a bush trail up ahead. The weather's cooled enough to enjoy it." Unless the conversation ended up too heated. What did she want to discuss?

The sky streaked in colors of russet, pale amber, and strawberry—unusual, but stunning. "Have you spent much time in Exmouth before?"

"Not really. Passed through when we were kids. We had a bus, and in the winter holidays often camped on the way to Broome. Cooked damper in the coals, held outreach meetings for the Aboriginal communities, and had a holiday at the same time."

"Wow. I would've loved that upbringing. Big family. Ministry focused."

"So, tell me more about your mother. Does she live in Los Angeles too?"

Just the mention of his mom caused a sick taste in his mouth. "No. She lives in Oceanside, about an hour from where I stay. Mom managed to get into a flashy senior apartment after dad passed. She's happy with the facilities and community there."

"Do you call her much?"

He scratched at the back of his head. "Um. Occasionally." Mother's Day. Christmas.

"I guess it's not as easy on the ship?"

"Mmm." He didn't find it easy at any time.

Beth angled her head and studied him. "Would you say you have a good relationship with her?"

Here it goes. Background check. So, this was what Beth wanted to talk about. Was she having doubts about him?

"We had a close mother-son relationship during my childhood. But as my faith got stronger—different to her reserved points of view, a distance formed between us."

"I'm sorry to hear that." Her eyes seemed genuine.

"Yeah. So am I." He swallowed hard. "As an adult, she's opposed a lot of my decisions to travel or minister. I can't talk about any revelations or insight on what the Lord is doing in these times. She doesn't get it." Muscle tension formed in his left shoulder. "Mom's not supportive in any way, so I don't tell her much about what I'm doing. I ask her about her life, but don't go into details of mine. Easier that way."

He glanced at Beth's frown. She seemed to have a close family connection, so this would be foreign to her way of life.

He scuffed his shoe against the red dirt bush trail. "In Mark, chapter ten, Jesus replied, 'and I assure you that everyone who has given up house or brothers or sisters or mother or father or children or property, for my sake and for the Good News, will receive now in return a hundred times as many houses, brothers, sisters, mothers, children, and property—along with persecution.'"

Beth's forehead lines deepened.

"I'm willing to give up anything for the sake of the gospel, and God will reward me with family and children in the future." He squeezed Beth's hand. "By following me to America and Jerusalem, you're giving up your family too. But God will reward both of us in time."

She nodded slowly.

"You wanted to talk to me. Are there other questions?"

Beth waved a fly away from her face. "If you don't mind." She connected her gaze with his. "I do trust you, Nick. I only want to understand you more and what's made you the man you are today."

Nick began to relax. That sounded fair. Her motivation didn't stem from suspicion, only genuine interest. "Ask away, then."

"On one of our dates in Fremantle, we talked about our past. I told you about Braydon, but that led to changing subjects about submission to leadership. You did mention about one serious relationship you had." Beth offered a small smile. "Can I ask more about why it didn't work out?"

"To be fair on Tracy, you're only going to hear my point of view. She may have other reasons of why we didn't stick together." Nick let go of Beth's hand and swung his behind his back. Another uncomfortable conversation that needed discussion. "Mom and Tracy became very chummy. She even called her Mamma Sue—the caring mother she never had." He sighed. He wouldn't let Beth get too close to his Mom. He wouldn't make that mistake again. "But Mom placed a lot of doubts in Tracy's head. She doubted my leadership and direction. Tracy broke it off and crushed my heart at the same time. More like she stomped on my heart, squished it into the dirt, wiped off anything to do with me, and cut me off completely."

Beth collected his hand and stopped their walking. "That's her loss, Nick." Her expression conveyed sincerity. "I would never crush your heart."

He placed her palm on his chest. "I trust you. And you aren't like Tracy. Your dad has raised you to be faithful and dedicated to ministry. We're on the same page. That's why our relationship will work."

She closed the distance between them and rested her head against him. He folded her into his arms and held her tight. Finally, he'd found a woman who would go the journey with him—one who'd trust his lead and partner with him in ministry. His Eve.

CHAPTER FIFTEEN

AFTER TWO WEEKS of jam-packed adventure, Beth needed a holiday from her holiday. Nick had loads of energy, able to handle a morning of intense training at the Navy base, then take her sightseeing all day, and beach walks in the evenings.

Beth placed the last of her dirty laundry in the washing machine, pressed the save water option, and start. She enjoyed her time in Exmouth, but it was nice to be back home. She collected her cane basket from the floor. Well, home for now. She wanted more detail on where they'd live in Los Angeles. Nick had been vague—his friend had a house they could use until they set out for travel. And when would that happen? She preferred to have a set plan.

It was a struggle to completely relax in Exmouth, knowing she had a mission to accomplish in organizing a last-minute wedding. She'd cut the time with Nick to get home sooner. The passport had been paid for on the day after the proposal, but no wedding dress picked out as yet. The next task on her long list. She glanced at her PJs—once she got changed, that is, and so headed to her bedroom.

Beth guessed that life with Nick would always be an adventure. Amazingly, he convinced her to go swimming with the whale sharks. She touched her throat at the memory. Oh, when that shark opened the widest oval-shaped mouth she'd ever seen, she nearly had a heart attack. Of course, they were at a reasonably safe distance. A school of mini silvered fish entered its mouth, quite gracefully, so she had nothing to worry about. Still, she had a few disturbing dreams since then, where it didn't end up so well.

Beth shook the image from her mind and scanned her unusually disorganized room. Two of her luggage cases laid open, covering most of the shaggy carpet. Her thick doona with swirly patterns of pinks and purples remained rumpled to one side of her double bed. She hadn't even tidied her room since seven a.m. when Nick woke her with a video call. He found it amusing that she could barely string a sentence together without her morning coffee.

She crawled over her bed and straightened the cover, starting from the far side. Pink wouldn't be appropriate once she shared a bed with Nick. Her stomach dropped. How would their wedding night go? Nick had kissed her on their beach walks and at the end of each night. There were no sparks, but it was nice enough. Comfortable.

Her mother often told her that the fireworks were just in the beginning, and marriage wasn't all about that. The foundation should be friendship. Cassie disagreed. On the phone last week, she said in the engagement they needed to build on the friendship, but a strong attraction was a healthy sign of compatibility, or why not just stay friends or ministry partners? Cassie believed marriage with a mutual attraction was important. At the end of the call, they agreed to disagree. In the Bible, there were arranged marriages, so not everyone in history had the privilege of choosing someone they desired. Hopefully, she'd grow in that attraction to Nick as time went on, and she wasn't so distracted by the many things she had to accomplish.

She fluffed her mauve throw pillows and stood back, admiring her presentation. Much better. Now, time to get dressed and meet her sisters at the bridal shop. Trudy said she could make it and hopefully Shanae as well. Amy opted for photos taken as she didn't want to bring Talicia in case the little girl pulled on expensive dresses.

* * *

"How about this one, Beth?" Shanae lowered the ivory silk gown from the display rack. "Simple but elegant."

The material shined from the chandeliers above. Thin straps attached to a gathered bodice, leading into a length of silk to the floor. Shanae held it up to her chin, then glanced at Beth for approval.

"It's gorgeous." Beth took it from her sister and studied it closer. "After the wedding, I could have it shortened for an evening dress for special occasions, since it has a cream shade to it, it could pass as a formal dress." Beth pulled out the price tag. Under four hundred dollars—within her small budget. "Let's hope it fits, so I don't need to wait for adjustments."

Trudy clapped her hands in delight and let out a small squeal. "This is so exciting." She ran her fingers over the other dresses on the rack. "I should pick one out for myself. Although, Michael and I haven't settled on a wedding date. We aren't fast movers like some." She winked at Beth.

"In normal circumstances, neither would I be in a rush." Beth placed a hand on her hip. "But I'm not young anymore. Thirty-three—its time."

"Wasn't Jesus crucified at that age?" Trudy grinned.

"Not funny." Beth feigned a scowl. "I'm sure marriage will include plenty of dying to self. But a lot of great things too."

"Like . . . the act of marriage." Trudy laughed. She quoted the book title that dad loaned to engaged couples. He hadn't offered her one, thankfully. That would be plain awkward.

Shanae giggled too. They were having a lot of fun at her expense. Should she tell them how nervous she was about it all? Beth shook her head and walked to the fitting corner of the private room. The classical sounds of a piano played through the speakers above.

She flicked the vintage curtain aside and glanced over her shoulder. "Nick doesn't focus on the physical side of the relationship. I have no idea how that's going to go. His love language mustn't be physical touch." She closed the curtain behind her.

Trudy called out. "Every man's language is physical touch. What are you talking about?"

Beth wriggled out of her jeans and continued to try on the dress. "Let's put it this way—I didn't have to worry about temptation in Exmouth."

"That can change." This from Shanae.

"I don't know how he feels, but for me, it's just nice to be loved. He's a good guy."

"But what about that other Navy dude?" Trudy asked. "You had it bad for him."

"Exactly. *Bad* being the key word. A sign that it wasn't right. What I have with Nick is based on our calling. We're meant to be together."

Silence fell amongst her sisters. Did they agree? She zipped the dress as far as she could reach, then stepped out of the fitting room. "Ta-Da!" As she twirled, her hair fell over her shoulders like in a shampoo commercial.

"Oohh. It's beautiful, Beth." Shanae rushed over and brushed the material between her fingers.

"Stunning." Trudy looked over her thin-framed glasses. "Nick will definitely speak another love language when he sees you in that."

They all laughed in unison. Deep down, Beth hoped so too.

* * *

"What do you mean the marriage license hasn't come?" Nick raked his fingers through his hair, paced Beth's floor, then turned to stare at her again. This couldn't be happening.

Beth raised her palms in the air, eyes bulging. "I checked the letterbox today, and it still hasn't come. Thirty days' notice had finished yesterday."

"Why didn't you tell me sooner?" Heat pulsated through his neck, rising to his cheeks.

She shook her head. "I didn't want to concern you unless the thirty-days were up. I hoped—"

Nick let out a frustrated sigh. "It's not your fault. Let's go to the licensing center and sort this out." He stamped his foot. "I can't believe the wedding is in two days and then I leave for the US. What was I thinking? Of course, delays happen." He ran a palm over his chin. "I'm sorry if we miss out on celebrating with your family."

Beth stepped forward and rubbed both of his arms. "It'll be okay. If we have to make it an engagement party, that's fine. We can get married in America. My family can watch via a video call."

"I wanted this for you. A woman dreams of her wedding day and wants to be walked down the aisle by their father. This is terrible." He gazed into her compassionate eyes, shining from a film of moisture. No denying this was important to her. Failure number one. He failed Beth—robbed her of a childhood dream to be a stunning bride for all her family and friends to see.

Footsteps came down the hallway. Nick stepped away from Beth, and he forced a smile for the young lady with peroxide blonde hair and steely blue eyes. Must be Melissa, the single mom.

"What's all the fuss out here?" She kept walking to the kitchen and called over her shoulder. "Having a lovers' tiff?"

Beth left him and followed Melissa. "The marriage license didn't arrive." Beth sat on the breakfast bar stool, placed her elbows on the table, and sunk her head into her palms.

Yep. It mattered. Beth tried to pretend all would be okay to him, but now her friend was here to bare her soul to, she showed how she really felt. Devastated.

Melissa's head whipped around, her hair slapping her mouth. "No! You serious? But you've paid all the deposits for the catering and reception. Will you get your money back?"

"Maybe some," Beth mumbled into her hands.

"Hey." Nick joined them and rubbed circles over Beth's back. "It could come tomorrow. Let's call the office first and see where it's at. We could be getting worked up over nothing."

Beth turned with a pink flush to her face. "You were the one getting all worked up over there." She flicked her head to the living room.

Melissa eyed him with suspicion. Rightly so. He did let his temper slide a little. Nothing like the past. In his twenties, he had an anger issue. The night he'd received a broken jaw sorted that problem out. A punch of reality. He pressed his chin—still numb from the surgery.

Beth slipped off the barstool. "You could be right. I'll find the paperwork and give them a call." She strode out of the room. Leaving him with feisty Melissa.

The woman grabbed a block of cheese from the fridge and slapped it onto the cutting board. Despite her stiff resolve, he straddled the bar stool and attempted some conversation. "So, I hear you have an adorable little girl. Hannah?"

Her thin brows daggered toward her nose. "What's it to you?" She placed a hand to her hip.

His eyes widened, and the corner of his mouth twitched as he tried to smile. "Just making friendly conversation."

She pouted her lips to one side. "I've met plenty of sailors in my time. They have the right words and all the smooth moves, but it's all a façade." She clicked her fingers. "Then they disappear, back to where they came from, breaking hearts at each port."

Nick straightened his back. "I'm sorry you've had a bad experience. I agree women shouldn't hook up with a sailor visiting a port. But I've proposed to Beth, willing to marry her. Surely you can see I'm not just any sailor?"

"Hmph." She wobbled her head. "We'll see." She continued to open the drawer and retrieved a cheese grater.

He hopped off the witness stand and waited in the living room for Beth instead. He could only take so much sass from the lady.

Beth's voice echoed down the hallway. "DeHann and Michaels." Her cell pushed to her ear as she strode into the room. "Yes. That's us." She sat on the sofa opposite him and crossed a leg over her knee.

Her brows furrowed. "Issued three days ago? Do you have a tracking number?" She scanned the receipt in her hand. "I didn't know it was an option. No, we haven't paid for registered post." She warily glanced at Nick.

He scrunched his forehead. Where was the document then? It was supposed to be next day delivery.

"What address did you send it to?" Beth swapped the phone to her other ear, deep in concentration. "Marriage celebrant?" She looked at her papers. "Oh, my dad. Winston Michaels. My dad is a pastor." She laughed. "That makes sense. You send it to the celebrant. Oh, I'm sure he has it then. No problem. Thanks for your time." She ended the call.

Beth tilted her head and smiled. "My dad has it." She let out a small laugh. "I must've got confused. Thought it came to us. My mind is a blur. Dad has Pastor Allen helping with the first part of the ceremony, so Dad's free to walk me down the aisle. But he will lead us in the vows and signing the papers."

"Great." He gestured to her phone. "Well, let's call him, just to be sure he has the license."

"Oh, yeah. Good idea." She blushed.

Beth speed-dialed her dad and placed the call on loudspeaker. Nick leaned forward in anticipation.

"Hi Dad, I called the marriage office, and they said you should have the license by now. Has it arrived?"

"Ugh, no. Not to the house or the church. Do you have a tracking number?"

Beth rubbed her temple. "No, we didn't realize it was an option, but I see on the copy of my form we didn't tick or pay for registered post."

"When did they send it?"

"Three days ago."

"Oh." Winston paused. "Maybe it's at my local Australia Post. I'll go down now and see if it's there."

"Okay. Let me know as soon as you've checked."

"I'll call back soon."

"Thanks, Dad."

Beth focused on Nick with concern in her eyes. "This is not good."

"Is it normal that documents go to the post office first?"

She frowned. "Not usually, unless it's registered post."

He slumped his head and splayed his palms over his jagged haircut.

Beth touched his shoulder, her voice soft. "Worst scenario, we have an engagement party here. Get married in the States, and your mother can be there."

His jaw clenched. He remained still, waiting for Winston's phone call. From the kitchen, the microwave tinged.

A mild aroma of melted cheese drifted into the living room, followed by open-mouth chewing. "Is everything okay in here?" Melissa asked.

"Not sure." Beth's voice sounded weak. "We may have to delay the wedding."

"Hmmm. Right." Melissa's chewing retreated to the kitchen.

Nick bet she had a smug look on her face. He slowly raised his head and studied Beth's worry lines, although she offered a consoling smile.

A few heart-wrenching minutes later, Winston called with the news—no document.

Beth took Nick's hand after she ended the call. "Oh, well. I guess it's been a rush. This way, I'll have more time to organize things better."

"You were doing a great job of pulling it all together. Everything's done. And you've paid those deposits."

"I'll get most of my money back."

Nick bit his lower lip. "There's no chance . . . that your dad . . . ?"

Beth crossed her arms over her peach blouse. "That he what?"

"Your dad likes me, doesn't he? He wouldn't?"

"I'm thirty-three. He wouldn't go to that extreme to stop us from getting married. He'd just give his opinion and let me decide."

"You know him better than me."

She gave him a stern look. "Yes. I do."

Oops. He'd touched a sensitive button. Beth seemed defensive about her dad. They were close. In a weird sort of way, like a married couple. She'd raised his children and partnered in running his church like a pastor's wife would. And that could be an extra motive for Winston to accidentally misplace the document. He shook his head. This frustration wasn't helping the situation.

"Sorry for bringing it up."

She leaned back into the suede sofa, arms crossed. Her lips remained thin. "All right."

He matched her posture. "All right."

CHAPTER SIXTEEN

LACHLAN SWUNG BACK his hammer and slammed it into the concrete encasing the rusted bathtub. A small crack formed. He brought it down again. Smash. A deeper break stretched across the sidewall. He wiped his brow with the back of his flannel shirt. Not an ideal job, but it gave an outlet to his frustrations.

Helping his brother renovate bathrooms wasn't his idea of the promised land. Slam. A chunk of concrete flew across the floor.

He'd applied for over twenty jobs in the last three weeks. No call backs. Nothing. His pastor had no leads—no word of ministry openings or any positions for a Christian counselor.

Whack. Whack. Slam.

His brother glanced over his shoulder with a frown that turned into a grin. "You having fun over there?"

"Just dandy." Lachlan rolled his eyes.

Mark chuckled and turned back to the cabinet he'd recently installed. He had already completed a row of tiles around the mirror above the sink. The customer wanted tiles to the ceiling.

Lachlan needed to get a move on so they could set the new tub in concrete at the base and let it dry overnight.

He hammered the floor around the bathtub like a woodchopper in a carnival competition. Sweat trickled down his back, his heart pounding in his chest. At least he didn't need a gym membership. This job gave him a healthy workout. The bathtub tilted, free from any support. He scuffed his steel-toed boot against the last bit of rubble from the base. He lowered his hammer to the floor in a squat and rose again, arching his back. Argh, he'd be sore in the morning. How did Mark work year in and year out in this industry? Intense.

Mark had a wall of tiles in place. "Ready for a lunch break?"

"Yeah, I'm ready to call it quits." Lachlan rolled his shoulders.

"Your muscles just for show, bro?"

"I've got no one to show them to. A sad, sorry story." He joked, but at thirty-two, single status and lonely evenings had long turned old and stale. Time for a change.

The owners of the house weren't home, so after washing their hands in the laundry room, they moved to the backyard to have lunch. Their clothes were too dusty to sit inside. Mark placed his lunch box on the glass patio table and unloaded homemade blueberry muffins.

Lachlan's mouth watered. "Care to share some of that?" He gestured toward the muffins. Mark didn't need three. Surely, he could share one of them.

With reluctance in his gaze, Mark handed one over.

Lachlan grinned. "I see the pain in your eyes, bro. But look at my pathetic bachelor lunch." He held up the pizza bread roll he'd grabbed on the way to work.

Mark smiled and continued to unpack two sandwiches, a container of trail mix, and a yogurt.

"Has Lizzy got you on a diet?"

"No, it's similar to the kid's lunches. Easy for her."

"Right."

The fresh, cool air was drying his sweat. Lachlan shivered. He'd need a jacket soon, but with his meager fare, he wouldn't stay outside long. Mark got out his phone and started scrolling. Lachlan took a bite of the moist muffin, and a blueberry squashed between his back teeth, filling his mouth with flavor. Freshly baked. Mmm. He used his free hand to grab his cell, more out of habit than having anything important pending. Unless an interview opportunity.

His photo app had a notification. This Day Two Years Ago. He clicked on the tab. Lachlan took in a breath, causing cake to lodge in his throat. He coughed and grabbed his water bottle.

Mark glanced his way. "You okay, bud?"

Lachlan's eyes watered, and he nodded, unable to speak. The image faded from the screen, and he tapped it again to see those captivating eyes. Bethany Michaels. A wide grin, delicate freckles, tendrils caressed her cheek—and behind Beth, a cute face of a Quokka with its nose in the air. Her head laid tucked under his chin. His eyes were bright—one of the happiest photos he'd seen of himself in a long, long time. He shook his head and whispered, "Bethany Michaels."

"Did you say something?" His brother gave him an assessing stare.

He took another sip of his drink and gulped hard as the memory hit his chest. He turned his screen to show Mark.

"Australia. This is when I went to one of the islands, found this cute creature."

A playful smile slid up Mark's face. "You dawg."

Lachlan retracted his phone and scowled. "The Quokka. A rare marsupial. Endangered species."

"Who's the woman?" Mark's crow's feet deepened.

Now it was his turn to smile. "She's gorgeous, isn't she? Wish Beth was mine. But there's oceans and oceans between us. Just a photo memory now." He clicked the side button and flicked his hard-cased phone to the table.

Mark ran a hand through his black hair. "Don't have her number? Friends on Facebook?"

"There's no point. I doubt Beth would move to the States. Her family and church seem to rely on her. And we didn't keep in contact. Only for a while."

"You seemed pretty taken by the photo. Did something happen between you two?"

Had something happened? They'd formed a friendship. Understood a spiritual connection between them. There'd been an undeniable chemistry reaction whenever they got close. His neck heated.

"You've taken too long to answer that question." Mark smirked. "Which gives me the answer anyway."

Lachlan gave a small laugh. "Nothing physical happened. I didn't want to pine over her for two years. That's why I brushed off her emails, didn't give her much response. She must've got the hint and moved on. Sounds mean, but I was saving us both a world of disappointment. It couldn't go anywhere."

"What about now? What's holding you here? You have no job, career . . . attachments." Mark took another bite of his sandwich.

"Thanks." Lachlan sat up and playfully rubbed a chill from his arms. "I've been back two months, and you're already trying to get rid of me." He huffed. "I belong here. With my family. Don't I?" Did he? He hadn't settled, but that had to be normal after being absent for several years.

Mark wiped some mayonnaise from his mouth. "Hey. I didn't mean it like that." He leaned forward and tapped Lachlan's shoulder. "We're always family. But things change. We move on. I've got my own family, Kayce has hers, and you need to start yours eventually."

Lachlan scratched at his one-inch beard. "I hope to meet someone in San Diego." He flicked a piece of pizza roll in the air and tilted his head back. Leaning right, he caught it in his mouth. "Surely I don't have to travel to Australia to find Mrs. Right."

"Chris did."

"Chris?" Lachlan frowned. "Oh, Chris Evanson. Yeah. He looks like one happy fellow. Got it made."

"He has now, but remember when his first wife cheated on him? Devastated. He didn't date for years. Traveled the globe. Then he met the Aussie girl."

"Cassie."

Mark's forehead lined. "You know her?"

"No, but Beth sees her as a mentor. She volunteers at the youth center. Well, she did when I knew her. Don't know what she's up to now. Beth was trying to get into journalism." He shrugged. "Maybe she's the one traveling now."

A dog barked from the neighbor's yard. Were they talking too loudly for others to hear? The houses were close in this street.

"You won't know unless you contact her."

"She's probably with someone by now." He rubbed the back of his neck. "Two years is a long time." But Beth hadn't mentioned anything in her emails.

Mark guzzled from his eco water bottle, then wiped his mouth with the back of his hand. "Chris has a restaurant. You could go on a working holiday."

A smile started at the corner of his mouth. "He did make me an offer."

Mark jumped in his seat and pointed at him. "There you go! What are you waiting for? You loathe bathroom renovations, and you have plenty of cash, anyway. Why not treat yourself to a trip to Australia?"

"It does sound tempting." And seeing Beth again was even more so. Why was his heart racing?

Mark slapped the table, sending vibrations across the glass. "Do it, man. Live life. Travel while you can. Before you're tied down with kids."

"Tied down?" Lachlan shook his head. "You love being a dad."

"It's the best. But if I didn't have 'em, I'd be making the most of my freedom."

He nodded. "If I don't get a qualified position soon, I might give Chris a call."

Mark scraped his chair back and stood. "Chris would be an awesome boss. Love that guy." He collected his lunch box. "We need to get back to work. Gotta set that new bathtub."

"I finished lunch ten minutes ago." He patted his empty stomach. But Lachlan felt full—full of excitement for the future.

* * *

The airport's intercom echoed flight numbers through the sterile white corridors. The hum of conversation filled the open space. Beth leaned down to her niece and engulfed her in a bear hug. "I'm going to miss you, sweetie. My favorite niece in the whole wide world."

Talicia circled her thin arms around Beth's neck, nearly choking her. "When will you come back?"

Beth pulled away a little and smiled, determined to shed no tears. "I hope to visit next Christmas."

Amy rubbed the little girl's back. "Come on, Talicia. Aunty Beth needs to get on the plane."

The little girl turned sad eyes away from Beth. She leaped into her mother's arms and buried her head in Amy's golden locks. Beth's heart tightened. She didn't want to leave her family. The skin under her eyes remained puffy from last night's crying session with her pillow. She wouldn't admit that to anyone. They saw her as the oldest and bravest, and she didn't want them to think any different of her.

Simon and Jacob hugged her next. She planted kisses on their cheeks, and they gave her awkward pats on the back. Typical of her brothers. But Trudy lunged toward Beth and clung like a koala. A laugh bubbled in her throat, but a clog of mixed emotions stifled any sound.

"Can you fit me in your suitcase?" Trudy said.

Michael tugged on Trudy's ponytail. "Hey, you're not going anywhere, baby." He wrapped his arm around his fiancée, and kissed Beth on the cheek. "And you make sure you return for our wedding."

"Whenever that is." Beth tossed her head.

The couple smiled and stood back so the next person could say goodbye. Dad. Beth touched her mouth. Tears stung the back of her eyes. Dad edged forward, dressed in gray suit pants and a buttoned-up shirt—always the pastor. He lifted his palms to her. Daddy's girl. His brown eyes shone, the overhead lights reflecting off unshed tears. She rushed forward, gave him a fierce hug, and nuzzled into his chest. Her lower lip trembled as she resisted a sob. A familiar place where she'd cried many a tear. When boys had broken her heart. As she'd shared frustrations and disappointments. And when church folk misunderstood her and spoke behind her back. Dad had been her rock to lean on, and she'd been his armor-bearer.

Dad stroked her hair. "I'm proud of you, Beth." His voice crackled. "Thank you for serving your family and laying down your life for us." He pulled back and cupped her shoulders, meeting her eyes. "Now, it's your turn to live out your dreams. Spread your wings and fly."

"Thanks, Dad. I intend to. I've learned so much from you. I'm your arrow, going out to set the next generation aflame."

"I believe it, my girl. I'll be praying with you all the way."

She kissed his cheek. He kissed her forehead, then let her go. Her flight number called over the speakers. Time to find her footing in the big wide world. Smiling, she turned slowly in a semi-circle, memorizing everyone's faces. Then she stepped backward and collected her carry-on bag. Several suitcases had been checked earlier. All she needed to do was board the plane. Nick would be waiting for her in Los Angeles. They'd go to the marriage office the next day and replan a ceremony. But first, she had to get through twenty-one hours of flying.

To her right, a long line of passengers formed at gate nineteen. Her gate. Oops. She flicked her head back to her family. "That's me. I'll message the group chat as soon as I land. And I'll send you the zoom link to the wedding ceremony as soon as I confirm the date with the registrar."

"Bye, Beth. We love you." Amy called.

One by one, they shouted their well wishes as she backed away, waving goodbye. Trudy's eyes glazed with tears. Dad kept a smile in place, but his eyes were bloodshot. He was a softie under all that stern strictness. He cared too much—that was his problem. But Dad trusted her to go and make the right choices. And she would continue to make him proud.

CHAPTER SEVENTEEN

BETH GAZED OUT the passenger-side window, taking in as much of L.A. as her heavy eyelids would allow her. Nick hummed to the radio, steering with one hand and holding hers with the other. Palm trees of various sizes lined the streets beside the glow of traffic lights. Cars filled wide roads with several lanes even at 9 p.m. They'd already passed the central area and cruised on toward Glendale. Wherever that was.

"Excited?" Nick said quietly.

She looked over to him. "Yes. It's different from Perth. Sydney is a bit like this, but L.A. seems to have no end. It's huge."

He grinned and faced forward. "There's no skyscrapers and traffic where we're staying."

"How long do we have at your friend's house?"

"Up to eight weeks of free rent. It's not a house either. A one-bedroom apartment."

Beth's stomach dropped. She pulled her hand away. "Oh." Where was she meant to sleep? Would he have to sleep on the sofa? She needed a bed for at least tonight. Exhaustion filtered through every muscle. She worked the kinks from her neck.

"The place isn't much, but it's only temporary, Beth. If I'd had more time, I might have arranged other accommodation, but I've only had a day here myself. I spent most of that scrubbing the place down. The unit must've been vacant for a while."

How bad was it? The apartment blocks looked quite clean and upmarket so far. The bright lights flickering in the cabin phased into a blur as she closed her eyes. She was too tired to stress over it. Tomorrow they would work things out.

Beth awoke to a gust of chilly air and the creak of the car door opening.

"Home sweet home, my love." Nick offered a hand.

She blinked to focus on his tall frame. Nick? America. Oh, she was here. Really here.

He smiled like a kid in a candy shop. What was he so happy about? Hadn't he said the place was a dump? Home sweet home?

She unclicked her seat belt and took his hand. "I'd be more enthusiastic if I didn't have jet lag. Sorry."

"We're here together. That's what's important. Don't worry about the unit. Glendale is a great place. Anyway, we're only here for a while. Onward and upward."

She stepped out into an undercover parking lot. Several concrete pillars with painted numbers dominated the small area. Nick unloaded her luggage and rolled two cases for her to take.

He stacked the rest for him. "I don't know how we're going to fit all this in the apartment."

"I packed as light as I could. There's still a ton of my belongings in Australia. Amy's sorting through some of it, selling what she can for me."

He hoisted a large canvas bag over his shoulder and tilted the handle of the luggage cases. "I'm sure you've done your best. I appreciate all you've given up to move here."

"Thank you." After some sleep, she might not be so grumpy about it.

She followed Nick to a ramp that led to the ground level. The outside of the building looked fine. Beige brick, cream railings, small balconies, and concrete steps crisscrossed in several directions. The middle strip between two buildings had an artificial lawn and outdoor potted plants neatly spaced apart.

Nick nodded his head to the left. "We're over there. Unit five."

When they arrived at their apartment, Nick opened the wooden door with a creak, and they stepped inside. The scent of dust and male cologne mingled in the air. Commercial-grade carpet covered the floor in the first room, which must be the lounge. Cozy, all right. She could take two steps in each direction and hit the walls. It held a vinyl loveseat, scratched coffee table, and a flat-screen TV. To her left, a round dining table sat next to a compact kitchen painted in black and white. At least it appeared functional and tidy. Nick said nothing as he continued down the short hallway. She followed him to the bedroom. A queen-sized bed with a gray and black striped cover and two red pillows took up half of the space. Her stomach knotted as she scanned the room. Mahogany wardrobes and matching chest of draws with bed-side tables filled the rest of the room. But where would her bags go? Nick lined them against one yellow wall, which left little room to walk.

Nick approached and rubbed her arms. "You okay? You look like you're about to fall over. The long flight is taking its toll."

"Yes," she mumbled as she released the handles of her luggage. Nick took the suitcases and squeezed them beside the others.

Beth shuffled to the end of the bed, turned around, and flopped backward onto the soft mattress. She closed her eyes and listened to Nick move about the room. An eye cracked open at the sound of a zip. He removed his jacket and placed it into the wardrobe, where an assortment of coats and shirts hung. He would let her have the room, wouldn't he? He'd need to hang his legs over the side of that tiny sofa. Maybe he could find a blow-up mattress somewhere.

"What's the sleeping arrangements?" She asked with the little energy she had left.

He hesitated as he looked to her. She sat upright. Her head whooshed with the sudden movement.

"About that. I'm sorry. I didn't realize this was a one-bedroom. You were on the plane. I couldn't call you to discuss what we should do." He ran his fingers over his short hair. "If you feel uncomfortable, maybe someone from the church could have you stay with their family."

"Who's sleeping on the couch tonight?"

"You want me to sleep on that sofa?" He grunted. "Have you seen how big it is? I could sleep on the floor if you don't want to share the bed."

Now, she felt like the moral police. She pinched the bridge of her nose. It was too hard to think.

"I'll keep my hands to myself, Beth. If that's what you want."

Her eyes flashed open. "What I want? What were you expecting?"

His head reared back. "Not much. I knew you would crash from your trip. I'm tired too."

She shook her head. "But what about the next few weeks while we organize the wedding ceremony? Did you expect us to share a bed?"

"It's up to you. I don't have a problem with it." He shrugged. "We're getting married soon."

Her eyes widened.

He quickly added, "We don't have to do anything. Just sleep." He raised his palms. "At thirty-eight, I'm not a virgin, Beth. But I respect that you want to do this the right way. Tell me, what do you suggest?"

Didn't he want to do things the right way too? This was not going to plan. And that was the problem. There was no plan. Nick seemed to be winging it. Would this be what it would be like to follow Nick around the globe? Not knowing where they would stay? Maybe she wasn't at his faith level to wait for God's leading for each step of action.

"I just want to sleep on a soft bed tonight. I feel bad that I'm making you sleep on the floor. But can you do it for tonight, and we'll work something out for tomorrow?"

Nick let out a sigh. "Of course. I've slept in sailor bunkers. I'm used to poor bedding options, so another night won't be too hard to get through."

"Thank you." She flopped back onto the bed and closed her eyes.

Some moments later, she flinched from the click of the bedroom door. Nick had left her alone with the overhead light off and a bedside lamp on. She stretched her arms above her head. Beth kicked her shoes off and crawled under the covers. Too tired to get changed. Must sleep.

* * *

The next morning, Beth woke to the clanging of dishes on the other side of the wall. A yawn expanded in her throat as she pushed herself up. On the pillow was a drool patch. Gross. Good thing Nick wasn't around to see. She turned it over and got out of bed. Her clothes clung to her from the body heat trapped under her jacket. She needed a shower fast—before Nick smelled her. Ew.

Beth collected a change of clothes and her toiletry bag, then sneaked down the short hallway, looking for the bathroom. Easy enough to find in a tiny apartment. The waft of bacon drifted from the kitchen. The rangehood whirled, and Nick sang off key to a Christian song blaring from his phone speaker.

She tip-toed to the bathroom and locked the door. Glossy black cabinets greeted her along with a round framed mirror. She jumped at the sight of herself—hair stuck out in every direction. Gray patches underlined her eyes. She stretched the pale skin over her cheekbones. Was she coming down with something? A shower would do her good.

Next to the sink, a drinking glass with a single garden rose tilted in some water. Nick must've placed that there. Sweet.

She showered as quickly as she could and slipped into skinny jeans and a rusty orange sweater. With her hair brushed and fresh breath, she was ready to greet her fiancé.

"Good morning." She trilled as she rounded the corner.

His smile stretched his cheeks. "Afternoon, my love." He winked as he leaned against the counter.

"Really?"

"Yes, I've been up since five. Gone for a jog. Had devotions. This is lunch for me." He bit a piece of his toast. "Yours is keeping warm in the oven. I didn't know how long you'd be in the shower."

"Thanks. What did you make me?"

"Bacon and scrambled eggs on toast."

"Better than airplane food. Sounds delicious." She pulled up a chair as he went to get her plate from the microwave.

He kissed her head before he placed her breakfast before her. "Enjoy."

The salty bacon and buttery toast delighted her tastebuds. Beside the dining room, she caught sight of a small outdoor area with potted ferns and one lemon tree. Cute.

"How did you sleep?" Nick hugged a mug of coffee.

"Wonderful. Thank you so much for letting me have the bed." She took another bite of egg with toast.

He grinned lop-sided. "I bear my cross daily."

She smirked. "So, what are we going to do about the sleeping arrangements?"

"It's all taken care of." He sat back in his chair. "I went to Target this morning and bought a single blow-up mattress. I'll move the sofa to the wall and sleep in the living room."

Beth took a sip of water Nick had set on the table next to the salt and pepper shakers.

"Okay. Don't tell my dad, though. He'd get the wrong idea."

"Where did he think you were staying?"

"I didn't know the details myself, and Dad didn't ask."

Nick nodded slowly. "Right." He leaned forward and touched her arm. "Sorry, it wasn't organized better. We thought we'd be married by now."

She patted his hand. "It's not your fault. If I'd made the time to volunteer at the church, I would've come across the marriage license envelope before you left Australia. Dad doesn't do admin. He left it all for me to handle, which I handed over to Sally, and she fell behind in processing the bills and mail while I was off swimming with whale sharks. Totally irresponsible. I feel terrible that I up and left everyone to take over my duties."

"You served your dad for years. He supported your wish to leave and start a ministry with me."

"True." She gave a small smile. "I'm sorry for seeming ungrateful last night. Now that I've had a big sleep, I promise I'll be in a better mood today."

Nick wriggled his eyebrows. "You can make it up to me by coming to the marriage office today."

Was there a rush to get married anymore? If she stayed with a church family, it wouldn't be urgent.

She cut into her toast. "Any progress with the Messianic Jews you connected with?"

"Yes. I had another zoom meeting last week." He sat up taller. "I shared the dream I had. They said to keep praying for the Lord's timing. But they're open to having us partner with them."

"That's wonderful, Nick." She touched his arm. "It's all coming together."

"Once we're married, I want to book our flights." He lifted one brow. "We could make it our honeymoon."

"All right. As long as we know where we'll stay before we leave." She half-grinned.

"You of little faith." Nick waved a teasing finger.

"Sometimes, I do feel like that with you. I like to make plans. This living-by-the-seat-of-our-pants deal is not my style. I know Jesus didn't have a place to lay his head, and the disciples were told to take nothing for their journey, but that's hard to do." She took another mouthful of food.

"Especially for a woman, I suppose. I'm used to the bachelor's life, so I've only been responsible for myself."

She nodded and swallowed. "I've already asked you a million questions in the first two weeks from when we met in Fremantle . . ."

"That you did." He chuckled.

"But I still feel I don't know much about you, and we're getting married so quickly."

His brows furrowed. "What are you saying? We've got our whole lives to get to know each other."

"There are things I need to know, like what's our financial situation?" She leaned back. "How are we covering our costs in Jerusalem?" She had some savings, but after paying for her flight, and losing pay to the Exmouth trip, her bank balance had plummeted. She also needed to pay half the rent until Melissa found a replacement tenant. How long would that take?

"I have savings from my Navy service. It'll cover our flights and about two months' living expenses, but after that, I'll need to get work if we don't receive missionary support. I'll be asking the missions director of my church if they'll sponsor us."

"Okay. I thought you'd have a plan." She smiled. "I just didn't know any of it yet."

"The last two months have flown by in a blur." He collected some of her hair and whipped it playfully. "But you trust me, right?"

"I trust you enough to follow you to America." But most of all, she trusted the Lord. If she didn't have any faith, this whole thing would be ridiculous.

CHAPTER EIGHTEEN

L.A. DIDN'T REQUIRE a thirty-day wait for a marriage license. After collecting the hard-earned paper, they headed to Nick's church. He enjoyed Beth's jaw-dropped expression as she took in the historical theatre building.

"This is the church you go to?" Awe filled Beth's voice. "It's beautiful."

He looked at her. "Very beautiful." He took her hand in his, and they crossed the street. The Tuscany-colored building towered above them, covered with intricate lacework and stained-glass windows.

Inside the grand entrance, rows of padded seating circled the main auditorium. A well-lit stage at the far end had two cameras on tripods and thick theatre curtains on either side.

"So, this is what they call a Megachurch?" Her voice became soft. "Massive."

"Four services on Sundays. Plus, Friday and Saturday night."

"New Life church only has two hundred members, one service. Once a month, Dad runs a worship night as well." Beth lifted her head and made a slow turn as she took in the amphitheater. "I've never been anywhere like this before."

"The world awaits you, dear Beth." He winked. "Let's find the pastors. There's eight of them on full-time staff. We need to see the mission's director, and if you want, we'll ask a pastor to do the ceremony."

Her eyes lit up. "Would we have the service here?"

He cringed. "I'd love to, but we'd need to book months in advance. Maybe a year. And there are costs involved. I thought a pastor could come to the marriage registry or an outdoor wedding. But with the video conferencing for your family, it's better indoors."

Beth's face fell.

It would be a very grand wedding, if held in this church. But he didn't have many friends or family to validate such a huge venue. And he didn't want to linger in L.A. any longer than necessary. God had things for him to do.

"The offices are this way." He gently tugged on her hand, and they walked down the dimmed corridor.

A modern-styled foyer came into view with a receptionist behind a plexiglass barrier. A mini bee-hive bun topped her head. It wobbled a bit as she tapped away and squinted at her computer screen, oblivious to their arrival. Nick cleared his throat.

"Oh, hello. Welcome to Oasis Church. How can I help you?" she said in a singsong tone.

"We'd like to meet with one of the pastors about booking a marriage ceremony."

She peered down her nose over her glasses. "Are you a member of this church?"

"Not officially." He switched his weight from one foot to the other. "I've been away with the Navy for six months, and I travel a lot."

"Which pastor would you like to see?"

"Is Garrison available? Actually, ask the missions director. I need to talk to him anyway."

"Okay. I'll see if Pastor Jeremiah is free to chat with you now. Please, take a seat." She gestured to a white leather sofa next to a water dispenser.

"Thank you," Beth said.

Ten minutes later, they sat in a small office with a world map mural on one wall. Pastor Jeremiah wore a dark blue knitted sweater with black-ribbed jeans and boots. All the pastors were super trendy here. A few of them had the same haircut, a slicked wave at the front, and a fade up the sides.

Pastor Jeremiah gestured to the two armchairs. He rolled his from behind the desk and positioned himself in front of them. "How can I help you?"

Nick touched Beth's knee. "We obtained our marriage license today, and we'd like a Christian pastor to marry us. Beth is from Australia, where we met, but the license didn't come in time before I had to leave. Unfortunately, her father, who is a pastor, was unable to give her away, but her family will watch on video. We'd like to get married as soon as possible, as we have plans to minister in Jerusalem."

Pastor Jeremiah's lip curled, and his brows furrowed slightly. "I see. How long have you known each other?"

Nick's heart skipped a beat. What did that have to do with anything? He'd already explained that Beth's father had approved.

Beth straightened. "We met seven weeks ago. My father has given us his blessing and feels this is God's orchestration. Nick visited our city while working for the Navy." Beth smiled at Nick. "Instead of a long-distance relationship, we decided to marry straight away. I arrived in America last night."

The pastor scratched at his trimmed beard. "At Oasis Church, we do pre-marriage counseling before leading a couple in marriage vows."

Nick crossed his arms. "I'm thirty-eight-years-old, Pastor Jeremiah, and Beth is thirty-three. We aren't twenty."

The Pastor nodded calmly. "Last month I counseled a sixty-year-old widow and widower who wanted to marry. They weren't offended by the idea. They embraced it."

Nick adjusted in his seat. "How many sessions do we need to have?"

"The standard is six, but since you have plans to leave the country, we could make it four."

Nick rubbed his head. Four. Would that be four weeks? He didn't want to waste time.

"Okay. Another subject I wanted to discuss with you is our ministry to Jerusalem. Can I share with you what the Lord has laid on my heart?"

"Certainly." The pastor smiled, and for the next fifteen minutes, Nick explained his dream and the contacts he'd made with the Messianic Jews.

"Nick, I appreciate your passion to reach out to the Jewish community. Here at Oasis, we have a large outreach portfolio. Our congregation gives generously to overseas missions. But we usually sponsor missionaries through an oversight agency. Have you considered contacting an organization like Mission Outreach?"

"I heard that training is required and often Bible college certificates."

"Yes, they prefer this and want accountability for funds spent."

"Right." Nick clapped his hands together and stood. "Well, thank you for your time, Pastor Jeremiah. You've given us some things to think over." He offered his hand.

The pastor stood and shook hands with both Nick and Beth. "You're welcome. If you decide to take up the offer for counseling, contact the receptionist."

"Okay." He turned to Beth and gestured toward the door. Nick couldn't wait to get out of the office and into the fresh air.

When they were out of the building, Nick let out a sigh of relief. "What a waste of time." He edged to the pavement, looking left and right for a clearing in the traffic. A mixture of diesel and gasoline fumes assaulted his nostrils. "Let's get out of here." He grabbed Beth's hand and rushed her across the street.

Once inside his Honda Civic, he clicked the gears into reverse and the wheels let out a squeal as he zoomed out of the parking lot.

"Nick, are you okay?"

He jabbed the gear shift into second. "How do you think it went?" A touch of sarcasm laced his voice.

"Made sense to me. Most churches follow that protocol."

"Rules and regulations. Policies and procedures. It gets in the way of following the spirit."

Beth wriggled in her seat. "Their church is full to the brim and supporting great work. I imagine with the dynamics of managing such an organization, there would need to be plenty of guidelines."

"Managing and organization are an interesting choice of words. They manage and control the people. It's not a business. It's God's church."

"If we ever run a megachurch, I guess we'll know more to pass judgement."

"Beth, we are going to do great and amazing things, and it won't be in the confines of a building."

She remained quiet. Did she think he was wrong?

He cleared his throat and looked to her. "The Hollywood sign isn't far from here. You want to see it?"

Beth's eyes lit up. "Sure. I've seen it on television for years, it will be surreal to see it in person. I still can't believe I'm in America." Beth's voice sped up. "I'd seen myself visiting Asian countries on mission trips, but never America. No reason for it. Do you think we could do a road trip one day? Travel around."

Her enthusiasm warmed his soul. He let out a breath. "With you by my side, I'd go anywhere. To the ends of the earth and back. I love you." He reached for her hand and squeezed it. "I thank the Lord every day for sending you into my life."

She smiled sweetly. "I love you too."

* * *

The weather wasn't too different from Perth. Although winter, a nice afternoon sun came through the clouds. The wind whipped hair around her face as she stood gazing at the famous Hollywood sign.

Nick had known the quickest way to get a decent view from Lake Hollywood Park. She'd taken a few snaps with her iPhone but it didn't look impressive on the small screen. Maybe she could buy a postcard somewhere and send it to Melissa. She'd be the only one interested. The Michaels family didn't care much for Hollywood.

"Beth, see how the 'D' looks farther apart from the other letters?"

She squinted. "Yeah. Why is that?"

"Apparently they are evenly spaced. But it doesn't appear that way. Not everything is what it seems." Nick became silent as he stared at the sign.

Her fiancé was the philosophical sort. A deep thinker.

He spoke again. "I believe that Hollywood will continue to unravel. With the internet making megastars out of ordinary people like YouTubers, and social media dominating screen time, the traditional ways will fall away." He stared at Beth with great intensity. "It's the same with the church. Megastar preachers will be a thing of the past. Ordinary people like you and me will not be limited by a single location. We can run our own online ministry. Reach millions for Jesus." He gripped her hand. "Do you see it, Beth?"

She blinked. See what? Nick and Beth becoming YouTube Evangelists? "Do you still want to go to Jerusalem?" Wasn't Israel the plan?

"No limits, Beth." He spread his arms wide. "No limits. God is showing me many things. Signs. They're everywhere, confirming I'm on the right path."

She raised her brows. "You are on the path or 'we?'"

He laughed and wrapped his arms around her waist and swung her in a circle. She giggled like a girl. Nick loved to kid around and made her feel young. Sometimes she felt older too, because she acted much more serious. She was a practical person. Nick was the total opposite. A dreamer. The optimist.

He held her close and pressed his lips firmly against hers. Then he rested his hands on her hips, and his eyes searched hers. "Let's book in a time and day at the marriage office. We'll have the ceremony in their hired registry room. We need to get married. Now." He kissed her passionately. The most he'd ever had before. It surprised her. She responded, liking the change in his affection. She wanted him to desire her, not for only a ministry partner.

He stood back. "There's more where that came from." He grabbed her hand and nearly yanked her toward the car.

This was a Nick she hadn't known before. Who was she kidding? Did she even know him at all? But it excited her to become caught up in his vision, Nick leading the way, and taking her places she'd never dreamed she would go.

CHAPTER NINETEEN

THAT EVENING, BETH made her signature dish, Sri Lankan Chicken Curry. They sat in the small dining room, listening to a podcast from Israel while they ate. Nick gobbled his food in minutes. She dipped the large metal spoon into the casserole dish, and scooped more of the bubbly, buttery sauce along with a drumstick and cubed potato. Waves of steam drifted in the air, as she poured it into his bowl. The whole room emanated cumin, cardamom, and paprika spices.

The sermon finished, and an Israeli song came next. Fascinating cultural music, but she had to bite back a smile when the singer pronounced her r's with a throat-curdling spitting sound. Nick was getting into the moment, and the likelihood that he would find her amusement disrespectful, made it difficult to resist turning into a giggly schoolgirl. In science class, she'd gotten into trouble when her friend had made some silly joke about Mr. Hennrison always wearing brown. How had she kept a straight face when she'd asked him, "Is your favorite color brown, sir?" They'd been shocked when he'd said nothing and just grinned.

Nick turned down the music. "What's making you smile?"

She blinked. "Oh, my mind drifted to another time. Nothing. It's nothing." She lifted another spoonful to her mouth.

He touched her hand. "Well, I'm glad you're happy—whatever it is that makes you smile."

She picked up a paper napkin and wiped her mouth. "Nick, when am I going to meet your mother? On the day of the ceremony?"

He leaned back and patted his belly. "That was an amazing meal, hon. Another talent of my beautiful wife-to-be."

She smiled.

His forehead wrinkled. "It's a long way for Mom to drive, so I assume she'll come the afternoon of the ceremony. I booked it for four-thirty p.m., the last slot before closing, which is seven-thirty a.m. for your family."

"Oh, that's why you made it so late. When you've got the links ready, I'll send it to my family's group chat."

"Beth, I haven't been in Los Angeles much the last couple of years and lost touch with most people." He rubbed his cheek. "I used to live in Oceanside near my mom. So, I'm not going to invite anyone to the ceremony. I'll post a link to a select group of friends on Facebook who want to watch the live video."

"Okay," She said slowly, then shrugged. "We're in the same situation then. I don't know any of your friends anyway. It'll be nice to meet your mother though."

"Mmm."

His mother couldn't be that bad. Beth cleared her throat. "So, two weeks from today, and we'll be married. Do we need visas for Israel?"

"No. Not American citizens." His eyes widened. "Oh, I better check that it's the same for Australians. I think a visa is needed for anyone who wants to stay longer than ninety days."

"Right. Well that's definitely something you should check before paying for any flights."

His chair scraped the tiled floor as he stood. "Let me take your bowl and I'll clean up the kitchen. You put your feet up. Relax." Nick stacked the bowls and spoons and headed to the sink—a total five steps from the table.

The sofa wasn't a place to sprawl out, so she retreated to the bedroom. She flopped onto the queen bed, stretched to the bedside table, and grabbed her phone. Time to catch up with the other side of the world. She'd never been much of a Facebook fan, but she intended to check it regularly now. She clicked on the notification bell and froze. Lachlan Peters had sent her a friend request. What? She clicked off her screen and faced the phone down.

He hadn't sent her a personal email in nearly a year, and now he wanted to be friends? They didn't have shared contacts, so he must have looked her up. How did he know which Bethany Michaels was her? She'd put a generic profile pic of the Fremantle shoreline. He must've recognized it. Hang on, he knew Chris, so maybe he friended Cassie, and then saw her name as a suggestion.

She grabbed her phone again, her heart racing. Why did this matter? Lachlan was a friend of the past—barely that. She opened the app again and clicked on his profile. Oh—still handsome as ever. A beard? He must've finished with the Navy. *Click.* She chucked her phone to the other side of the bed. She couldn't accept his request. Even if Facebook offered a way of indirect and limited communication. She wasn't even Facebook friends with Nick yet. And if he found out she'd recently friended a Navy guy, he might ask questions.

Was Lachlan's profile picture recent? Totally free from the Navy? Two years had passed. Had he signed another contract?

Beth sat upright. Why was she even giving Lachlan two seconds of her time? He'd made it clear she wasn't worth his. Five-word sentence responses to her long emails. She needed a shower. That always cleared her mind and helped her relax.

* * *

When Beth entered the kitchen, she found a note on the Laminex counter. "Gone for a prayer walk." Without her? Couldn't Nick wait for her to finish in the shower?

She huffed out a sigh as she opened the freezer. Ice cream for one then—more for her. She took out the cookies and cream gourmet dessert and spooned three scoops into a wine glass.

Was it safe to walk the streets here? Her eyes widened. People in America had guns. She covered her mouth. Did Nick have a gun? He'd been in the Navy and would be comfortable with one. Was it here in the apartment? Did he take it with him? Panic flashed through her as she dropped her spoon. She raced to the bedroom and checked the bedside tables, then under the mattress. She'd never seen a gun in her life, only a replica old-fashioned one at the Ned Kelly exhibition years ago.

Taking deep breaths, she chose not to become overwhelmed. Nick knew what he was doing. He would walk around the block and have a lovely time praying. Something she needed to do more of. And she needed to keep things in perspective. Her body would be out of whack with a fifteen-hour time difference, twenty-one hours of travel, all the rushing around the following day—no wonder she couldn't rationalize. She needed more sleep. After a Bible study and a catch-up nap, she'd feel a lot better.

* * *

Hours later, Beth sleepily reached toward the bedside table where the lamp remained on and tapped her phone. 3:17 a.m. Oops. She rolled on her back, then flinched when she saw a body next to her. Nick! He lay on top of the doona with the same clothes he'd worn that day and his shoes still on. What time had he come home?

He must've been exhausted to have skipped changing. Although they'd be married in two weeks, she felt strange to wake up beside him, to be in the same bed. It would be more special if they waited until they were married, even though he'd promised to keep his hands to himself.

She quietly lifted the covers and slipped out of the room. Fumbling in the dark hallway, she ran her hands along the smooth wall until she found a switch in the living room. The mattress leaned against the wall and a folded blanket lay on the coffee table. She set herself up and snuggled under the thick, gray blanket, ready to sleep. The blow-up wasn't uncomfortable. Maybe they could alternate who got the bed from now on.

It took her a while to fall asleep. Some time later, she woke to the scent of coffee and scraping of metal. Nick stood in the kitchen. The slightest glint of morning sun shone through the blinds behind him.

"You're up early." She croaked from the living room as she wobbled, sitting up.

He scooped sugar into his mug and stirred. "I don't need much sleep. Going to go for a jog after this." He lifted his coffee and took a sip.

"What time did you get home last night?" She flicked off the blanket and made her way to the dining table, smoothing out her unruly hair.

"Late." He took a seat opposite her.

"What were you doing? Isn't it unsafe to walk the streets alone?"

He chuckled. "Glendale is okay. But I did come across a homeless person outside a seven-eleven. I sat talking with him for a long time."

She rubbed her eyes. "Witnessing?"

"Yes." He scratched at his unshaven cheeks. "I also deposited some money into his account."

Beth was suddenly more awake. "You asked him for his bank account details and he gave them to you?"

"Yes." He laughed. "He needed the money."

"How much did you give him?"

"Two hundred dollars."

"Nick, he might spend that on alcohol and drugs. You should've bought him food or gave him a voucher."

His face scowled. "The Lord led me to give him the money."

"Sure. But in my experience, when our church ran a food program and helped pay bills for those struggling, we never gave cash." She shook her head. "It's too much of a temptation for them to get high."

Nick thumped his mug to the table. "Not everyone ends up on the streets because of an addiction."

"I'm aware of that." She crossed her arms. "But how do you know if they tell you the truth? Druggies lie and cheat to get a fix."

He waved his hand in dismissal. "You sound like a Pharisee, like Pastor Jeremiah. Rules. Procedures. No yielding to the promptings of the Holy Spirit."

She blinked owlishly. "Excuse me?"

"You heard me," he raised his voice. Nick flicked back his chair and dumped his coffee in the sink. "I'm going for that jog." He walked out the door with a slam behind him.

Beth remained dumbfounded and frozen.

Her mind whirled for several minutes as she tried to understand. She needed to talk to someone. Cassie.

In the bedroom, she sat with a red pillow on her lap and waited for Cassie to answer the messenger call.

"Hello, Beth! How's life in the U.S.?"

Emotion clogged in her throat, blocking her voice.

"Beth?" Cassie paused. "Can you hear me? You there?"

"Yes." She managed to squawk out.

"Are you okay?"

"No."

"Oh, honey. What's the matter?"

Beth squeaked a high-pitched whisper. "Sorry. I'm emotional from the jet lag, and I'm missing home."

"Oh. That's okay. Take your time. Breathe. I'll go somewhere quiet. Chris is watching T.V." The sound of swishing came through the speaker.

Beth wiped her cheek and exhaled a shaky breath.

"Is everything going okay with Nick?" Cassie asked.

"He's very . . . spiritual. Sometimes, I'm not sure if it's sound. Do you know what I mean?"

"Can you give me an example?"

"There are lots of those." She went on to explain what just happened.

"Mmm." Cassie waited for a moment. "What's his church like?"

"He's not that connected with them. We met a pastor to see if they'd do the wedding ceremony, but Nick didn't want to do the pre-marriage counseling. And he's angry with them for not wanting to support our ministry in Israel. The pastor said we should go through an over-sight mission agency."

"That's wise advice."

She swiped an escaped tear. "I thought so too. But Nick wants to be led by the Holy Spirit, not a man."

"That sounds grand and all, but not everyone has accurate discernment with every decision. Sometimes it's our own ideas, so it helps to have accountability. And if you feel uneasy by Nick's words or actions, you should be able to voice your opinion without him calling you a Pharisee. That's a red flag to me. If he's irritated and snappy at you when you're genuinely concerned, then that's not working as a team. Is that how you want him to lead you in a marriage?"

She reached to the bedside table and grabbed a tissue. "Of course not."

"Beth, can I be honest with you?"

"You're always honest with me." She sniffed. "I called you for help, so tell me what you think I should do."

"Delay the wedding. Insist that you do pre-marital counseling. And bring up these situations with the pastor."

She swallowed. "You're right."

"Did I ever tell you about the time when my friend, Chantelle, met this super-spiritual guy?"

"No."

"He seemed amazing when I first met him. I encouraged her even." She hissed. "He proposed to Chantelle within a few weeks. She didn't say yes, but oh, it took her months to untangle from his web. He had some strange ideas, and she was confused for a while, but eventually, she knew something wasn't quite right."

Beth swapped her phone to the other ear. "Nick's a nice guy. He's got a good heart, Cass. I don't think it's exactly the same as your friend's situation."

"Nick can be a great guy and still get things wrong. I'm sure he genuinely wants to serve God. That's not in question here."

A click from the front door sounded.

"Cassie, I've gotta go. He's back."

"Okay. I'll be praying. Stay strong."

"Thanks for the talk." She hung up and plugged her phone into its charger.

CHAPTER TWENTY

NICK WENT STRAIGHT to the shower upon returning from his jog. With a towel around his waist, he entered the bedroom. Beth wasn't there. Good. She'd probably have a fit if she saw him like this. But his clothes were in the wardrobe. What was a guy to do? At every corner, she resisted him on some level. Keeping her distance. Not connecting with him spiritually. She didn't even ask to pray with him. He hadn't seen her read her Bible yet. Although, it had only been a couple of days, and the Bible lay on the bedside table. Was it for show? How had she ministered in New Life church when she hardly prayed?

He put on his jeans and a Nike sweater and scuffed his hair with the towel. Beth had freaked out about him giving money away. What if she knew how many people he had witnessed to until the early hours of the morning? And about the other people he had given money to? God would replace the money somehow. But Beth wouldn't have the faith for that. He felt compelled to help people. He had the answer, and they were going to hell if he didn't stop them.

Time to face her condemnation again. He went out to talk with Beth, barefooted.

"Hey." He leaned on the wall at the entrance of the living room, arms crossed.

"Hi. Feel better after your run and shower?" Beth tucked her legs under her thighs on the sofa.

He wouldn't fall for that seductive look she was giving him. What if she had a Jezebel spirit? Controlling and using her sexuality to influence him. A distraction to God's purpose and calling.

She patted the space next to her. "Wanna sit down and chat?"

His eyes narrowed. "No, I'm good here, standing." He flicked his head back. "What's up?"

Beth moved her feet to the ground and placed her hands in her lap. "Is everything okay between us?"

"You tell me."

Beth took a deep breath. "Nick, I think it'd be a good idea to take the pastor's offer for counseling. It seems we aren't on the same page with some things."

With his shoulder, he pushed off the wall. "Is that so?"

She frowned. "Are you in a bad mood? Did I do something wrong?"

He forced a laugh but didn't answer.

"I've been adjusting to the new time zone and sleep pattern. Today will be much better. I should've gone for a jog with you." She fiddled with her cross necklace. "How much sleep did you get last night?"

His arms dropped to his side. "Maybe two hours. I haven't slept much this last week. Lots on my mind. I haven't stopped since I got off the ship. It's hard to stay still, wanting to get on with obeying God's voice." He stared into space, unfocused. "I must go to Jerusalem soon. I feel an urgency in my spirit." He turned to face her.

"I can see you're passionate about serving God. That's admirable." Beth tucked some hair behind her ear. "It would be good, while we're here in the U.S. to drum up some sponsorship. Maybe the small groups within the church will support your vision."

"Maybe."

"Um. I need to get some milk and eggs from the corner store. Do you want to come for a walk?"

"No. I'm making a quick call to Malachi. I need to share with him what the Lord has shown me this morning."

Beth blinked. "Oh. Okay. I'll make you some breakfast when I get back."

He nodded, although he didn't want her to cook for him. Not now.

* * *

Beth entered the brightly lit convenience store. Neat rows of colorful fruit in crates somehow lifted her mood. She could do with some healthy treats. She lifted a pineapple and read the sticker. The store must've imported all these tropical fruits. Nick would love the variety. She grabbed a blue shopping basket and put in the pineapple, then added figs, apricots, and strawberries.

A lady moved through the narrow aisle, wearing a polo shirt with the store's logo above the pocket. "Good mornin', ma'am. How are you today?"

"I'm well, thank you. You?"

The woman's brown eyes widened. "You from Australia?"

"That I am." Beth smiled.

"I don't meet many Australians around these parts, but I'd know that accent anywhere. Just like Nicole Kidman."

Beth couldn't help laughing. "I'm not as well-spoken as Nicole, but thank you for the compliment."

The stocky lady bent down and adjusted the cartons of juice, bringing the back ones to the space at the front of the lower shelf. "How long are you staying in California?"

"A few weeks." She added two apples to her basket. "I haven't met anyone yet. Not a proper conversation with any of the locals. I've only been here for a few days, and I'm feeling homesick already. Never been out of Australia. I'm from a close-knit community. Small population."

"People keep to themselves here. But, if you get involved in the activities, you'd meet lots of friendly folks. We have a notice board in the window. You should check it out. Yoga classes, Zumba, mother's groups, there's something for everyone."

"Thank you." She hesitated. "I'm Beth, and your name is?"

"Sally." The African American woman stood, her hip leaning to one side. "You look like a homey-type-a-gal. Would you be interested in a craft group at the library? I go on Tuesday mornings, my day off."

"Really? That's nice of you to invite me. What crafts do they do?"

"People bring their projects and morning tea to share. I crochet. Some paint, scrapbook, dress jewelry, art, anything you like."

Beth swapped the basket to her other arm as it weighed heavy. "That sounds wonderful. I'll talk to my fiancé about it."

Sally raised a brow. "You need permission to visit the library?"

Beth let out a small laugh. "No. He may have other plans for us that day. That's all."

"Well, I hope he can rearrange any plans so you can have some time with the ladies. It'll do you good."

"I'm sure it will." She felt better already. "Which building and what time?"

"Library Connection. Ten o'clock."

"Wonderful."

Beth continued to meander around the store. Self-serve dried fruit, nuts, and snacks lined one wall, and she couldn't resist her sweet tooth for chocolate-coated almonds. In the meat section, she scanned the options; salmon fillet, lamb liver—yuck, Red-Trout, Quail? In a corner store? Fancy-pansy. She picked up the salmon and placed it into her overflowing basket. Oh, she needed to get back to the apartment. Nick would've settled for cereal by now. She'd taken much longer than she'd intended.

Beth paid for the goods and thanked Sally once again for her friendship.

* * *

When Beth returned to the unit, the door remained slightly ajar. That suited her, with arms aching from the two shopping bags full of groceries. After using her hip to bump the door, she entered.

"Honey, I'm home." She'd always wanted to say that. Beth grinned as she placed the food on the counter.

She called out again, "Nick, do you want to see what I bought? So many yummy options down there. Sorry, I took so long."

He must've fallen asleep. He'd only had a few hours last night. She continued to unpack the groceries, humming a tune that played in her head.

Before she started on the fruit salad, she would check on Nick, in case he'd woken from her calling out and wanted to join her for breakfast.

She slowly creaked open the bedroom door. The covers were pulled aside—no Nick. Had he gone out again? Not even a text? She slid out her phone from her back pocket and checked to see if he'd called. Nothing.

Beth called his number, frustration building inside her. In their counseling session, they needed to address the topic of communication. The call rang out. Maybe he was driving. He'd call back soon.

* * *

By ten in the evening, Beth was a wreck. She sat rocking on the bed with her arms wrapped tightly around her legs. Why wouldn't he answer her calls? Had he had a car accident? No one would know to call her. Was he still angry with her because she'd questioned him about his decision to give the homeless guy two hundred dollars? If so, it was unfair to punish her like this and avoid her calls. She didn't know anyone here. He had the only door key, and if she left the apartment, their things could get stolen.

Beth picked up her cell and checked the time for Perth.

10:15 p.m. Los Angeles, 1:15 p.m. for Perth. She dialed Cassie's number.

"I've been thinking about you. How did Nick take the news?"

"He's not here. I don't know where he is. I walked to the corner store in the morning, came back, and he was gone. Nick won't answer my calls."

"How long since you last saw him?"

"Thirteen hours." She was about to burst into tears. But she'd already cried most of the day and her emotions were spent.

"How could he do this to you? Oh, Beth. I'm so sorry this has happened." Cassie growled. "I should've spoken up more. I didn't want to come across too strong, but I worried that the engagement had happened too fast."

"I didn't even get to tell him that we needed to slow it down."

"So why did he leave?"

"I don't know what's going on in that head of his. He's been a bit out of character. Nick is usually caring and loving. But he was annoyed this morning. He wouldn't even sit next to me on the sofa."

"Let's back up. Tell me everything you said to each other before you left for the store."

Beth recalled word for word, which wasn't hard as they hadn't spoken long.

"So, who's Malachi?"

"Nick's contact in Israel."

"So, he hasn't slept much for days, and he urgently needs to get to Jerusalem. Beth, has he taken any of his clothes?"

"Do you think he's left me for good?" Her voice shrilled.

"I don't know. Are all his things still in the apartment?"

Beth flung herself off the bed and yanked the wardrobe door open. "Oh, my goodness! This is not happening. No."

"Beth?"

She ran her hand over her face. Her heart pounded in her eardrums. Nick didn't have many possessions or clothes, but nothing remained. The top shelf where he'd crammed his duffel bag was empty too. "The worst possible scenario."

"The worst scenario would be marrying him. You've found out before it's too late."

She ran a hand through her knotty hair. "But . . . I love Nick."

"Do you? In two months, you deeply love him?"

"I thought I did." She swallowed. "But I don't really know him . . . do I?" She reached out to the wall to steady herself and slid to the floor.

"Oh, Beth. I'm so sorry this has happened." A little child's voice spoke in the background. Johannah. Cassie whispered. "Mummy is on the phone, sweetie. Here, have a cookie." The sound of plastic crumpling came next and a cute "tank you" from the toddler.

"Sorry." Cassie returned. "Do you know anyone there?"

"The lady at the corner store," she said weakly. "Maybe she'll be there tomorrow morning on shift. She invited me to a craft group."

"How long do you have the apartment for?"

"A month or two. But I don't have the key. I think." She jumped off the floor and searched the house while Cassie kept asking questions.

"I can't find it. Nick left the door open this morning. It's his friend's apartment. I don't even know who that is."

"This is terrible." Cassie sounded annoyed. Rightly so.

"I can't stay here. I won't be able to lock the door. What if I came back and a robber was in here, or my things got stolen?"

"Beth."

"Yes?"

"You need to come back to Australia."

CHAPTER TWENTY-ONE

BETH PRAYED DURING her shower and came out feeling a touch better. She repeated God's promise from the book of Hebrews. "I will never fail you. I will never abandon you." At least, she wasn't close to nervous break-down anymore.

She grabbed an apple and her phone and sat at the dining table. As she flicked through airline ticket prices with her left index finger, the engagement ring sparkled from the fluorescent light above. The ring. She needed to return it, but how?

The crunch of the apple between her back teeth was the only sound in the apartment. No T.V. or radio, and the thick walls drowned out any sound from the neighbors.

Alone in America. Knowing not a soul. No car. Not even a key to the front door. She didn't belong here.

An email notification popped up on her screen. A piece of apple jammed in her throat when she gasped. Lachlan? She coughed into her fist, then clicked the message.

Hello Beth,

I'm sorry I haven't kept in touch lately. I've recently finished my deployment and returned to San Diego. Not much is happening here, just working for my brother. But, I've been talking to Chris Evanson, and he offered me a position at Bayside Manna. It sounds like a great opportunity to see more of your amazing country and spend time with my Australian friends. That includes you, of course. That is, if we're still friends? Did you get my Facebook friend request?

How have you been? What's happening in the small town of Fremantle? I would love to hear from you.

Bye for now,

Lachlan.

Beth laid the phone back on the table and stared until the screen dimmed. She touched her cheeks. San Diego. Where was that? How far from L.A.? He'd just emailed, so maybe he could talk on messenger tonight. She could tell him—oh, how embarrassing. Shameful. Dumped in the U.S.A. Sounded like a song title. *Dumped in the U.S.A. yeah, dumped in the U.S.A., yeah.*

She clicked on Facebook and accepted Lachlan's friend request. She hadn't posted anything for months, but she wanted his friendship—even though he'd shunned her for almost a year. Opening the messenger app, she typed in his name and sent a message.

Hi Lachlan,

Thanks for your email. I'm available to talk now, can I call you on messenger?

The three dots waved as he typed. A smile appeared on her lips. He was in America. She had a friend in America.

Lachlan replied that she could call. One tap later, she held her breath and waited for his voice.

"G'day, mate," He said in a poor attempt at an Aussie accent.

"Oh, Lachlan. It's so good to hear from you."

He laughed. "Really? That's nice to know. Wow, I can't believe I'm talking to you after two years. Your photo appeared on my memories' notification the other day. The one with the Quokka."

She laughed. "Oh, I love that photo."

"Yeah. That was a great day."

She wriggled in her seat. "How's Wally? How did he weather the rest of his training?"

"Ugh, he didn't last much longer."

"Right." She swallowed. Her stomach dived, taking the plunge to ask him more. "So, you live in San Diego. How far is that from L.A.?"

"Two hours. Why's that? You know someone in Los Angeles?"

"Yes." She bit her lip. "Me."

"What? You're in L.A.? Are you joshing me? Serious?"

A bubble of joy rose in her belly. He sounded happy.

"So, I don't have to fly to the other side of the world to see you?"

She giggled. "Were you going to fly to Australia, just to see me?" Her tone turned sassy.

"It'd be worth it. What are you doing in L.A.? Did you hit it bigtime in journalism?"

Beth didn't know if she should laugh or cry at his comment. Now she had to tell him why she sat in an L.A. apartment, alone. Oh, it was so nice to forget, for just one minute.

"Beth, you there?"

"I have a sorry tale to tell." Where to start? "I'm embarrassed by how foolish . . . I . . ." Too late to chicken out, she'd contacted Lachlan—told him she was in America. He was a counselor—a safe person. Beth bit her fingernail. How would he feel about her falling for another sailor? Would he understand?

"I'm listening. No judgment here." His voice had not a trace of worry. Yet.

"True? I needed to hear that." She released a breath. "Thank you, Lachlan."

"So, how did you end up in the States?" he said in a singsong tone.

She started from the beginning, only two months ago. Lachlan listened, asking an occasional question. "Nick said he had an urgency to get to Jerusalem, and when I returned from the corner store, he was gone. Took his things. And I'm left here in an apartment with no key."

"He abandoned you? After you spent all that money, gave up your life in Australia, after a few days, just left you?" He whispered, "Beth, you poor thing."

"I am poor now. I've wasted so much money. On a wedding that didn't happen in Fremantle, then a flight to L.A. But I do have money to get home. Thank goodness."

Lachlan asked more questions about Nick's odd behavior.

"Beth, I've seen things like this happen before. My neighbor once had an episode where he couldn't sleep and had an urgency to tell everyone about his spiritual experiences. He wasn't even a Christian. Have you told Nick's family about what happened?"

"He only has his mother and doesn't speak with her much."

"Does she live nearby?"

Beth startled from a crash of metal outside. "Um. Somewhere on the coast, an hour from here." She crept to the peep-hole but found no movement nearby. "In an over-fifty-five villa or something."

"Newport Beach?"

Her legs became weak as she made her way back to the table. "No, but it's something beach."

"Longbeach?"

"No, I was wrong." She plonked herself into a wobbly dining chair. "It has the word ocean in it."

"Oceanside?"

"Yes, that's the one, and she's in a fancy retirement place. Hard to get into."

"And her last name would be?"

"DeHann."

"We could track her down."

She bit her fingernails again. "But Nick wouldn't want me to contact his mother. He doesn't believe she supports him, and they don't get along."

"His mom needs to know that her son is unwell. She's the next of kin."

"You're right. Poor lady, she'll be worried sick when she finds out."

"She can confirm if this has happened before. Because if it's what I think it is, this wouldn't be the first time."

Beth glanced at the diamond on her finger. "I hope we can locate her. I want to return the engagement ring before I leave the States."

The line went quiet. What did Lachlan think about her rash engagement? Disappointed?

"Beth, I'm sorry Nick left you. Remember this is about him, not because you aren't worth sticking around for. After the shock wears off and your life settles back in Australia, you'll recover when this is all in perspective."

"Thanks, Lachlan. It helps to have a friend who's a professional counselor." She smiled, and her shoulders relaxed. "I feel so much better knowing I'm not alone." She swallowed. "You did say 'we' when you said, 'we can track her down,' which I hope means you're going to help me."

"I'd feel awful if I didn't. I'm only two hours from L.A. Are you okay to stay in the apartment tonight? I can pick you up in the morning, and you can stay at my parents' house until you fly back. They have a spare room you can use. You shouldn't be alone, Beth. My folks are very hospitable, and it'd be no problem at all."

"You sure?"

"Certain. And Oceanside is only forty-minutes from me, so once we locate Nick's mother, we can visit her and explain the situation."

She let out a breath. "You're an answer to prayer and messaged me just when I needed you."

"I'm glad to help. Send me the address, and I'll be there by ten o'clock tomorrow."

"Okay."

"Get some sleep."

"I might be able to now. Bye, Lachlan. See you tomorrow."

"Look forward to seeing you again." He sighed. "Although I wish it were in better circumstances. Night."

* * *

The next morning, Lachlan woke early, had a light breakfast, and jumped into his exercise routine. He hadn't rested well after the phone call. He'd gone into counselor mode while she'd explained all that had happened. Emergency response. But it did pain him to know she'd fallen in love with someone else. Got engaged! And it could've been him. If he'd kept in contact and built on their friendship over the last two years, he would be the one organizing a wedding with her right now.

He paused his sit-ups and took a swig from a water bottle. His stomach ached from pushing himself hard—he wanted to punish his stupidity. In the Navy, he'd justified brushing Beth off because every time she made contact, he'd think about her continuously until he replied a day or two later. A polite, quick answer seemed to keep her at a distance. Eventually, he'd resorted to adding her to his group email list. She must've got the hint, and then what happened? Nick.

He stood, strode to the press machine, and adjusted the weights. He nestled onto the padded seat and held the bars. Taking even breaths, he counted in his mind, blocking the taunt of his regrets.

When he finished, he hopped in the shower. At this rate, he could get to Beth an hour earlier. What would it be like to see her again? He had squashed all feelings for her the last two years, and he'd need to do it again. The circumstances weren't right for Beth to consider him more than a friend. And he needed to get over the thought of her wanting another serious relationship. Casual ones weren't ever his style—he was all in or not at all.

Although she'd only been in the apartment with Nick a couple of nights, it made him wonder what level of intimacy they'd shared. The first day he'd met Beth, she'd spoken openly about her abstinence. As if that would turn him off to her, but it'd had the opposite effect.

Lachlan moved about on autopilot—dressed, shaved, and switched on the coffee machine. Beth's situation turned circles around his head. He smacked the old coffee grinds into the bin and scooped in a fresh batch. He needed to wake up to reality. He cringed at the memory of the last words he'd said on the beachside in Fremantle. "Beth, if we meet again, I promise you, I'll kiss you like there's no tomorrow." He jammed the coffee holder into place. Argh. He hoped Beth didn't remember those words. Boyish dreams that a woman would wait two years for him, while he served in the Navy. It hadn't worked before. And he guessed this wasn't too far from the same feeling he'd experienced when Laura broke up with him to date someone else.

The smell of Italian coffee licked his senses as the brown crema filled the bottom of his mug. Well, at least he and Beth could be friends. She came from a Christian family like his. Although her dad seemed stricter than his parents, Lachlan respected that. She'd make a good friend, and Beth needed him. He wanted to help her and would do everything he could to get her through this terrible time.

* * *

Lachlan worked up a smile as Beth swung open the door. Her eyes widened, and she flung herself at him. "Lachlan, you're here."

He stiffened and patted her back. Completely opposite the feeling he'd experienced the last time he'd held her. "I said I'd come." He mumbled into her hair. No coconut scent this time.

Why did he remember what she used to smell like? He stepped back.

"Come in, come in." Beth swooshed her hand and welcomed him into . . . a box.

He scanned the dull surroundings. The place lacked color. Lacked floor space. "You're going to appreciate my folk's home. Much cheerier."

She laughed. "I know, right. More like a prison than a—" Her voice trailed off as she flapped her arms, circling the living room. A sadness shadowed her expression. "I don't want to stay here a minute longer than I need to. I'm all packed. Hadn't unpacked in the first place."

Lachlan flicked a glance to the mattress against the wall, then looked back to Beth, hoping she didn't notice.

Her jaw dropped, and she stuttered. "I didn't share a bed with him, Lachlan."

His cheeks heated at his wrong assumptions. But relief flooded him at the same time. "That's none of my business."

"Just for the record, I want you to know that nothing in the slightest happened between Nick and I." Her ponytail flicked in the air as she spun and strode to the kitchen.

Beth's indignation and sassy ways were still as strong as ever.

She collected her phone and handbag. "All the luggage is in the bedroom. There's a lot of bags." She turned and gave a magnificent smile—one that warmed his heart. Man. Helping Beth wasn't going to be easy.

CHAPTER TWENTY-TWO

BETH CLIMBED INTO Lachlan's Ford Ranger and released a long exhale. The click of the back door signaled he'd finished cramming all her luggage. Good thing he had a Four-wheel-drive.

She clicked her seatbelt and waited as Lachlan hopped into the driver's seat. "You don't know how much this means to me—not having to face this alone." She offered a smile, and he returned a compassionate glance.

She bit her thumbnail. "When we meet Nick's mother, I'll let you start the conversation."

"First, we need to locate her." The engine roared to life. Lachlan flicked on the turn signal, and pulled into the narrow street. "If we can't, we'll stop at a police station and ask them to contact her. If Mrs. DeHann wants to speak with us, she can call."

Lachlan merged into a highway bearing five lanes of lined-up cars. Busy for a Saturday.

"I remembered her name this morning—Nick's mother. He had a girlfriend who called her Mamma Sue."

Lachlan gave a solemn nod. "Susan DeHann."

"Are your folks okay with me staying?" She frowned. "You didn't guilt them into hosting me?"

Lachlan chuckled and changed gears. "Not at all. They're having a family dinner tonight with my sister and brother and their children. But if you want to skip that, I can take you out for pizza until they're all gone."

"No, that's okay. I would like to be around people. Maybe if you don't tell your sister and brother the details of why I'm here, it'd be less awkward."

"Sure." Lachlan turned on the stereo.

A familiar song, 'Way Maker,' began to play. Beth closed her eyes. The steady high-hat beat, accompanied by gentle piano, calmed her soul. The melody washed over her, and peace settled within. Her head fell back upon the headrest as the music climbed, the base kickstarting her heart back to life. She hummed the chorus, the words reminding her that God had her back. She dropped her hands to her side, surrendering control of the future.

Upon the next song, her eyes fluttered open. The mid-morning sun filtered through the cloud cover, warming her face. "I needed that song." She smiled at Lachlan.

"You seem more relaxed."

"I find it amazing how listening to worship music can clear the cobwebs almost instantly. It's like going to another place or gaining a different perspective on life. I can imagine Jesus standing in my boat, commanding the waves of worry to still."

"Yep. And the storms do come. There's no avoiding them. Life has trials."

She looked at him curiously. "Have you had any major trials?"

"Not anything uncommon for someone my age. But I've seen the effects of trauma in others. It's not always easy to distance myself from their pain. Often, I'd be disturbed for days until I gave the burden to God. Eventually, I learned to do that sooner than later. The emergency relief projects can take a toll emotionally. During the action, I'm fine responding, remaining calm for the people I help. Then there's the aftermath, and I can't believe what I've witnessed. Especially when it's small children. Breaks your heart."

Her dilemma seemed insignificant in comparison to what Lachlan spoke of. Another reality check. She'd get through her heartbreak. And she'd be wary of another man pushing her into marriage so quickly. How did she not see the signs? She proved her naivety—trusted too much. But that would change now. Next time, she'd have her security walls ready.

An hour later, Lachlan paralleled parked the Ford close to a beach.

"Is this Oceanside?"

"Not quite. We're in San Clemente. I need more coffee, and the stop will give me a chance to look up Susan DeHann's details. Then we have another twenty minutes to get there."

Beth stepped out of the car and stretched her legs. The wind flapped palm leaves that topped trees as tall as ten people. A rickety pier stretched out to the ocean.

Lachlan stood beside her and shielded his eyes. "Remember the Rottnest Island jetty? You looked like you'd struck gold when you got off the ferry."

She laughed. "Do you remember me throwing up on your shirt?"

"I recall the smell, yes." He bumped her shoulder with his.

"Ew." She grimaced. "What an introduction. Amazing you stuck around for the day."

Lachlan didn't answer but scratched the back of his neck. "Wanna come with me to get coffee? Or you could take a walk on the beach while I make some calls."

She wrapped an arm around her waist. "A walk and fresh air sound perfect."

"Okay. See you in ten minutes." He turned and crossed the road to the three-level SeaShore Apartments. A take-away coffee vendor stood next to a shop lined with surfboards.

Beth made her way down a staircase and crossed railway tracks to reach the pier. Several blue umbrellas bordered a restaurant and bar, but she continued down another level to the bottom step. Slipping off her shoes first, she stepped into the cool sand. Bliss. How could this be winter? An urge to run and let the wind turn her hair into a kite filled her imagination. A strange sensation of freedom flashed through her soul. She'd nearly married Nick, and there would've been no return. Her upbringing taught her marriage lasted for life.

A child played close to the water's edge, making a sandcastle while the mother sat on a beach towel, reading a book.

Beth strolled along the beach, appreciating the sparkling reflection of sunlight on the water and waves. Diamond dust. The diamond ring had a safe place in her handbag, ready to give to Mrs. DeHann. Why hadn't Nick asked for it back? The money would've covered his expenses in Israel. His impulsive behavior baffled her—one day proclaiming their destiny, the next day gone. She kicked at some sand and edged toward the water to test the temperature. Didn't Nick see that his actions contradicted what he'd said God told him? And what was that? More importantly, what had the Lord shown her? Cassie had urged Beth to quiet her soul and listen to the Holy Spirit. Had she even had time to do that before being swept into Nick's plans and rushed to another world? She'd left everything she loved to follow an empty promise.

Beth dipped her big toe, and a chill ran up her leg. Thank goodness she hadn't let Nick sleep with her. That first night, he'd mentioned he wasn't a virgin, and it didn't matter to him if they waited or not. When they had first met, her innocence had attracted him, but later, he hadn't cared—and she'd felt undervalued.

"Beth!" Lachlan's voice called from a distance.

She turned, and above the rocky cliff, Lachlan stood behind a rail and waved. His hair had grown from his Navy days. He wore it ungelled, and it had a curl to the ends, tossed about in the breeze. His white cotton shirt rippled across his sculpted chest and stomach. Her breath hitched as she waved back and headed to the staircase. Lachlan Peters. If only he'd contacted her two months ago. Too late. He wouldn't want her now. And he'd showed no desire for a relationship with her the last two years. Chasing after a sailor, impulsively giving her heart to a stranger had tainted her reputation, leaving her no chance.

By the time she made it to the blue Ford, she'd lost her grip on the relaxed state she'd achieved. Knots formed in her belly.

"You okay?" Lachlan frowned.

The sick disappointment must've shown on her face. "As can be expected."

Blip. He unlocked his car with a remote. "Sorry."

"You didn't do anything. You're my good Samaritan."

He grinned. "Get aboard the donkey then." He opened her door and closed it behind her.

As he reversed out of the parking lot and shifted to first gear, he glanced her way. "I have an address for a S.A. DeHann at Pacific Senior Village. It's in Oceanside. Want to head on? If she's not there, we can call and schedule a time to see her. I'd rather explain in person if we can."

"Agreed."

* * *

Susan DeHann placed the china tea set on the white-laced table, her movements fluid and unhurried. A fountain trickled in the corner of her delightful backyard, and wind chimes tinkled nearby.

"This is a lovely place you have here, Mrs. DeHann," Beth said.

"Please, call me Sue." The corners of her mouth creased as she smiled. "I've made many friends in the complex. I didn't feel alone during the Corona lockdown, either. Neighbors would chat from the balconies, and there's lots of park space and gardens to enjoy." A little tremor shook her hands as she unloaded the cups and saucers. She must be in her seventies. Waves of thin silver hair touched her drawn cheeks. Although her shoulders rounded, Sue could reach five foot, ten inches.

"How long have you lived here?" Lachlan asked.

"Eight years." She poured the tea into three cups, then sat. "Help yourself." She gestured to the cookies.

Lachlan lifted the milk jug and raised a brow at Beth. She nodded, and he added milk to her tea, and placed a chocolate-chip cookie on the saucer.

"So, you have some concerns about Nicholas?" Susan asked.

Beth flicked her gaze to Lachlan, and his eyes told her to be brave.

"Sue, I was engaged to your son. A swift engagement, mind you, but we had planned to get married in two weeks. Did he send you the details?"

"No. Nicholas is very protective of his personal life. He doesn't like my nagging." Her hazel eyes saddened. "You said, 'was' engaged. He's done it again, hasn't he?"

Beth straightened in her chair. "He's broken an engagement before?" She blinked. "Oh, Tracy. I didn't know they were—"

"Married. She filed an annulment, and the court accepted her reasons." Susan's tone held no emotion.

Lachlan squeezed Beth's hand under the table. He leaned toward Sue. "May I ask on what grounds it was approved, Mrs. DeHann?"

"Unsound mind. He became unwell and ended up in a hospital, a month after they were married. But he refused to stay on the medication when he got out, and Tracy couldn't handle his moods. They hadn't been together long before he'd proposed, and so the court could see, she didn't know he had mental health issues prior to the marriage. He hadn't told Tracy about past episodes."

Beth's pulse quickened. "He hadn't told me either. I didn't even know he'd been married before."

"Annulment is as if the marriage hadn't existed." Susan sighed. "But he should've told you. You can understand why he wouldn't, though?" She shook her head. "Nicholas denies he has an illness."

"I'm a qualified counselor, Mrs. DeHann. I'd imagine this has been difficult over the years, worrying about your son's welfare?"

Sue's eyes became glassy. "Yes. It breaks my heart. But he won't listen to me. Says I'm judgemental and critical. At twenty-three, he first had clinical depression, and he wanted help then. But when the mania occurs, it's a high he enjoys—until he crashes. And he will, eventually. Then I'll get a phone call from someone. Pay for the damages or a hospital bill."

Beth touched her lips. "I'm so sorry, Sue." She gulped. "He's in Israel, I think. That's the last conversation we had of his plans. Then he disappeared. He wouldn't answer my calls, so I don't know for certain of his whereabouts."

Sue forehead wrinkled. "He's visited there before, five years ago. But he ran out of money and begged me to pay for his flight home. I couldn't say no. He didn't sound well, and I worried he'd have an episode over there with no insurance."

Beth bit her lip. Would Nick become unwell in Israel? She glanced at Lachlan. Concern lined his face too. He knew more about these things than she did. Lachlan had seen his neighbor go through it.

"We'll keep him in our prayers. I hope he'll be okay." What else could she say? Was it okay to ask more questions?

Sue took a sip of her tea and carefully placed the rose china cup onto its saucer. "God will look out for him. He always does. It's too much for me in my old age to worry about him. My hands are tied. Until he humbles himself enough to listen to the professionals or those that come to care about him." She raised her palms. "So many people have tried." She shook her head.

"My neighbor has Bipolar. Medicine helps him manage it well. If Nick found a good psychiatrist willing to journey with him, it could change his life."

A budgie chirped from inside the house. The calming sounds of the wind chime and fountain also did little to alleviate the heaviness from the conversation.

"Nicholas doesn't like the way the medicine makes him feel. By the time he's ended up in a hospital, the doctors have to give heavy doses to stabilize the mania."

"My neighbor looked like a zombie his first day in the mental ward. Heartbreaking to see him that way. He had to have several adjustments before they found the right medicine for him. It's not perfect, but he holds a job and has a lovely family. No one would know he has Bipolar. He's stayed well for eight years now."

"Nicholas is a caring man. So many good qualities. And he does love the Lord. I know that's real. He'll do okay for six months, then the signs start showing. A few weeks or a month later, he becomes driven by grandiose ideas, and soon he can't sleep at night. And his mind crashes. Sometimes he burns those around him. Usually, that's me."

Sue met Beth's gaze. "If he tries to get back together with you. Don't accept him unless he's on reliable treatment—for a year, at least. He can't keep going off his medicine and breaking hearts."

How many girlfriends had Nick had? "I'm not planning to stay in the States. I'll be booking my flights back to Australia soon."

"Of course. I understand completely, dear." Sue brought a cup to her mouth, sipped her tea, then leaned back.

"I wanted to give you the ring before I leave. It must be worth a lot of money. He didn't hold back in splurging on me."

"That's another sign he's becoming unwell. He spends a lot when he elevates."

Beth's mouth went dry. When would his money run out? How much did he have left before he'd need his mother to come to his rescue? She gulped hard. "Nick gave two hundred dollars to a homeless person the night before he disappeared. In itself, it doesn't seem a bad thing, but in the middle of the night? I was concerned for his safety."

"During mania, he'll be invincible in his eyes," Lachlan said.

Beth collected her handbag from under the table and gave Sue the Pandora bracelet and the engagement ring. "I'm sorry. I don't have a message to pass on. I thought I did, but in light of what you shared today, knowing Nick wasn't well, I—" Tears stung the back of her eyes.

Lachlan rubbed her shoulder. Then he looked at Sue. "Can we pray together—for Nicholas?"

"Yes. I'd appreciate that." Sue reached out one hand to Lachlan and the other to Beth.

Beth took her frail hand in hers. Lachlan kept his other hand on Beth's shoulder.

"Lord, you know where Nicholas is right now." Lachlan paused. "You know the state of his mind, his confusion, and brokenness. God, have mercy on him. Protect Nick. Lead him home, and we pray he'll be open to receiving help this time."

Beth added. "Jesus, help Sue during this time. Give her peace and restore her relationship with Nick. May this situation bring them back together, and we pray that he'll see that his mother has always been for him, not against him. Bless Sue. Thank you for this beautiful place she lives in and her friends around her. Continue to bring support and love through her church family and neighbors."

Sue prayed next. "Thank you, Lord, for Beth and Lachlan." She squeezed Beth's hand. "May Beth feel free to move on, with no guilt or shame. Heal her heart from any disappointment and pain that Nick unknowingly caused her. Bless her travels as she returns to her country. And bless Lachlan for helping her through this time. In Jesus' name, Amen."

CHAPTER TWENTY-THREE

THE SMELL OF parmesan cheese, garlic, and bacon mingled in the air. Beth stood comfortably in the Peters' kitchen, peeling apples. At least she could be helpful. Cooking had become second nature, growing up in a big family. Judging by the number of dishes on the counter, Lachlan's family must be large too. When all five of her siblings eventually had children, family get-togethers would become a massive affair. Her niece needed some cousins.

A perfect spiral of unbroken apple skin dropped into the bowl. Hmm. Who'd be the next sibling to have a baby? Perhaps after Trudy got married, Beth would have another baby shower to organize.

"How many more apples do you need?" Beth looked to Mrs. Peters, who had opened the oven and retrieved another ceramic dish.

"All of what's in the bag. Thanks, darling." She placed the meatloaf on a heat mat.

"No worries."

Mrs. Peters let out a small laugh.

Beth smiled. "Did I say something funny?"

She shook her head, grinning. "I just love your accent and the Australian phrases you use."

"Oh, should I say, 'no problem' instead? We use that term also."

"Don't change a thing. You're perfect the way you are, dear." Mrs. Peters covered the dish with aluminum foil.

She'd welcomed Beth into her home like an old friend. Not a single condemning word or action for the predicament Beth had found herself in. Girly knick-knacks had transformed the spare room. Fresh flowers dazzled in a vase on the dresser, and guest soap topped fluffy towels positioned at the end of the bed.

Lachlan strode into the room. "Smells delicious, Mom." He placed his arm over his mother's shoulder and kissed her cheek as he picked a buffalo wing.

"Lachie! Hands off until the guests arrive."

"I am a guest." He tore a piece of meat with his teeth.

"You'll keep."

That was where Beth had heard the saying. She caught it from Lachlan two years ago and adopted it as her own.

The doorbell rang. "I'll get it." Lachlan made his way to the front room.

Beth slipped the apron over her head and used her palm to smooth her hair back

"Don't be nervous." Mrs. Peters smiled. "They'll adore you as I do. I'll finish the apple pie. How about you put drinks on the table?"

The calming effect Lachlan had on people must come from his mother. Mr. Peters seemed super relaxed too.

Beth fetched the carafes from the double-door fridge. The kitchen gleamed under the downlights. White marble counters, glossy white cupboards, and stainless steel appliances told her that their real estate business was doing well. Beth carried the jugs to the walnut square dining table. A ten-seater. Leather padded the high-back chairs, adding to the opulence.

Girly giggles came from the entrance, and Lachlan put on a funny voice. He came limping into the dining room, a little blonde girl clinging to his leg and another hanging from his shoulder, squealing.

"I seem to have lost someone. Beth, have you seen a cute girl in pigtails anywhere?"

She played along. "No. Maybe she's under the table." She bent down and pretended to look intently. "No little girls here."

Lachlan continued to limp toward the kitchen. "Kayla, where are you?"

The girl sitting on his shoe eyed Beth and mouthed "shh," as if Lachlan remained oblivious to her whereabouts. Beth gave her a thumbs up and followed them.

Mrs. Peters gushed over the grandchildren, unwinding Kayla from Lachlan's leg. Beth turned at a new voice. Kayla's mother?

"They've been hyped up from the moment we got in the car." The woman looked at Beth. "Hi." She glanced at Lachlan, her eyes full of questions.

"Kayce, this is Beth. My friend from Australia."

His sister's green eyes widened. "G'day." Kayce offered a hand.

Beth smiled as she shook it. "Y'all are so friendly—speaking my language." She drawled her words. "I'll have to come back here, right now."

Kayce raised a brow and burst out laughing. "Nice try."

"I'm better at British impersonations."

"Lachlan met Beth on an island off Australia's coast two years ago, and they kept in contact." Mrs. Peters explained. "We offered for her to stay a few days while she's visiting the States."

Kayce's blonde head nodded. "Mom's an awesome host. She literally had to kick me out of here when I turned twenty-five. The cooking is that good."

Mrs. Peters waved her hand and huffed. "I did not kick you out. But, yes, you needed to leave the nest."

Kayce crossed her arms. "Mark stayed 'til twenty-seven."

Mr. Peters walked into the room, tall and broad shouldered. "When will Mark and Lizzy arrive? Smells like dinner's almost ready."

"They're on their way," his wife answered.

The second blonde girl hid behind her grandmother, peeking at Beth. Lachlan seemed to notice and swung his niece onto his hip. "My friend won't bite you, Sasha." He winked at Beth. "She sounds kinda strange, but she's really nice."

Beth gave her sweetest smile to the girl. "Nice to meet you, Sasha. I'm from Australia. Do you know where that is?"

Sasha straightened her neck. "Where kangaroos come from?"

Beth clapped her hands. "Yes. That's right. Clever girl."

A man's voice boomed around the corner. "And Quokkas, I've heard."

"Uncle Mark!" Sasha wriggled out of Lachlan's arms.

"I see I'm not the favorite uncle." Lachlan crossed his arms.

A shorter, rounder version of Lachlan entered the room, followed by a woman and three kids.

Mark collected his niece and nodded at Beth. "I've seen you before, on Lachlan's phone's screen saver."

"She's not on my screen." His face flushed as he slid out his phone and flashed it to Mark.

Mark chuckled and mumbled something like "was." His wife stepped forward and bumped into her husband. "Ignore him. I'm Ann." She gestured to the older children. "This is Samuel, Esther, and Jonathon."

"Hi, kids." Beth waved.

"Well, dinner's ready." Mrs. Peters called. "Everyone in the dining room! Children, wash your hands."

Once they were seated, Mr. Peters blessed the food and started handing the dishes in a clockwise direction. Across the table, snippets of conversation rose with steam from Pyrex dishes. Beth wasn't sure about eating meatloaf or Brussel sprouts. On the American sitcoms, children complained about having to eat them. She'd do her best not to offend the cook and take small portions. Lachlan handed her a platter of cubed yellow cake. Dessert with dinner?

He smiled, amused. "Cornbread."

"Oh. Thanks." She took a piece and passed the plate to Kayce.

Lachlan leaned close. His spicy aftershave made her heart skip a beat. "You okay with my crazy family?"

She tucked some hair behind her ear. "No crazier than mine. I like them."

"Good." He turned and took another dish from Ann beside him.

To Beth's left, Kayce struggled to please the girls' complaints about the healthy options. The girls won, their small plates holding only cornbread, one buffalo wing, and a scoop of macaroni and cheese. No greens.

Amazingly, the whole family fit at the one table. Lachlan's arm often brushed hers, sending unrelenting shivers over her skin. Why did his closeness always have that effect on her? Truly annoying. Nick never caused tingles or flutters. They'd founded their relationship on ministry, and that had ended as an airy-fairy fantasy.

Instrumental jazz played from a sound system in the living room. His parents had style. They must be rich too. French doors to a separate theatre room connected to the living area. And the bedroom she was staying in had an adjoining bathroom with a spa bath. Lachlan mentioned they owned a real estate business, so it made sense they had immaculate home décor.

Once her plate was full, Beth carefully cut the smallest amount of meatloaf and placed it in her mouth. Lachlan gave her an appraising glance.

The flavor, similar to meatballs, spread over her tongue, and had the texture of bread. Unusual, but delicious. She nodded her approval to Lachlan. His eyes wandered to her mouth, then flickered elsewhere. He began a conversation with his sister-in-law to his right. Beth wiped her forefinger across her lips, hoping she hadn't left crumbs.

She scanned the people around her, animated in conversation. Did they use cutlery to eat the buffalo wings? Mr. Peters had one in his hand, so she collected her piece and nibbled as gracefully as she could, using a napkin at regular intervals. The marinated sauce had a kick to it, but she wanted another. Before she'd finished, Lachlan added a second one to her plate. He seemed quite observant of her tastes. Mark too. He flicked a glance between Lachlan and her, then grinned. He obviously didn't know she'd just come out of an engagement. And had Mark joked about Lachlan having their Quokka photo on his screen saver? At least for a while? Lachlan had mentioned the photo popped up as a memory. Had that been the reason he'd accepted Chris's offer? He'd said he wanted to see her when he came to Australia. Would he still want to, after she'd fallen for another man?

She bit into another wing. Had she really loved Nick? She cared about him. Still worried about him. But that wasn't the same as love. True love.

"Can I pour you a drink?" Lachlan interrupted her thoughts.

"Yes, please. Lemon soda."

His chiseled hands held her glass firmly, and she became entranced by his movements, the liquid fizzing, and his low voice as he whispered, "Here you go," and placed the soda between them. She met his gaze through her lashes. "Thank you."

"My pleasure."

She pulled at her sweater. Was it warm in here, or just her? Likely, Lachlan's unmerited kindness not only warmed her heart, but did crazy things to the rest of her body too. Sitting so close to him wasn't a good idea. Who had placed her next to Lachlan? She glanced at his mother, who flicked her gaze elsewhere. Did Mrs. Peters notice how she responded to her son? Women had that sixth sense, and a mother even more so. Beth ground her back teeth. She needed to get a grip on reality and focus elsewhere. For the rest of the meal, she did just that—kept her back to Lachlan and chatted with Kayce and the girls.

* * *

After the extended family left, Lachlan scrubbed the oven dishes while his mother stacked the dishwasher. Beth helped until Lachlan dismissed her to make the necessary phone calls to her family.

Mom clicked the dishwasher door closed and pressed start. Then she grabbed the lemon spray and wiped the counters. "I like her, Lachlan."

"What's that?" His hand slipped, and a splash of soapy water hit his arm.

"Beth is a lovely girl."

"I know. She comes from a good family. Her father pastors a small church. Beth was very involved too." He placed a Pyrex dish on the rack. "Surprised her dad encouraged Beth to marry a guy after no more than a few weeks of being acquainted."

"He likely got caught up in the grandeur as well."

He glanced over his shoulder. Mom wiped with circular strokes, causing the marble to shine.

"Must have. I remember him seeming suspicious of me when I visited their church. He was very protective of his daughter." How would he act around Lachlan now, knowing he'd also come from the Navy?

Mom placed her cloth next to the sink. "I can tell you have feelings for Beth."

"What?" He scrubbed harder. "I'm just helping her out. Couldn't leave her abandoned in a country she's never been to before, not knowing a soul—except for me."

She crossed her arms and cocked one eyebrow. "True. But the way you look at her and how she responds is adorable." She chuckled.

"I'm glad you're amused by it all." He gave a wry grin. "I'll keep my distance from Beth in the future, so you don't get any ridiculous ideas."

She touched his arm. "Lachlan, look at me, son."

He frowned. "Yes?"

"Beth will get over Nick and this drama as quickly as it started. She'll be ready in good time." She tilted her head. "Do you remember telling me about Beth two years ago?"

"I told you about her?"

"Yes. You said you'd met a sweet Christian girl and it was refreshing to know some women still held the same principles as you." She hesitated. "Well, months after that, I had a dream . . ." Mom looked to the floor, then cleared her throat. "All I can say is . . ." She met his eyes. "Don't miss the opportunity again. She's worth waiting for. You're what she needs, Lachlan. Faithful. Dependable."

Footsteps echoed from the hallway, the sound bouncing off the high ceilings. Mom pulled away and got busy in the kitchen.

He turned to Beth. "I'm nearly done."

She walked over and straddled a bar stool behind the counter.

Mom touched her forehead. "Oooh. I'm feeling fatigued after all that cooking and cleaning. You can finish up, can't you Lachlan? I need to lie down for a while." A curl to the corner of Mom's lips started to form as she left the room. Beth didn't seem to notice.

Lachlan pulled the plug and let the water swirl down the drain. He gave the sink a quick wipe and put the dishtowel aside.

"So, how'd your family take the news?"

"As you might expect." She shrugged her rounded shoulders.

"Shall we go in the living room and talk it over?"

She gave a solemn nod and followed him to the front room, barely lit. Saxophone music played on repeat. Not the atmosphere he was going for. He turned the light up a touch and changed the track to one of Mom's classical piano albums.

Beth sank onto the white three-seater sofa. "Dad projected a mix of fury and disbelief."

"Not surprised." He slumped into a single-armchair and squared a leg over one knee. "It's only natural for him to be angry at himself for not seeing through Nick's grandiosity."

"Dad said to thank you and your parents for looking out for me. He's relieved that I have people to support me until I return home."

"It's the least we can do. Who else did you call?"

"Amy, my sister. She liked Nick too." Beth shook her head. "She can't believe it." Her voice cracked on the last words, causing his own heart to splinter.

"This might be inappropriate to ask, but if I were in Australia, I'd have my sisters, my friends, or my dad to comfort me. Someone to hold me and say, 'you'll get through this. It's going to be okay.'" Her almond-shaped eyes implored him with innocence and vulnerability. "I remember being on the island, flustered and upset about my lack of progress on the Quokka story. But in your arms, I felt peace." Her gaze swept up, meeting his. "Lachlan, can you hold me?"

Should he dig his grave now and hop in? This woman would kill him. Beth spoke of the island hug, but what about on the foreshore, the day he'd left? That simple hug undid him, flicked

209

on every switch and awakened desire. How could he keep it together, and pretend holding a beautiful woman didn't affect him?

He opened his mouth to make excuses, but out came, "sure, of course." He stood, and Beth came to him. He hugged her stiffly, making sure he didn't hold her close enough to feel her soft body, but rubbed her back with rapid swipes.

What next? Should he change the words she wanted him to say and make it personal?

Beth pulled away. "Um, Lachlan, it's okay. It's not really working." She smiled, but a tear hung in the lower lid of her eyes.

"Sorry." He needed to keep it real, be himself, and share his heart. Lachlan gently held her shoulders. "Beth, I'm here for you. I'll stay by your side, accompany you to Australia—face your family and friends. Defend you if anyone asks why this happened." He softly squeezed. "It's not your fault. You got caught up in someone else's dream, and it wasn't real." His gaze turned intense. "Forgive yourself."

Her lashes swept up, and her eyes became round. "Do you forgive me, Lachlan?"

He blinked, surprised that she would even ask that question. "Yes. I do."

"That's all I need to know."

He wiped a tear from her cheek. "Now, how about a real hug?" He opened his arms wide and grinned.

Beth's face softened. Without hesitation, she embraced him and rested her head against his chest. He had nothing to be afraid of. Lachlan relaxed his arms around her and enjoyed the bond between them.

He held her until she made a move to separate, and they sat together on the sofa.

"Shall we look at our flight options?" he asked.

"You're really coming to Australia to work for Chris?"

He turned to face her, leaving ample space between them. "I'd like to. Do you mind?"

She raised a brow and angled her head. "It's not my country to refuse you."

He laughed. "Well, it matters to me. If you feel comfortable with me hanging around." His voice faded. "After what nearly happened last time I was there."

Beth let out a small laugh. "Yeah, you said next time you saw me, you'd kiss me like there's no tomorrow."

His face heated. "Oh, you remembered. Boyish dreams." He rubbed the back of his neck. "Anyway, I can't fulfill my promise given the circumstances."

She smiled. "But this morning, I did hug you like there was no tomorrow. I was so glad to see you. Thank you for coming to my rescue."

"I should add 'hero' to my resume." He chuckled. "Seriously, it's no problem. That's what friends are for."

CHAPTER TWENTY-FOUR

THE WARM WINTER sun soaked through Beth's cotton sundress as she strolled beside Lachlan's mother, Nancy. She refused to be called Mrs. Peters, and since Beth would stay another week to get the cheaper flight, Nancy had created a schedule of entertainment. Today, she'd taken Beth to La Jolla outdoor mall. Tomorrow would be spent with Ann, the next day with Kayce, and then Lachlan would have the rest of the week free from work.

They passed an artistic display of massive, steel balls. Water cascaded down the spheres, into a boxed pond. Music changed from store to store. Deep bass notes pulsed from meters away, while other more tranquil tunes invited shoppers to linger.

A red sign forming the words "Cotton On," was the only familiar shop name. Although she'd heard of Macy's, Beth hadn't been to the American store before. Where did Nancy intend to take her?

Two children pulled on their mother's arms. A group of teenagers dangling various bags from their wrists skipped by. Garden pots projecting vibrant colors of violet, burnt orange, and white, backdropped seating areas shaded by yellow umbrellas.

Nancy waved her into a clothing store featuring a sales sign, "new arrivals." Metallic-colored mannequins showcased dresses in delicate fabrics. Nancy had great fashion sense and looked young for her age. She wore a medium-length pencil skirt, a flowy, off-the-shoulder number, and wavy hair curved around her cheeks.

The outfits hanging from rough textured walls looked expensive. More than happy to window shop, Beth would resist any purchases and save her last pennies. Next day flights doubled the price, so it made sense to wait a week and at least see one part of America. San Diego seemed perfect for tourists—clean, endless things to do, and she couldn't complain about the weather.

Nancy flicked dress after dress on a circular rack as if on a mission. Did she have a real estate event soon? Lachlan's mother shook out a shimmering midnight blue dress with a scoop back of gathered satin. Wow, Nancy liked the racy numbers. She had a trim figure to pull it off though.

Nancy stepped closer and held it under Beth's chin. "Perfect."

Her brows rose. "You want me to wear this?"

"You'll look stunning. Try it." Nancy's face beamed.

Beth took the hanger and peeked at the price tag. Her eyes widened. "It's way out of my budget. 'Cotton On' is what I can afford right now."

"I'm paying." Nancy patted Beth's arm. "You can't visit San Diego and miss out on the experience of a five-star restaurant with an ocean view."

"Oh. Which evening are we going out for dinner?"

"Lachlan will take you one night. I'll make sure he does."

How could she explain to Nancy that this wasn't the type of dress she'd wear out—on any occasion? "Nancy, I don't—"

"Just try it on." Nancy shooed her to the fitting room. "Go. I want to see it on you. You'll look great."

Beth did as she was told and squeezed into the dress. Since her shoes didn't match, she kept them off and stepped out to the catwalk.

"Gorgeous!" Nancy oozed. "Turn around." She waved her finger in a circle.

Beth's cheeks warmed. She twirled quickly, the swish cooling her naked shoulder blades.

Nancy's gaze meandered from her toes to her waist. "You've got great legs, Beth. You should show them off more." She crossed her arms. "I have spider veins and find stockings too warm." Nancy stood back, assessing her further. "Before you have children, you should take advantage of your thin waistline. You look amazing. It's perfect. Let's get that one."

Beth blinked. "Oh. Please, don't fuss over me. This is way too much."

"Think nothing of it. You need some pampering after what you've been through. Lachlan can take you out and treat you like a queen. That's what you deserve."

"I'm not sure he'll be as keen as you to take me out to a fancy restaurant. Sounds more like a date."

She waved away the comment. "He'll be happy to. Lachlan cares about you and would want you to feel special. And you are. So, let me buy the dress."

Beth fingered the hem. When she got back to Australia, she could lower it two inches and raise the back scoop. The material was exquisite, and it would be a shame to only wear it once when it cost so much. "Are you sure?"

"Positive. Let's find some heels and accessories next."

Beth swallowed and gave in to Nancy's generosity. It was so much easier to give than receive. Beth needed to work on that.

* * *

Lachlan had finished a vigorous day of bathroom renovations and yearned for a relaxing night at Mom's. She had other plans for him. Said Beth wanted to experience fine dining on the waterfront. Mom had already made reservations. Apparently, she wanted to bless Bethany and would pick up the tab. His parents were always generous, but he preferred to pay the bill. Beth was his friend, and if she wanted a fancy dinner in San Diego, he'd make it happen.

Lachlan put on the suit pants he'd last worn at a friend's wedding. Workouts on the ship left the material a little tight around his thighs. He'd have them adjusted for the next time. On his bed, he laid out the two dress shirts he'd bought since he'd come back. The long-sleeved white Jameson would go best with his Prussian blue jacket.

Next, he added a touch of hair wax and a splash of Wild organic cologne his sister brought him last Christmas. Then he headed to his parents' house to collect Beth.

The front door was locked, so he pressed the bell. The door swung open, and the sight of long legs nearly knocked him over.

His gaze cruised bare slender arms, and a dazzling dress that highlighted all her curves. Was this really Beth? He blinked.

"Whoa . . . you dressed up. I should've worn a tie."

She clung to her purse. "It's a bit over the top, isn't it?" she whispered.

He leaned forward. "Why are you whispering?"

"Your mother picked this from the mall today and insisted I wear it tonight."

Now it made sense. Beth was conservative. "Where *is* my mother, by the way?" He angled his head to peer past her, then glanced at his watch. "Don't worry about it. I'll take care of her later. We've got a reservation at seven. Let's go."

After he opened the car door for Beth, he hopped in his side and remembered his manners. "By the way, you look amazing."

She adjusted her dress, pulling at the end as if to make it longer. "Your mother had a ball picking out accessories. She insisted on paying for everything. Such a sweetie."

He bit back a laugh. Oh, mother dearest. Playing the matchmaker. He shook his head as he switched on the radio.

Ten minutes later, they rode the elevator. Lachlan read the poster about Atlanta Cosmo. *Perched atop a skyscraper on the brink of downtown, the restaurant offers the most outstanding dining experience in San Diego.*

Beth studied the photos a foot away from him. "The view will be breath-taking."

His gaze wandered over her figure once more, and he agreed. How in the world would he focus on friendship with Beth dressed like that? Torture. At least at the table, he wouldn't have to see those long legs. He raked his hand through his hair, willing the elevator to hurry up and get to level twelve.

As they entered the restaurant, a gush of air-conditioning hit his face. Good. Maybe Beth would get cold, he could offer his jacket, and cover some skin. He smiled to himself.

They checked in and followed the waiter to their table. Beth walked in front of him, flashing a bare back and shapely hips. He flicked his glance at the skyline. City lights of white, red and pinks, flittered through the floor to ceiling windows. The sky reflected shades of rich, eggplant purples onto the water of the bay. Mom had picked a classy place.

The tuxedoed waiter pulled out a padded Carolina blue highback chair for Beth. Lachlan drew back the chair opposite her. Perfect. He could gaze into her alluring eyes all night. Should he message his meddling mother and thank her for the setup he didn't need right now? Surely Beth wasn't interested in a romantic date. What was his mom thinking?

The waiter poured water into the goblet wine glasses and said he'd be back soon to highlight the specials.

Beth smoothed her hand over the white tablecloth. His mind ran away with a fantasy of her palm doing the same to his cotton shirt. He blinked to shut out the image.

"Are you okay?"

He pulled at his collar. "I'm finding it a little difficult to relax. Intense day at work—started at six-thirty in the morning, and we didn't finish until an hour ago." He rubbed the back of his neck. "I don't usually drink, but I might need a red wine tonight. Did you want anything?"

She flicked the menu over and traced her finger down the list. "A pine-orange for me, please."

"I'll go and order it from the bar, so we don't have to wait." And he could go to the bathroom first, and splash water on his face.

When he returned holding the two drinks, Beth faced away, admiring the view. Her hair looped in curls on top while a few wispy ringlets kissed her neck. She wore dangly diamante earrings which Mom must've bought to match the sparkling dress. When he cleared his throat, Beth turned with a megawatt smile that kicked his heart into overdrive. He might as well raise a white flag and surrender now.

Lachlan handed her the juice glass and sat down. "Picked anything from the menu yet?"

"It all looks delicious. Shall we go for the chef's degustation?"

Dominated by French and Californian cuisine, the menu listed the impeccable eight-course sample dishes. If they chose this option, they'd commit to a long night. He searched Beth's face. The candlelight flickered across her skin and brightened her eyes. Why should he hesitate? They were both single. Sure—not the right timing for him to make any moves, but she had seemed open to the idea of him going to Australia. And he'd made it clear he wanted to spend time with her. Mom could be right. Beth might come around eventually, and he'd be there waiting when she was ready.

"Good choice." He let out a contented sigh and leaned back into the admission that he'd allow his heart to fall in love.

* * *

Beth placed an empty mussel shell on her appetizer dish and collected another crumbed-baked Provencale. She forked into the garlic and parmesan herb filling and let it tantalize her tastebuds.

"Mmmm. The flavors are exquisite. I must try to bake these back home. We have an abundance of fresh seafood in Fremantle."

Lachlan propped an elbow on the table and leaned into his palm. "So, you love cooking, huh?"

"I enjoy cooking for my family and church dinners. Not much for myself."

Lachlan gazed dreamily at her. "I like how you've done your hair tonight." He reached over and gently tugged a lock. The brush of his fingers against her cheek sent tingles down her neck. "How do you get it to curl like this?" He let it bounce back into shape.

"I have a natural wave. If I scrunch it while it's damp, my hair goes curly. The locks form when I twist my fingers through."

He collected another lock. "Like this?" He swirled his finger through the strands.

She smiled. "Yes, like that." What was going on in that head of his? All of a sudden, Lachlan was studying her intently and making her heart thump. Why?

"When I let my hair out later tonight, it will be springy. Then by the next day, it calms into a nice wave."

"Your hair is beautiful however you wear it. Cute in a ponytail."

"Thanks." Was that what she should say? His undivided attention and compliments unnerved her a little. Had Nancy put him up to this? Treating her like a queen? She liked it, nonetheless.

The waiter approached, refilled their water glasses, and collected their empty plates.

Lachlan thanked the waiter, then turned to her. A serious expression came over his features. "I have an apology to make." He laced his fingers.

What now? Had he changed his mind about coming to Australia? She gulped air.

"I should've kept in contact with you. I could have . . . even video called regularly." He flicked his gaze at the patrons nearby, then back to her.

"Go on. Why didn't you?" She leaned in with full attention to every word.

Lachlan placed his hands under the table and leaned his chest against the edge. "I found you to be a big distraction." His cheeks reddened. "And I've been hurt before. I should've given you the benefit of the doubt. I feel so bad that we lost hope in us. Then you moved on . . . and Nick took advantage of your trust. Now, you'll probably be like I was, disbelieving . . ."

She touched his arm. "I still believe it's possible to meet a faithful guy. I'll just take my time before making any life-long decisions."

Lachlan let out a loud sigh and sat straighter. "Well, that's out in the open. Let's get on with enjoying the night." He lifted his wine glass and took a sip.

"Thanks for explaining." She tucked a curl behind her ear. "I did wonder why you went cold. Makes perfect sense." She smiled. "And it's my stupid fault for trusting Nick." But perhaps things would've been different if she'd known there was a possibility of more with Lachlan. Too late for regrets.

The music changed from a slow jazz to an upbeat funky bass. A good distraction to lift her mood. She did a silly jig in her seat, and Lachlan laughed.

"Do you like to dance?" He raised a brow.

"I like to groove in my car with the stereo loud—when no one is looking."

"There's a dance floor between the restaurant and the casual bar around the corner." He grinned. "I'd like to see your moves."

She threw her head back and laughed. "They aren't that great. I'd win the daggy dance competition if there was one."

He stood and approached her side of the table, holding out a hand. "Would you like to dance?"

She fluttered her lashes in surprise. "Now?"

"Why not, between courses? One dance won't hurt." Irresistible—the warm sparkle in his eyes.

"All right." She took his hand and stood. They passed the bar, and Lachlan told the staff to hold their next entrée for a while.

They stepped onto a small stage floor that had a disco ball circling above. No one else danced as it was early in the night. A few glances came from distant patrons, but they continued eating or became engrossed in conversation.

The music slowed again, presenting more saxophone and piano. Lachlan slipped his hand around her waist, and her breath hitched as he drew her close. The mesmerizing scent of something like geranium and musk emanated from his shirt collar. He held her other hand and bent his elbow, closing the space between them. Oh, she could melt in a puddle right now. *Lachlan Peters, what are you doing?*

He swayed her side to side in time with the music, and her eyes drifted to a close. A flute flowed into the mix, and she relaxed into Lachlan. His head dipped slightly, pressing his short beard to her cheek, allowing his warm breath to caress her neck.

They danced the whole song like that, then another jazz number played.

A deep feminine vocal began, *"I never knew what real love was, the kind a girl dreams of . . . love that lasts and never ends . . ."* Oh, no. This would make her cry. Lachlan's hand slid a little above her waist, snapping her focus toward his fingers brushing her skin. He hugged her tight, conveying security and strength. Was he trying to tell her something from the way he held her? He wasn't one to let her go.

The lyrics continued, *"searched all of my life . . . then you entered my world . . . I struggled to believe . . . could it really be?"* Lachlan placed her hand on his shoulder and palmed her waist, embracing her in an intimate hug. She laced her arms over his shoulders. He nuzzled into her neck, a touch below her earlobe, sending tremors down her spine.

The saxophone soloed for a few beats, then the woman sang, *"Stuck by my side . . . showed me true love . . . I can't let you go . . . now I found you. . . you're the man of my life . . . I can count on you."* Oh, she wanted to believe it. But could she?

Lachlan's thighs brushed hers as he led her in a slow semi-circle. She'd never danced with someone like this. Back in high school, she'd accompanied friends to the balls, and had once gone with a guy from youth group, but they hadn't danced together. Nick hadn't taken her dancing. They hadn't been together long enough. Was this what it was like to be on the rebound? The thought of Nick didn't ignite feelings of guilt and longing. Once she'd sighted Lachlan, all of that disappeared. Only the dread of facing her friends and colleagues back home remained. What she'd felt for Nick hadn't been real love.

The last lingering notes of the song cued the end, but she didn't want Lachlan to stop holding her. Would he stay for one more dance? They should get back to their meal.

He whispered, "That was a long song blended into two. But you seemed to enjoy it."

His breath tickled her ear.

"I'm the only one who enjoyed it?"

"Okay, I did as well. Too much." He withdrew in a sudden movement, clasped Beth's hand, swung her in a twirl, and pulled her back into his chest. "That's the extent of my groovy moves."

She giggled. "Nice."

His grin came easy. "Shall we resume our dinner?" He offered his hand.

She placed hers in his. "We shall."

CHAPTER TWENTY-FIVE

LACHLAN TILTED BACK, all five inches the airplane chair allowed. The nighttime take-off had gone smoothly, and the plane leveled. So far, no turbulence. The captain dimmed the cabin lights, and the static hum of the engine clogged Lachlan's ears. An unusually quiet Beth sat beside him, her eyes shut. He wanted to hold her hand, but sitting close was good enough for now.

In the last few days, Lachlan hadn't found a reason to touch her, only at the ice-skating rink. She'd seemed impressed when he'd faced her, skating backward, and guided her around the arena. The other opportunity came when he'd steadied her once, holding her waist. Unplanned, but satisfying. He grinned to himself.

Strange, how they practically dated all week, but neither of them had pointed it out. On the last day, they'd crammed in as much as they could. Walked the treetop bridge, eaten messy tacos at Salud, rode a double-seated go-cart from waterfront rentals, and played arcade games at Coin-up. Sleep should come easy enough during the flight. But who could sleep with twenty-one hours of one-on-one, side-by-side, uninterrupted time together? He was as giddy as a kid on their birthday morning—should be sleepy but bursting with energy.

Beth adjusted her travel pillow and faced him, eyes closed. A wisp of copper eyeshadow remained from the day. No use trying to pry his gaze from her, not that he wanted to. He angled toward Beth, tucking a hand under his head. Who would've thought he'd be following this beautiful creature back to Australia? Should he take a photo for Mark? He stifled a chuckle.

Beth's lashes swept up, and she blinked. "How am I to sleep with you watching me?" She smiled, her face only a few inches from his.

"How can I sleep with you being in my personal space?" He circled his finger between them.

"I think you're actually in my space, mister."

His gaze flittered to her lips, and he longed to brush his thumb across her mouth, and more.

"Lachlan." She feigned a frown. "Close your eyes. Sleep."

"Yes, dear." He loved to tease her. Anyway, once she drifted off, he could watch her again. He closed his eyes and grinned, and she softly giggled.

A few moments later, he cracked one eye open, to find those aqua blue eyes of Bethany's holding a nebulous gaze.

"Now, I can't sleep," she said.

"That makes two of us." He winked. "What's on your mind?" Him, by chance? Beth wouldn't admit it, even if it were true.

"I'm a little apprehensive of facing everyone." She bit her bottom lip. "I'll eventually go back to Youth Connect and face my students. They'll be glad to see me, but it's embarrassing after the speech I gave them."

Lachlan's heart ached for her. It would be humbling.

"Then I'll visit the *Fremantle Herald*. I'm not sure if they'll let me return. Likely, they've found a replacement. My boss is a grump and he'll make me beg to get the same position."

"Do you have to work there?"

"I will need to find some work. Dad might increase my days at the church. I did a lot of extra hours for free, which is typical for part-time pastors." She rearranged her pillow. "How many shifts will you work with Chris?"

"My working visa starts in two weeks. But I'll earn my accommodation. Chris has a granny flat, and he made it part of the package."

"Melissa used to live there. When her daughter grew into a toddler, she wanted more space, and we got a rental together. Thankfully she hasn't found a boarder." She tucked a loose wisp of hair behind her hair. "So, do you like working in a restaurant, or it's just something to do for income?"

"I'd rather use my other qualifications as a counselor."

"Youth Connect may have some work for you. Chris's wife runs the charity. Cassie."

"Cool. I'll be living in their backyard, so I'm sure I'll get to know Cassie. Maybe the subject will come up."

"She's a great woman. Only ten years older than me, but she's like a mother figure. Cassie was probably the only one who warned me about rushing things with Nick. And the first person I called when I was abandoned in L.A."

"A good friend."

"The best," Beth said.

He gave a lop-sided grin. "And I was the second person you called."

"The second best." She sniggered.

"I hope to change that. Become first place."

She gave a cautious smile. "That won't be hard if you stick around long enough."

"I'll stay as long as you want me to."

Her gaze searched his. "Do you mean that?"

He traced his finger down her cheek. "Actions speak louder than words, so I'll have to show you. Then you'll trust me."

"I do want to trust you."

"I know. It's okay." He grazed her chin. "I understand."

Beth gave him an affectionate smile and let her eyes drift to a close.

"Sweet dreams," he whispered.

* * *

Blurry vision, fuzzy teeth, and clammy armpits summarized his state of affairs twenty-one hours later. Lachlan got in line at customs and blinked in a daze. The Australian accents from airport staff told him he was the odd one out now.

The security personnel acted way friendlier than any airport staff he'd encountered before. Lachlan placed his backpack and cell in a tray. He glanced over his shoulder. Beth unloaded her laptop, half-asleep. Invasive artificial lights lit up every part of the open space. Shiny white tiles gleamed without a speck of dirt. Other than the beeps of the scanners and murmurs from staff, lack of a crowd left Perth airport particularly quiet.

They'd left San Diego around midnight, but due to travel and a fifteen-hour time difference, it was early morning, not bedtime. He would be asleep before noon.

They meandered the corridors, glass doors opening and closing behind them like a 'Get Smart' scenario with his sidekick, Ninety-Nine, behind him. The clomp of his boots and the click of Beth's sandals bounced off the walls. He rounded the corner. Clusters of family members and partners waited to greet loved ones.

Lachlan scanned the faces. Chris! He wore a contagious smile on his tanned face. An older gentleman stood next to him—Beth's father.

A boost of adrenaline increased Lachlan's strides. His long-lost buddy, the man giving him another opportunity to win Beth. Boom. They knocked shoulders and fist-bumped, the high-school handshake they'd done a thousand times in a by-gone era.

Chris scuffed Lachlan's hair. "Mate! Good to see ya."

"You say, 'mate,' now? How long have you lived here, bro?"

Chris laughed. "You've gotta become like the natives." He winked.

Beside them, Beth plunged a hug into her dad. Winston swayed her, cupping her head, whispering consolations in her ear. It warmed his heart to see they had a great relationship. Chris thinned his lips, shook his head, and whispered, "A shame." Beth would likely get a lot of such reactions. Chris wouldn't know the extent of Lachlan's interest in Beth, but it wouldn't take long for everyone to figure it out.

Tears shone in Beth's eyes as she pulled back. "Dad, you remember Lachlan, don't you?"

Winston clasped Lachlan's hand and gripped his arm. "Thank you so much, and thanks to your family for looking after my girl." Genuine appreciation emanated from his warm, hooded eyes.

"Our pleasure. My sisters and mother adore Beth, and I think your daughter had a fun week of distractions touring San Diego." He winked at her. "Am I right?"

She gave a mischievous grin. "Yes, I had plenty to distract me." She faced her father. "I'm so glad to be home. I love my simple life back here. Why did I get caught up in bigtime ministry and travel?" She shook her head. "I don't know. That's not even me."

Winston rubbed his daughter's shoulder. "That's all behind you now. Left in the States. His mercies are new every morning. It's a new day."

"Amen to that," Lachlan added.

Beth smiled and hitched her laptop strap, then they all made their way to the baggage claim area.

Twenty minutes later, when Lachlan had no reason to stay, he reluctantly said goodbye to Beth. An emptiness hung in the pit of his belly. Although, she'd stayed at his parents' house, he'd spent every spare minute he had with her. Beth would be busy this week, putting her life back together. He promised to accompany her to church on Sunday and answer any questions people might have about Bipolar and what had happened with Nick. He'd studied a myriad of personality disorders and mental health illnesses. While working alongside a Christian Psychologist, one lady diagnosed with Bipolar told them God had healed her sixteen years ago and she no longer needed medication. Her folder of legal action and incident reports said otherwise. Would Nick admit he needed help? Could Nick convince Beth to give him another chance?

Lachlan dismissed the thought and rolled his luggage bags into warm sun rays. He gazed into the crisp blue skies. Good morning, Australia.

* * *

Bayside Manna worked like a Navy ship. Chris had worked in kitchens around the world and must've merged the best systems and structure ideas to create a seamless flow in the back of house.

Lachlan zipped the rosemary needles from its stem, then rubbed them into the oil-coated lamb shank. He didn't mind starting as line cook this week. It had been years since he'd worked in a commercial kitchen. Chris had done him a favor by sponsoring him to work in Australia. Once other opportunities opened, he could change direction then. But that'd only be viable if a relationship with Beth developed.

"Order up!" Kyle called through the server window.

Emily, a waitress, swished past Lachlan's back carrying a pile of dirty dishes. She stacked them next to a junior at the wash station.

The noise level became hectic. Kitchen hands chopped produce, the grill sparked and spit dangerous obscenities, waiters buzzed in and out like wasps to a nest, and two chefs barked continuous orders.

Lachlan was more than happy to stay out of the way and focus on the mundane task of prepping meat. His second shift was almost done. What would Chris have in mind once he went full-time?

Another rub of rock salt and Lachlan added the aluminum tray to nine others lined against the white-tiled splashback.

He called over to Marcus. "Chef, twenty lamb shanks here, ready for the oven." It astounded him how Chris had trained troubled youth into award-winning chefs. Marcus, only eighteen, had won the Golden Chef's Hat award last year. Impressive.

Marcus ordered a kitchen hand to take the meat for roasting. The young chef towered over everyone in the kitchen and could pass as a wrestler. The neck tattoo added to his authoritative dominance. When they'd chatted earlier, Marcus seemed like a gentle giant. He'd professed Chris as a spiritual father. Maybe Lachlan would eventually build friendships and touch the lives of Australian teens.

Chris burst through the swinging doors. "Right, lunch rush is nearly over. How's dinner prep going?" He glanced at Lachlan.

"Twenty lamb shanks are slow cooking. How many more do you need?"

Chris strode toward him, his black beret slightly off-center. "Another forty."

Lachlan blinked. "Bayside must be doing well."

"I'm talking to my head chef, Samuel, about branching out to the northern suburbs. Kyle and Marcus can go with him, and I'll take on more apprenticeships here." He gripped his shoulder. "There's plenty of work for you if you want it. Line-cook is only temporary until you get familiar with how we do things here."

"Good to know." He grinned. "I'll take care of these shanks."

Chris moved to another station, inspecting stock levels. Kyle approached Lachlan, packets of raw shanks in his gloved hands. He heaved them onto the stainless steel counter.

"You finished the last lot pretty quickly. How long have you been working in kitchens?" Kyle leaned his skinny frame against the edge.

"I haven't for eight years. I'm a qualified chef but changed career paths. It's great to have this trade as a backup." He unloaded the meats. "What's your story?"

"That'd take a long time to tell. Cassie believed in me and landed an apprenticeship here when I was fifteen. That's before Chris swept Cassie off her feet." He chuckled. "One day, I'll run my own restaurant. I have a five-year savings plan." He pushed off from the counter. "Gotta keep moving." Kyle nodded in Chris's direction. "Catch ya, later."

Lachlan could imagine Kyle being a scallywag at fifteen. The ginger hair and freckles added to his charm and ambitious ways. Youth Connect must have some great testimonies. Friday, he'd pop in and check it out. Beth volunteered that day, so maybe he could take her to lunch during her break. Cassie seemed open to him offering counseling services for the interns. Opportunities were starting to unfold. Who knew what his life would look like in six months? God did, but it'd be nice if He shared more of the details.

CHAPTER TWENTY-SIX

BETH POISED AT the edge of her seat, spine stiff, and hung on Cassie's every word.

"As humble as this may be, teens can learn from our mistakes. We are mentors, but it doesn't mean we never fail or stumble. They will feel encouraged by your story if you turn it into a life lesson." Cassie gave a gracious smile. "You'll seem more human. They place the leaders on a pedestal sometimes, and that's not healthy either."

Beth took a sharp breath. "Maybe you should explain the situation. Your words have more weight."

Cassie gathered papers on her desk and placed them to one side. "I think you're old enough to handle this one on your own. Their hearts are like sponges. They aren't like some judgemental churchies." Cassie winked.

"Lachlan's going to stand by me on Sunday, to answer any tough questions."

Cassie gave a wistful sigh. "Oh, he's so—what's the word I'm looking for?—endearing and romantic—following you to Australia."

Beth settled into the vinyl office chair and swiveled. "He'd already planned to come work with Chris. A working holiday. Before I even spoke to him about my situation."

Cassie's hazel eyes widened. "Is that what you believe? That's not what Chris told me."

Beth halted her chair's rotation and perked up. "What does Chris know that I don't?"

Cassie playfully jiggled her necklace. "We're not one hundred percent certain, but we worked out the timing of when Lachlan first contacted Chris about sponsoring him. Chris hadn't heard from him in two years. From what you told me about the Facebook friend request, it happened around the same time. When you called me to say Nick had left you, Lachlan called Chris an hour later, and made arrangements for the visa application."

Beth's pulse quickened. Could Cassie be right?

"He's here for you, Beth." Her grin slid up her cheeks. "Not a holiday."

"Lachlan has hinted that he's interested in something more." Like on the dance floor when her legs nearly gave way from the intensity of his embrace. And when he held her tighter as the words of the song washed over them.

Cassie gave a sideways grin. "What happened in San Diego? You're reminiscing, aren't you? Did you kiss him?"

"No!" But she might have if he'd tried. "Lachlan wouldn't bust a move on me after I'd just been dumped. He's very self-controlled, but the attraction between us is the same as two years ago. Undeniable—excruciating." She'd get hot flushes just thinking about his nearness.

Beth flinched at the sound of tapping on Cassie's glass door. Lachlan waved from the other side. Had he just heard any of that? Beth covered her mouth and turned toward Cassie. They exchanged a bug-eyed look and burst out laughing. Lachlan lowered his arm, his cheeks turning pink. Cassie rushed to the door. "Oh, sorry, Lachlan. You just caught us in a moment." She tugged on his wrist. "Come in, please."

He shuffled inside, filling the space of the small office.

Beth touched her neck. "It's okay. We weren't laughing at you, we're laughing because Cassie was gushing at how kind you've been by escorting me back home. We would only say good things behind your back." She winked.

Lachlan stood taller and let out a whistled breath. "I'm glad about that." He rubbed the back of his neck, his lop-sided grin melting her heart. "You sure know how to make a guy nervous."

Cassie swung her hands behind her back. "So, are you here for the tour, or to take Beth to lunch?"

Lachlan looked between them, still a little unsure. "Whatever suits you."

Cassie bit back a smile, and Beth suppressed a giggle in her throat. Lachlan usually seemed so confident. His uneasiness around women made him even more attractive right now.

"How about you tour with Cassie first. I need to chat with my students about why I'm back already."

His forehead lined. "Do you want me to come with you?"

"Cassie said I should handle this one alone. They'll respect me more."

Lachlan nodded. "Okay. Come and get me when you're done, and we'll grab a bite to eat."

"Sounds great."

Beth left them to it and headed down the hallway. As she approached the main workstations, animated conversations became louder. She poked her head around the corner, and one by one, they stopped gas bagging, jaws ajar.

"Hi." Beth gritted her teeth and waved. "I'm back," she said in a singsong voice.

"Get out of town." Chelsea slapped her ripped jeans and jumped to her feet. "You're back, miss?"

If that meant Chelsea was happy to see her, Beth would take it. "I am."

Nigel stood, his chair swinging in his absence. "I have Sushi in the fridge, ma'am."

She chuckled. Oh, she loved these kids. "Group hug." She opened her arms wide and rushed toward them. "I'm back for good. I missed you guys."

Gothic Luke, Sanguine Ruth, Sushi Nigel, and Sassy Chelsea engulfed her in devotion. Why had she feared their response? They would never judge—only love on her, and she adored them right back.

* * *

The grumble of trucks and cars swooshed past as Beth and Lachlan approached the Dome café. Western Australia didn't have Starbucks, and in Beth's opinion, Dome had the better décor and atmosphere.

Lachlan put his hand to her lower back as she stepped up the stairs and entered the building. She savored every touch from him.

Although they remained at friend status, Lachlan's affection hinted they'd be more one day. And from what Cassie had confirmed, it wasn't just Beth's imagination.

The delicious aroma of coffee beans and oven-baked pizza stimulated her appetite. They could share a large vegetarian. A pizza date. A pizza-friendship-date. She smiled to herself.

After they ordered at the counter, they slid into an emerald leather booth, and faced each other. She wanted to reach out and hold his hands, but it was too soon. *Slow down, girl.*

Chips of amber sparkled in Lachlan's eyes from the light coming through the window beside them. "I missed you these last few days."

Her stomach flipped at his words. Lachlan sure wasn't afraid of showing his feelings.

But she tried her best not to reciprocate too soon. Even though he seemed the real deal and she'd met his family. His sister, Kayce, couldn't stop singing his praises when she'd hosted Beth for a day. Still, more time was wise. She'd played the fool and wouldn't again. "I've been so busy. It's as if nothing got done while I was away. Church volunteers are great and all, but paying for admin equals performance in my experience."

"I'd offer my help, but you're right. I'd just goof around and distract you."

Beth had become very aware of his distracting capabilities of late.

"How's Bayside Manna? Busy?"

"Chris is transitioning me into the workload. He's a great boss. My brother is jealous that I'm spending so much time with his old buddy. He and Mark hung out in the old days. I was the annoying little brother, always trying to keep up. I think Chris and I will be great friends."

"That's great. Cassie's always bragging about him. He's a doting father to Johannah."

"Oh, she's a little sweetie. I hear her playing on the swing-set next to the granny flat each morning, singing made-up songs. 'I love Jesus. I love my family, love daddy and mommy.' Too much cuteness."

Her ovaries swelled. "You like kids, then?"

"Hope to have a bunch, one day." He flashed a smile that quickly gave way to seriousness. "You?"

"Definitely. Not six, like my parents. Too exhausting. Plus, my time is running out."

He wrinkled his brow. "You're thirty-three. Plenty of time."

"Not for six children. I don't want to be over forty and pregnant."

"Cassie managed."

"There's a story behind that."

His eyes widened. "Oh."

She leaned back into the padded booth. "How many kids do you want?" She bit inside her cheek. Too late, she'd asked.

"Depends on my wife, I guess. I don't have to give birth to them. Three would be nice."

She smiled, satisfied with his answer. Three would be perfect.

He gave a lop-sided grin. "What?" The word stretched with his accent.

Oh, she couldn't hide the smile playing about her lips. She didn't want to talk about kids with Lachlan, but it was nice to know they were on the same page—just in case.

She fluttered her lashes in jest and gave a cheesy grin. "Nothing."

"Something."

"None of your business." She wobbled her head.

"You sure?" He paused, but she wouldn't give in to answering. "Women." He huffed, his playful smile growing. "Who understands them?"

"We don't understand ourselves, Lachlan. So, you have no chance." She laughed. Flirting with Lachlan was so much fun. And she felt safe to do so. He respected boundaries and respected her.

A waitress in a black Dome apron gracefully placed their half-vegetarian, half-meat-lovers pizza between them.

They agreed on the number of children, but not pizza toppings. No deal breaker.

The lady collected their table number flag and left them to devour the goodness before them.

She held a slice high and let it come into a landing, not allowing any melted mozzarella cheese to drip over her chin. Cooked mushrooms and tangy pineapple ignited her tastebuds. The combination of barbeque sauce, avocado, and oregano added to the decadence.

"Hungry, are you?"

"This is so good." She covered her mouth as she spoke. "How's yours?"

"It's meat-lovers. Can't go wrong."

How he liked pepperoni, she didn't know. "To each their own. Wanna bite of mine and see how it is possible to enjoy a pizza without meat?"

"Absurd." He mocked her. "But being hand-fed from you somehow sounds delicious." He gave a cheeky grin.

Her face warmed. Lachlan mastered the flirting game. She stretched across the table and let him take a bite.

He nodded. "Not bad. So-so. Could use some bacon, then it would be perfecto." He pinched his finger to his thumb.

She rolled her eyes.

They finished their pizzas in comfortable silence. Lachlan wiped his mouth with a paper napkin. "Chris wants me to work Saturday night. Lots of reservations. Can you pick me up for church Sunday morning?"

"Sure. It'll be around eight, as I need to help set up the auditorium."

He straightened. "I can help you."

"That'll be nice. Thanks."

Lachlan edged forward. "Are you nervous about facing your church family?"

"You know small churches. Word gets out pretty quickly. I've had a few sympathy calls. Mrs. Morrison brought over a lasagna. Sweet old lady."

Lachlan leaned into his palm. "Well, that's good, isn't it?"

"Most of them will show understanding. I've grown up in the church, so I'm very loved. I'll get a few strange looks. Ones of pity. Maybe a scolding from Nan Betty. Oh, and Tina—she's fifty-two—she'll give her unwelcome opinion. She does that about everything. Thorn in my flesh." She covered her mouth. "Ooh. I shouldn't say that. But if you stick around long enough, you'll see what I mean."

He raised his brows. "Oh, I plan to stick around."

"So, you keep telling me." She couldn't hold back her wide smile.

CHAPTER TWENTY-SEVEN

LACHLAN FILLED THE communion cups, placed the welcome cards on every third seat, and straightened the nursery books.

Soon after, he paced the back of the auditorium, wearing a path in the old ruby carpet. Why hadn't he thought about how it'd look for Beth to come home with a different American sailor? Chris was already teasing him about being smitten with Beth. Apparently, everyone else was picking up on his feelings as well. Here he had plans to defend her against any attacks from cynical church members, but it'd just occurred to him that his presence would cause more angst for her reputation. Would they remember him from two years ago—a navy chaplain? He rubbed the side of his face. The first Sunday wasn't the day to make his comeback.

A singer stepped too close to the guitarist, and the sound speakers shrieked. The drummer twirled a stick in his hand, whistling to himself. A laid-back bunch of teens, the band kept to themselves and didn't whisper or stare at him or Beth.

Perhaps Lachlan should sit with Beth's brother-in-law. He'd met him briefly while helping set up this morning. Beth would understand it was for the best, or would she? He promised her he'd stick by her. Better not back out now when he needed to gain her trust.

He scanned the room to find Beth. She stood at the open doors, to distribute women's ministry pamphlets, and smoothed down her long skirt. He strode over and whispered in her ear, "Beth."

She startled. "What's up?"

"Do you think it's a good idea, us sitting together on the front row? Would it encourage people to talk?"

Her eyes widened. "You're right. Maybe just come straight over after the last song. Then I'll introduce you as Chris's friend . . . and mine."

"Right. Good." He scurried away to find the brother-in-law, what's-his-face. Remembering names wasn't his strong point

* * *

Beth clapped to the beat of the bass drum, stepping from side to side in her church shuffle step. Swirls in her belly spun faster and faster, like a mini-cyclone ready to take her through the ceiling. The service was ending. Time to face the wrath of—

"Tina! How are you this morning? Love that color on you." Beth enthused. She glanced past Tina's shoulder. People started to merge to the breakout area. Where was Lachlan? Was he being held up? Since he was a new face, he'd get swarmed with welcomes.

Tina grabbed Beth's wrist, demanding attention. "Dear Beth. I heard what happened with that sailor. Beth, darling, how shocking!" Her lips shaped an "O", jaw hanging.

Beth swallowed. "Yes. I was in shock. Let me tell you."

Tina grabbed her other wrist and drew her to the padded seats. "Do tell. I want to know everything, dear."

A throat cleared. Lachlan stood before them, a charming smile on his face.

She nodded rapidly, thankful for the rescue. "Tina, let me introduce you to a newcomer to our church. Lachlan, this is TINA." She widened her eyes, emphasizing the words, hoping he'd remember their conversation. This was the one. Warning, warning.

"Oh, Tina, is it? Lovely name. I knew a Tina once, in high school."

The woman's face scrunched. "You're American."

"Guilty as charged. I'm friends with Chris Evanson. Also, an American." He nodded his head slightly to the side in a gentleman bow. "I'm working at his restaurant, here on a visa. But I happen to know Beth too. She stayed with my parents after the Nick fiasco."

Beth wrinkled her brow. Was fiasco the best word to use right now?

"As a qualified counselor, I explained to Beth that the behavior her ex-fiancé showed lined up with mania. Unfortunately, Nick's mother confirmed he wasn't well."

Beth nodded and waved her hand for him to continue.

"When a person becomes elevated, they project a drive and passion for grand ideas and ambitions. It's easy for those around them to get caught up in their excitement. It's not sinister at all. A biological impediment on the brain confuses a person with Bipolar."

"Bipolar? My friend has Bipolar type two. I'm familiar with it." She tilted her head toward Beth. "Oh, that's understandable, Beth. No wonder your father didn't see it. Did Nick become very spiritual in the end?"

"Yes. Very much. An urgency to see people saved and to leave for Jerusalem. So that's where he went, I assume." She shrugged.

The woman's jaw dropped. "You haven't heard from him?"

"No. I tried to call him several times, but it's over."

Lachlan snapped his attention to Beth, eyebrows raised.

Didn't he know it was over? Of course, it was. She couldn't go back to Nick, even if he asked her. His mother's stories told her it was no use, and Beth had peace that it wasn't her responsibility to fix Nick.

Tina tapped Beth's hand. "Well, now you know. Don't go rushing into any relationships in future."

Beth nodded and gave her a fake smile. Thanks for the obvious advice.

Lachlan pointed over his shoulder. "Beth, can you introduce me to the connect group leaders?"

"Let's do that."

* * *

Lachlan smiled at the sight of his mother's face lighting up his iPhone screen.

"It's been two weeks, my boy, why haven't you called? Too busy romancing Miss Australia?"

He cackled. "Mom. Stop it."

"So, what's the latest? How's it going between you two?"

He walked to the fridge and grabbed a cold soda. "I'm having a blast here. And I've seen Beth every day, mostly in group settings. Her church or family."

"That's good."

"Yeah, it is. There's a newlywed couple from the church that we hang out with, and her sister is engaged, so we've had dinner there twice. When I have a night shift at Bayside, I'll see Beth for lunch." He took a breath. "That's been great. We're becoming good friends. Best friends."

"Oh, that's so sweet." Mom's face bounced on the screen as she walked around her house. "Things are progressing. Perfect. Now, that brings me to a question I have."

"Yes?"

"We've had an inquiry from a potential tenant. They want to lease your unit, but not for six months. A year."

Lachlan cracked open his soda, and fizz burst out. "Twelve months? Mmmm."

He gulped his drink.

"So, if things don't work out between you and Beth, and you come back in a few months, you'll have to live with us for a while."

"That's not likely to happen."

"You don't want to live in our house?"

"Not that. Beth and I will work out. It is already." He sat at the small dining table. "But if I lease the place for twelve months, I'll be tied into a contract and won't be able to sell it and buy a house here, if we get married."

"Married?"

He chuckled. "Wasn't that your plan, Mom? You practically arranged the marriage."

She laughed, and excitement sounded in her voice. "What are you talking about, son?"

"The sexy blue dress. I'm ashamed to say that it worked." He teased her.

"Oh. The Seaview restaurant date. That's not an arranged marriage." She scoffed.

"You practically told me to follow her to Australia and wait until she says yes."

"Mmmm. I did say something like that, didn't I?" She grinned. "So, you're actually taking your mother's advice for once."

"That I am."

"Good. I like Beth. She'll make a wonderful daughter-in-law."

He laughed. "And wife for me."

"Yes, that too." Mom angled her head away from sight. "Did you hear that dear, Lachlan's going to marry Beth."

Dad's voice murmured something.

"When's the wedding, Lachie?"

"Mom. We're not officially dating. We are, but we're not. If you know what I mean."

"Right. Got it. Well, I want weekly updates from now on."

He saluted. "Yes, ma'am."

* * *

Lachlan wiped sweaty palms down the sides of his suit pants as he walked through the doors of New Life church. Winston Michaels had been vague about the reason for the unexpected meeting, but he assumed Beth's dad had concerns about the unmistakable relationship that had developed between him and Beth. In the last two months since he'd arrived in Australia, she'd invited him to every family dinner, church meeting or social event. They barely left each other's sides and he didn't mind the teasing from her sisters. He was in love—big time. No point hiding it.

He climbed wooden stairs to the mezzanine level of the industrial-style building.

The receptionist took off her glasses and stood when he rounded the corner. Her pleasant smile gave him a burst of courage. He could do this. Come what may with Beth's father, Lachlan would validate his concerns and respect what the man had to say.

"Mr. Peters, you're nice and early. Pastor Winston is free to see you now. Follow me." She waved.

"Thank you." He couldn't place her name. It would come to him, though. While serving on the stewards' team each Sunday, he learned at least ten new names a week.

The middle-aged woman clipped a brisk pace down the corridor, her bobbed chestnut hair bouncing along. He passed three offices on the left with clear doors and windows. The youth leader studied his computer screen intently. Another door down, the pastoral care co-ordinator chatted on her cell using animated hand gestures. The third office was empty. Beth worked at Youth Connect on Fridays and he'd join her later. He hadn't bothered telling her about this meeting. He wanted to see what it was all about and avoid Beth's attempts to protect him from her dad's interrogations. Lachlan had nothing to hide.

A compact kitchenette lay to the right, and an old-fashioned table decorated by a swirly pink surface and steel edging. The receptionist halted on the next step to Winston's office and tapped on his glass door.

She turned to Lachlan, smiled big and nodded. "Good to go." She headed back down the corridor, humming a tune.

Beth's father opened the door, offering a polite smile, but a hint of something else shadowed his expression. Melancholy?

Winston shook his hand clasping his free hand over Lachlan's wrist, as always. The gesture conveyed a deeper desire to connect. "Lachlan, thank you for coming." He pointed to a high-back leather chair. "Please, join me."

The jittery sensation in his throat calmed as he sat and released a breath. "I like the personalized touches you've made to your office." Lachlan pointed to the embossed painting of a lion and lamb framed in antique brass.

Winston turned to the wall. "Amy painted that."

"Wow. She's very talented." The lion had a penetrating gaze. Even from Lachlan's angle, the lion peered into his soul, knowing all. Surprisingly comforting instead of creepy. The warmth of bronze blends in its fur, which blew in a breeze, created a majestic countenance. Jesus.

"Beth's sister went to art school before she married. She'll return to her career once Talicia is in school." He gave a warm chuckle. "Unless another grandchild comes along. I won't be complaining." Winston swiveled in his chair and faced Lachlan. "I would love her to paint a mural on the side of the church wall. A big project, but I know she has the gifting to do it."

Lachlan nodded at the painting once more. "I agree."

Pastor Winston threaded his fingers together. "So, you must be wondering why I called you in today?"

He squirmed in his seat. "I have some idea, I believe."

Winston's brows rose. "It's not about Beth."

Lachlan's spine slumped and the tension eased. "Really?"

Winston gave a deep, rumbling laugh. "It's obvious you care for my daughter. But that's not what this meeting is about." His smile widened. "Beth may think I'm overprotective, but it's not my place to direct her future." Winston's smile dropped. "The Nick situation proved that. I did a terrible job." He shook his head. "And that is why I wanted to ask for your help."

Lachlan perked up. "Help?"

"Yes. I've done some soul searching and have concluded that I don't have all the answers." His booming laugh returned. "Took me to sixty-one to realize that."

The man's transparency refreshed Lachlan. He gave his full attention. "So, how can I help you, sir?"

"You aren't in the Navy anymore, Lachlan. Winston is fine." He grinned. "As a qualified Christian counselor, I figure you know far more than I in regards to mental health." He rubbed his weathered chin. "I admit, I have spiritualized situations in the past. I acknowledge that prayer and faith does not solve every earthly problem." He adjusted in his seat. "Some of us have a thorn in the flesh. I won't understand it fully this side of heaven, but up 'til now, I've been narrow-minded in my ministry approach."

"I'm sure what happened with Nick has certainly raised some questions." He cleared his throat. "From what I've heard, Nick had a genuine relationship with the Lord and a passion for the lost." A heaviness hung in his gut. "I haven't stopped praying for the guy. I hope things work out for him and he gets the help he needs."

"Me too." Winston's face became somber. "Unfortunately, I'm not the only pastor in my city who's missed the signs." He shook his head and stared at the mahogany desk before meeting Lachlan's eyes. "A megachurch in Perth had their music director commit suicide last year."

The wind sucked out of his chest. Speechless.

Winston rubbed the back of his neck. "The churches are close in our city. We have a lot of unity. All of us were affected by the news." He shook his head again. "That's not the only suicide we've seen in the churches of late. Three pastor friends have gone through similar situations. It's shocking. Devasting for the families." He thinned his lips. "And the youth." A sigh came next. "They don't handle the news well. Life altering."

"I can only imagine." Was all Lachlan could say at the time.

Winston intensified his gaze. "You can help us, Lachlan. Not only from your training, but your insight into what happened with Nick also shows me you're a vital member of the Body of Christ. Pastors need a balanced ministry. You can assist with your understanding of the biological aspects of people. Body, soul, and spirit. Believers need all parts to be healthy. I'm a teacher in theology, which does help the psychology of a person, for sure, but in Nick's case, he needed a biological solution." He leaned back into his chair. "And I didn't see it to help the man."

"Don't feel guilty about that. You probably haven't seen mood elevation to that extent before."

The pastor shook his head. "Reflecting over my years of ministry, several faces come to my mind that I now believe had a form of mania. It's not easy to discern between the flesh and the spirit sometimes, but there's been the occasion where something just didn't sit right, and I avoided a confrontation. Usually, they were church hopping and left before I got to know them properly, but I've seen some odd behavior in prayer meetings. But the fruit of the person makes it clear. If their life is still a mess, and they keep repeating the same mistakes, it makes you wonder." He gave a sad smile.

"It does. For sure." Lachlan folded a leg over one knee. "So how do you think I fit into the picture?"

"We have a spare office here at the church. For the benefit of our members and the wider community, I'd like to have you on staff for two days a week. The other days, you are welcome to use the office to bring in other paid clients from other churches and any referrals you receive."

Lachlan sat straighter. "Sir. I mean, Winston. That's—just what I'm looking for. What I prayed for. Cassie has me on one day a week at Youth Connect, and I have as many shifts as I want from the restaurant. But my heart is for counseling." He jumped out of his chair and grabbed Winston's hand in a firm handshake. "I accept your offer. Thank you. This is—fantastic."

Winston stood, grinned wide, and continued to shake his hand. "Wonderful. Welcome to the team."

Beth. She was on staff at the church most of the week. He would be working alongside Beth. This was too good to be true. He let go of Winston's hand. "Does Beth know about your offer?"

"No." He smirked. "I'm sure she wouldn't object."

"I hope not. So, you trust me enough to work with your members, does that include . . .?" He shifted his weight to one foot.

"Like I said, Beth needs to find her own way." He raised his palms. "I'm staying out of her love life." His laugh lines deepened as he dropped his hands. "But, if she asked for my opinion, I would tell her you have my blessing to court."

Lachlan grew an extra two inches. "Well, that's good to know." He'd like to say a lot more, or burst into song or something. The excitement in his belly was bubbling over. *Thank you, Lord. You were in this, me coming to Australia. Meeting Beth. Thank you, Father.*

Winston stepped aside from his desk. "So, when do you want to start?

* * *

Bethany floated around her office, totally distracted now that lunchtime approached. Lachlan was counseling in the next room, then he'd come and take her out to lunch. She placed the missions outreach folder into the filing cabinet and let out a contented sigh. Life just got sweeter and sweeter.

Her mojo was back. Ideas for transforming New Life into a thriving church came with ease. Lachlan loved to brainstorm and helped her with the twelve-month strategic plan. The goal included reaching country towns that had no pastor. Dad had invested his time over the years visiting remote places, but the technology of today would allow them to integrate into the fabric of church life too.

Her mobile trilled and vibrated on her desk. Hopefully, this wouldn't be a long call. Lachlan would knock on her door any minute now.

She swiped at the green symbol. "Hello, Bethany speaking."

"Beth Michaels?" An older man's voice crackled through the speaker.

"Yes, that's me."

"It's Sergeant Andrews from the Fremantle police."

Oh. What had she done? Or had someone been hurt? Her throat constricted. "How can I help you?"

"I'm giving you the heads up that the Quokka poisoning case has reopened. We have witnesses against the two directors at Pacific Master Builders."

Blood in her veins pumped faster. She clutched at her necklace. "Really? Who's the witness?"

"A young Caucasian male, seventeen, came forward last week. He worked on the island with his uncle who runs the general store. He said US Navy officers questioned his Uncle two years ago. The boy was hiding in the storeroom at the time, but ever since, he's been having frequent nightmares of submarines and helicopters surrounding the island to come and arrest him." He chuckled. "Too much *Call of Duty* gaming, I reckon." Sergeant Andrews cleared his throat. "His school psychologist encouraged him to come forward with the information. Since he's a juvenile, he will probably only get a slap on the wrist if he confesses. He's suffered insomnia, obviously guilt-ridden that he'd assisted the developers in poisoning the Quokkas."

"He what? How did he do that?"

"The land developers gave the boy pellets resembling a cat biscuit, which housed silicone-like balls full of plastics. They wanted it to look like waste-pollution had killed the Quokkas. He still had samples, and the lab results came back showing the same chemicals found in the carcasses."

"Oh, how terrible. And they convinced this boy to do their dirty work? I'm glad you've caught them."

"Only because you sent your American contacts to interrogate the locals."

She gave a small laugh. "They were meant to coax the information out of people, so I don't think they would've demanded anything. I guess the military uniform scared the boy. But they were touring for the day. Thank goodness they changed *after* talking to the general store staff."

"The boy panicked and told the directors the military were scouring the island and collecting evidence. That's why the developers backed out. They offered to pay the teen to collect all the bait immediately. He refused the money and told them he had to do it to clear his conscience."

"That'll work in the boys favor, that he refused to take more money and showed remorse."

"For sure. So, your boss will be very happy with you."

Beth walked around her desk. "Ugh. About that. I'm not working for the local paper anymore."

"Well, this is bigger than Fremantle news. I'd imagine it would be of national interest. Over four hundred and sixteen dead Quokkas is a significant number since there's a minimal population of them. Approach the *West Australian* and *The National*."

Her pulse quickened as she picked up a pencil. "When's the court hearing?"

A shovel of papers sounded through the speaker. "The court case is on the thirtieth. We have enough evidence, but expect it to be a drawn out process."

She flipped a page of her notepad. "Have you issued a press release yet?"

Lachlan appeared and tapped on the glass door.

She pointed her pencil at her phone, then waved him inside.

Sergeant Andrews continued, "Our media liaison officer is working on the statement. But I wanted to honor your work and let you know before the press release date next week. I'll send some documents that you can forward with your submission to the papers, to validate your article."

Lachlan crept to the corner of the room and studied her selection of books in the shelves.

"Sergeant Andrews, thank you so much."

Lachlan swung to face her and raised his brows.

"Thank you, thank you. I'll get onto it straight away."

"I'll send the email now. Good day to you, Bethany."

"Fabulous. Bye now."

She threw her phone and pencil onto her desk, ran and lunged herself at Lachlan like a torpedo. She swung her arms around his neck. "I love you!" And smacked a kiss on his cheek.

Lachlan stumbled back, wide eyes.

Drats. She didn't want to be the first one to say it. "And Wally. I love you and Wally." She bounced on her toes.

His brow furrowed. "Wally? What are you talking about?"

She squeezed his cheeks and when he grimaced, she let go. Too much.

"You're heroes!" Beth pitter-patted her palms in front of her chest and let out a little squeal. "You and Wally scared the heck out of a teen boy on the island that day. He's had nightmares ever since and finally confessed. He played a part in poisoning the wildlife."

Lachlan blinked.

"The Quokkas!" She grabbed his hands and swung them side to side. "And you got the name of the builders. All the information I submitted lines up with the boy's statement."

He let go of her hands and flashed an amused smile. "Great. So you're going to become a big name reporter?"

She waved her hand and scoffed. "Nah. I'll use a pen name. Especially for this. A tad dangerous. I don't care about fame. I'm just glad they caught the men who did it. Justice has been served." She high-fived Lachlan and he laughed.

He smiled generously. "Well, let's have a quick celebration lunch, and get you back here so you can get onto that article."

She plunged into Lachlan, giving him a bear hug. "Oh, you're so wonderful. Understanding."

He hugged her back, then slid his palms down her arms, capturing her hands. A storm brewed in his intense gaze, then his delicious-looking lips curved at one side. "Wonderful and understanding. And you even said the three words." His eyebrow twitched. "In the same sentence of the name Wally? A little disheartening, Beth." He stepped closer.

Oh, no. Not here. She glanced at the office windows, where church staff could walk past any moment. The ones that made sure no shenanigans went on in the church building. The cave on Rottnest, may have been a romantic place for a first kiss. The foreshore of Fremantle—even better. Under the disco ball and before San Diego skyline views—perfect. But here? The church office? Not romantic.

She pressed her palm to his chest. "By the look in your eyes, I'd say you're willing to give me an exclusive interview."

"You and me? Exclusive." He grinned and moved closer. "I'm ready to commit."

She flicked her head toward the see-through doors. "Let's not get you fired in the first month." She stepped back. "Time for lunch and fresh air."

Lachlan waved his index finger. "You'll keep, Bethany Michaels."

She pretended he had no effect on her and skipped to her desk and collected her things as her heart did a victory dance inside. She'd won the Quokka story and the hero with it. Could her week get any better?

As she swished around, Marnie, the receptionist tapped on the glass. Phew—close call. Beth nodded for her to come in.

Marnie glanced at Lachlan as she opened the door, worry lines creased her forehead.

What had she seen? "We were on our way out for lunch." Beth's voice remained chirpy.

Marnie held out a handful of envelopes. "Some mail to sort through." She flicked her gaze at Lachlan once more and dipped her head to the ground. "One addressed to you, Beth—from overseas."

Beth's stomach dropped. Lachlan's tanned face whitened a shade.

Taking the mail, she pivoted and headed to her desk. "Thank you, Marnie." She nodded her dismissal, without looking over her shoulder. Mail from overseas? Could it be—? Her breath hitched at the pile in her hand. Junk mail, junk mail, bill . . . airmail. The envelope screamed to be opened. Her hands shook as she flipped it over. No—not now.

CHAPTER TWENTY-EIGHT

THE NEXT EVENING, Lachlan couldn't shake off the uneasiness flowing through his veins. Working on a busy Friday night at Bayside should've been a perfect distraction, but instead, he'd dropped an expensive platter, overcooked a Sirloin, and messed up two orders within the first hour.

Kyle and Chris huddled in the corner of the kitchen, heads tilted together, having discussions. Kyle's beady eyes flashed toward Lachlan and back. Chris nodded and flipped his cloth napkin over his shoulder and headed toward him. Lachlan swallowed. Here goes.

He grabbed a towel from the stainless-steel counter and wiped his hands. Kyle barked orders toward a junior at the sink. Rangehoods whirled, and steam rose from the main griller. All six staff worked flawlessly—all but him.

Chris approached with compassion in his eyes. He gripped Lachlan's shoulder. "Dude, what's going on?" His brown eyes bored into his. "Something up with you and Beth?"

Emotion clogged his throat. "How'd you guess?"

"Usually, you've got a love-struck grin on your face. Did you break up with her?"

He shook his head and scuffed the tiles with his boot. "We're not even a thing. Nothing official."

"You guys have a thing going on all right. Everyone can see it." His brows drew together. "What happened?"

Lachlan shifted on his feet. "Nick sent her a letter."

Chris's eyes rounded. "What? After two months, he finally decides to contact her." Chris clenched his jaw. "What did the mongrel want?"

Lachlan raised his hands. "Steady on. We don't even know the guy."

Chris's neck reddened. "Anyone who abandons his fiancée in a country she doesn't know is a flamin' idiot. What's in the letter?"

His chest tightened as he shrugged. "Beth hasn't told me yet." Why hadn't she?

Chris bounced back an inch and frowned.

Marcus interrupted with a tap on Chris's shoulder. "Chef, Jensen called in sick. Who do you want me to ask to replace him?"

"Um. See if Sam doesn't mind coming in. If not, I'll cover it." Chris focused on Lachlan as Marcus strode through the swinging doors. "How come she hasn't told you?"

"We were headed out to celebrate her upcoming article for the *National*. Then the receptionist handed her Nick's letter. Beth didn't want to ruin our lunch date, so she put the mail aside." He scratched at the back of his hairnet. "Some celebration. We barely touched our food. When we got back, her Quokka story needed attention, and I had appointments all afternoon. Last night she led the women's Bible study, but she didn't call afterward. Every night we video call if we haven't seen each other. No matter how late."

Chris's mouth lifted on one side. "Sweet."

Lachlan let go of a smile. "Yeah, but—"

"But—you have nothing to worry about. She's into you, man." Chris leveled his gaze. "Nick's in the past. You are her future."

Lachlan rubbed the back of his neck. "Beth has a compassionate heart. What if Nick has asked for another chance? Promised her he'll work on his issues. I don't know how close they were. Maybe she really loved him and still does."

"Buddy, why are we talking about this? Ask her. Put yourself out of your misery. Have the rest of the night off. Go see Beth."

Lachlan shook his head. "You're understaffed as it is. I can't leave you in peak hour."

"Bro, you're breaking my best dishes and burning my premium cuts." He chuckled. "I'll save money. Go see your woman. Sort out your love life."

Lachlan untied his apron and lifted it over his head. "Since you put it that way—I will."

* * *

Once in his Barina, Lachlan sent Beth a text. *Got off work early. Can I come see you?*

He clicked his seatbelt and drove toward the outskirts of Fremantle. At the next traffic light, he tapped his phone. The message remained unread. Maybe she was talking to Nick? Had she been messaging him all last night? A sick sensation swelled in his belly. He glanced at his speedometer and took his foot off the pedal to slow down. *Breathe. Beth isn't going anywhere.*

When he reached Beth's front door, Melissa answered his knock. "Hey, there." she blew her bangs from her eyes. "Beth's not here." Her Australian accent was strong.

Lachlan shoved his hands in his back pockets. "Do you know where she is?"

Melissa leaned against the doorway. "Said she was visiting her dad." Melissa's penciled eyebrows rose. "Are you okay? Your skin is a little patchy on your cheeks. Coming down with something?"

He rubbed his chin. "Maybe." He stepped back. "I'll give Beth a call. Sorry to disturb you."

Melissa smirked. "All right. Take care, then." She closed the door.

As he strode to his car, he whipped out his phone and speed dialed Beth.

She answered straight away. "Hi, Lachlan. Are you on break?"

He slowed his pace. "Haven't seen my message?"

"I mustn't have heard my phone ding."

"I've got the night off. Wanna catch up?"

"Um. Hang on a sec." Muffled voices came next. Winston and maybe her sister. "Okay. Let's meet. Where do you want to go?"

"How about South Beach? We can go for a walk on the foreshore."

"Argh—"

Was that uncertainty in her voice?

"All right. I can be there in ten minutes."

"Great. See you soon." He popped his trunk and grabbed his suede jacket. Spatters of grease covered his pants, but there was no time to change now. Inside his car, he rattled the contents of his glove compartment, searching for deodorant. Where was it? Papers fell to the floor along with other junk. He really needed to clean out his car. Life was busy with working at the restaurant a few nights and the church during the day. He sniffed his armpit. Not bad. Next, he angled the mirror and fixed his hair. If he got it cut, he wouldn't need a hairnet at work. But he enjoyed having it a touch longer for once. With the same style for five years in the Navy, it was a welcome change.

He turned the key, and the engine hummed as he exited Beth's driveway. How would tonight go? Should he tell her he was in love with her? Beg her not to go back to Nick? Mints. Peppermint candy should be here somewhere. Wrappers crunched under his fingers as he patted near the gear stick. He found Extra chewing gum and popped one in his mouth, just in case. If he confessed his love tonight, he didn't want to turn her off with garlic bread breath.

* * *

Lachlan spotted Beth at the water's edge looking out to the deep blues of the ocean. The rhythmic pounding of waves on the shore didn't soothe his soul as usual. The salty air brushed his face, the temperature slightly cool. A slight glow from the sunken sun remained on the horizon, but the parking lot lights lit the sand and the shoreline.

"Hello." His voice echoed across the beach.

She twirled, and his heart missed a beat as he made his way down the sandbank. One day without hearing from her and he was a wreck.

The wind flapped a creased paper in her hand. He sucked in a breath. The letter.

Vivid blue eyes implored him, so he stepped closer. It was hard to read her expression. Reluctance? Was she going to announce she'd take Nick back?

"How are you?" His voice came out breathless.

"A little frazzled. A hectic couple of days."

He scratched at his beard and stared at the paper. "Nick's letter?"

A tear stained streak glistened on the side of her cheek as she nodded.

"Can you read it to me?"

Beth's gaze shot to the ocean and she hugged the letter to her chest.

She was going to read it to him, wasn't she? Beth owed him that much. Hadn't he picked up the pieces of her shattered heart and escorted her back to Australia. Put his life on hold, waiting for her to fall in love with him. All for her to go back to—what? What had Nick promised?

"Can we sit?" Her whisper was barely audible over the crashing waves. The breeze played with her long hair. Beth's heavy eyelids showed she clearly hadn't slept. That made two of them.

He sat with his forearms resting on bent knees.

Beth nestled into the sand and angled toward him. "Nick didn't make it to Jerusalem."

Lachlan's eyes widened. "Is he okay?"

"I'll read you the letter." She cleared her throat and held out the crinkled paper. "My Darling, Beth."

Oh, he could puke right now. Surely, she hadn't fallen for this.

"Last week, I finally got out of hospital, so please, forgive me for not contacting you sooner. I'm so sorry for leaving you that night. The biggest mistake of my life. I misunderstood you, but my mind is clearer now.

After I left the apartment, I street witnessed in L.A. for two days and nights. On the second night, a homeless guy stabbed me in the leg, and I ended up in hospital. The staff recognized that I wasn't doing well mentally, and finally, I permitted them to call my mom."

"Whoa. That's terrible he was stabbed. But good Nick ended up in a hospital, and the red flags went up."

"Yes." She sighed.

"Sorry, go on." He waved his hand.

"They transferred me to the mental health unit, but the mania was out of control by the time I made it to Emergency."

Wow. He admitted he had mania.

"After some treatment, my mom visited me at the clinic. My heart broke when she said you returned the ring. Everyone in my life abandons me when things get tough."

Hold on. Nick abandoned her. How had Nick twisted this around to be all about him?

She continued reading. "Beth, I need you. I will listen to the doctors this time and stay on the medicine. God brought us together. You must believe it too because you pledged to marry me. Doesn't that mean anything to you?"

Lachlan's fists clenched and his jaw hardened. How could Nick hold her to a "pledge" when he'd left out vital details about his past?

Beth swallowed. "Tell me what I need to do for you to give me another chance. We can take things slow. It was wrong of me to rush you before. I can show you I've changed. Please pray about it. I trust God will help you to forgive me and we can start over. Yours truly, Nick."

Lachlan whistled through his teeth. "Wow. He sure laid it on thick and heavy."

Beth looked up at him with unshed tears.

No—she'd fallen for it. His gut turned in knots. Surely her dad was opposed to this. Wasn't Beth confiding in him tonight?

He was scared to ask, but he had to. "So, is that it? You're going back to him?"

With narrowed eyes, she tilted her head "Lachlan . . . I made up my mind before I even opened the envelope."

Of course, she had. Beth would feel obliged to keep her promise to Nick.

"Right back when we met his mother." She touched his leg. "I'm not the one to rescue him. If I had married him, then it would be a different story. But as you said—I was caught up in someone else's dream. One that wasn't real. I belong here." A tear trickled down her cheek. She wiped it away. "This whole thing has helped me see the deepest part of my motivations. Sad to say—it wasn't pretty."

Lachlan faced her completely. She had his undivided attention.

"Exposing my flaws to you isn't easy. God waited patiently for me to get the a-hah moment."

She cupped some sand and let the granules seep through her fingers. "I've always lived in Dad's shadow. Even at conferences, other ministers referred to me as Winston's daughter—not the assistant pastor at New Life. I grew up in one church and never left. I was a bridesmaid three times, never the bride. But I had responsibilities and no time to partner. Simon needed help with his homework in the evenings. I ironed uniforms, packed lunches, and motivated the kids to do their chores. I was the mum." Beth gave a small smile. "When things got easier, I helped with church admin and facilitating conferences or women's events."

"It's one of the things that drew me to you, Beth. On the island, I was amazed how much you sacrificed for your family and the church. None of that was wasted. Your brothers and sisters are great people. You were the glue that held your family together."

"I love my family. I have no regrets. I even enjoyed running the household. But it cost me. One day, I looked around, and all the good guys had been married off. It was too late. By the time I was free, no one was interested." Her fingers drew in the sand, and she mumbled, "There was Braydon but he—wasn't who I'd expected." She shook her head. "Would lead worship on Sundays but compromised the rest of the week."

Beth tucked her knees under her chin. "When Nick came along, I allowed my vulnerability to open the door for irrational behavior. No way would have I accepted a proposal in two weeks in my twenties." She glanced at Lachlan and smiled. "I was Mrs. Responsible. How far had I slipped? Totally desperate."

He touched her arm. "You're being way too hard on yourself. Nick presented that he had it all. You thought you hit the jackpot. There're studies that show people around someone who's elevating get caught in the excitement. Even the silliness and joking are contagious until something doesn't seem right, and before they know it becomes scary. That happened to you. Things didn't add up in L.A. It could have happened to anyone, Beth."

She wiped another tear away. "You're too kind, Lachlan. Thanks for believing the best of me."

He took her hands. "You are the best. I—love—being with you. My rare treasure. The one I want to protect and make sure you don't get hurt again."

"I won't get hurt again. Or even consider giving Nick another chance."

"So, what did you decide to say to him?"

"I thought you could help me word it with sensitivity. Can we go for that walk?

"Sure." He stood first and helped Beth up. Then he brushed the sand off his pants. Lachlan shivered and rubbed his shoulder. Beth had a blue cardigan on, but it looked thin. "It's starting to get cold. Do you want my jacket?"

"I'm okay."

Lachlan circled her back briefly with his palm. "If you say so." He dropped his hand, and they headed toward the yacht club. He let out a loud sigh. "Man, I so was worried about you."

"Sorry I didn't call you last night. Bible study finished later than expected. Then I was on a long call to Cassie."

"She's still number one for a go-to."

Beth grabbed his hand and stopped him. "Hey. You're my best friend, Lachlan. But you've got to admit—you'd be biased in this situation."

He smirked. "Is that so?"

Beth raised a brow but said nothing.

"I drafted a reply to Nick." She dug into her cardigan pocket, retrieved her iPhone, and opened the app. "Let me know if it comes across too harsh." Beth wriggled her nose and walked as she read.

"Dear Nick,

Thank you for reaching out to apologize. I'm glad to hear you're getting help. I was concerned about your safety. I assume you didn't tell me about your diagnosis before because you didn't agree with the doctors in the past. But you chose to leave out the details that you had married Tracy and why she really left you. How can I trust you after that?

In L.A., you weren't open to receiving good counsel and advice from the pastor. If you'd allowed doctors, pastors, and your mother to help you, we might have had a chance to make things work. But, it's not my place to make sure you take your meds and worry about you taking off impulsively. I tried to speak with you about your decisions, but you dismissed my concerns. If you're going to treat your illness seriously, you need to listen to those around you. Sometimes you won't be aware that you are going off track. Like this time.

I'm sorry, but I can't take you back, Nick. Not only because I would need to see long term change, but I realize that the life you want is not what I want. Living in my small hometown and serving my church fulfills me. I don't need a title or a spotlight on my name. It's clear you want to help people know Jesus. An international ministry might be your calling, but it's not mine. I'm okay with being a hidden part of the body of Christ. A team player, simply loving on people.

I hope you continue to seek professional help and become the stable person that your future wife needs. The perfect woman is out there for you. You're a great guy. I don't regret what happened because it revealed so much of myself. God used the situation to instil a greater understanding of His simple truth. Love God and love others. I have no other ambition.

All is forgiven. Our family continues to pray for you. You have a good heart and can have a successful life and ministry with the right support around you.

Take care,

Beth."

Lachlan raked his fingers through his hair. "That must've been a tough one to write. It's good. You need to tell him the truth. No use pretending. He needs to stick to his medicine and receive professional help. He could've been stabbed in a vital organ. Susan's prayers have kept him safe all these years."

"No doubt."

He shook out the cold from his arms. "Want to head back to the cars?"

"Yeah. I need to turn in early. I'm zonked."

"I'll be able to sleep tonight too. I shouldn't have worried, but I was afraid I would lose you."

She bumped her shoulder into his. "I'm not going anywhere, Lachlan"

He dipped his head and held her gaze. "Neither am I."

CHAPTER TWENTY-NINE

FINALLY, A NIGHT off work, both of them free from any commitments. Lachlan planned to up the romance factor and treat Beth to a night in Perth city—candlelit dinner for two at Coco's restaurant, a night stroll by the Swan River, and ice cream.

He pulled into Beth's driveway and hopped out of the Holden Barina he'd purchased three months ago when he'd first arrived in Australia. The click of his Cap Toe Oxfords echoed on the pavement. He shrugged his dress jacket into place and held a single-stemmed rose behind his back. That would set the mood for the type of evening he intended. So much more than friends.

A neighbor's dog barked as he approached Beth's door. *Rap-a-tap-tap.* He stood back in the spotlight of the bulb above.

Lachlan held his breath. The Tasmanian oak door opened, and Beth flashed a radiant smile.

"Hi," he managed to croak out.

Beth gave a little laugh that tossed her unbound curls about her slender shoulders. "Just hi?"

He cleared his throat as his gaze dipped to her vibrant red dress and black heels. "You look elegant tonight."

"And you look very smart. Even shaved. Must be an important announcement you're making." She raised a brow. "Do I have to wait until dinner's served to find out what we're celebrating?"

He took a step back. "You'll find out soon enough."

Beth wouldn't jump to conclusions that he'd make a surprise marriage proposal. Not after the loud statement at Trudy's last week how she wouldn't accept one until she dated the guy for a year first. Then she repeated it to make sure he'd heard, no doubt. He had no problem waiting. He was a turtle when it came to relationships. Slow and steady wins the race. He just wanted to press start to the dating timer she'd set. Tonight.

Oh, the rose. Smooth Romeo. "And I brought you this." *To symbolize my love for you? Too cheesy. Come on, relax, man.*

"Aww, thank you." Her silver bangles jingled as she smelled the flower, then placed it with her iPhone. "Let's go. I'm starved."

He grinned at his gorgeous best friend, soon-to-be-girlfriend, by the end of this night. A man could dream, and his dreams were often of her.

Lachlan opened her car door. As she brushed past him, the mingled scent of jasmine, vanilla, and musk heightened his senses. Beth smelled and looked incredible. She'd taken it seriously when he said, 'dress to kill.' The deep red satin dress wasn't as seductive as mom's man-bait choice, but the color against her skin gave Beth an angelic glow. Whatever she wore, he found her irresistible.

The sound system connected to his Bluetooth and shuffled a playlist. An oldie but a goodie, came on, *Jesus at the Center*. Yes, he wanted that foundation for their relationship, and he had no doubt she needed that too.

He boldly placed his palm face-up, next to her lap. Beth glanced at his hand and threaded their fingers. Her eyes sparkled, her smile radiant. Relief flooded his soul, and his breathing calmed. Peace enveloped him.

The engine reverberated to life, along with his heart. Lachlan raised their joined hands and kissed the back of hers, looking up at her through his lashes.

He reversed out of the driveway and drove toward the city. Fifteen minutes up the Kwinana Freeway, the Swan River mirrored lights from the skyscrapers. Streaks of violet, pinks, amber, and tungsten ripped over the waters.

Hand in hand, they walked into the restaurant. When the booking attendant spotted their listing, his eyes lit up. "Oh, yes, come this way." Chris knew the head chef and had asked in advance for V.I.P service for the evening.

Beth's delicate heels clicked over the Roman-like marble tiles. Several wine glasses and coolers glinted from the tables they passed. Couples and clusters of patrons spread out throughout the spacious restaurant. On several tables, delectable chef creations added color to the neutral mocha tones of the décor. King prawn stacks, lobster, and steak fillets beside beetroot puree, were a few that stood out. The poached pear on a chocolate tart caused his mouth to water.

The waiter pivoted and waved his palm. "Your table." He gave a slight nod. A private booth tucked in the corner faced the city lights. There couldn't be a better choice for the night he'd planned. The high-back curved booth blocked out the majority of observers. They had front row seats to Perth's majestic city skyline.

Beth scooted across first, and Lachlan slipped in next, so they were side by side, but angled enough to face each other in conversation.

The waiter had a cloth napkin draped over his arm as he poured water from the carafe. "I'll leave you to browse the menu."

"Thank you," Beth touched the edge of the table, gazed over her surroundings, to the view, and into his eyes. "This is very secluded, isn't it?"

"Is that okay?"

"More than okay." The corner of her mouth lifted.

He faced her squarely. "Now, I can tell you one of the reasons why I've asked you to fine dine with me tonight." He swallowed. "I received an offer on my house."

Her eyes widened. "You're selling your home in San Diego?"

"I mentioned to Mom that I'd want to sell it eventually if— things progressed here. When she did a routine inspection this week, my tenant asked how much a house like mine would be. He wanted to get a feel for San Diego before buying."

"So, he loves the area then?"

"Yes, and my place suits his needs. Mom told him that I'm open to selling. She suggested a price and encouraged him to make an offer."

Beth jumped an inch. "Have you accepted?"

"Not yet." He grinned. "I wanted to check with you first."

She blinked. "Me?"

He gently squeezed her cheek. "Yes, you." He collected her palm and placed it over his heart. "This is all about you, Beth. I'm here because I want to be with you. The open doors to work have paved a way for me to stay. But I don't want to go back to that lonely house in San Diego." He tapped her fingers against his chest. "You're in my heart now, and I want to be where you are. Australia. Where you call home."

Her gaze searched the depth of his. "I want you to stay too."

He inched closer, slid his arm over her shoulder, and kissed her temple. "I'm glad."

Beth threaded her arm around his waist and rested her head on his chest. "Mmmm. You've got that delicious cologne on. How am I to resist you?"

He chuckled lightly and brushed her cheek. "You're very honest."

Beth snuggled in more, and he savored the warmth of her closeness. The view mesmerized him as much as the beauty in his arms. They should look at the menu before the waiter returned. But he'd rather fast forward to dessert. He inched away and tilted her chin to meet his. Her gaze roamed his face, and his eyes whispered over hers, then dipped to her mouth. "And the second reason for tonight . . ." His voice became thick as honey. He brushed his thumb over her bottom lip and gently, ever so gently, parted her mouth. He glanced at the invitation in her eyes. "Can I kiss you?"

"More than two years is enough waiting, Lachlan." She smiled mischievously. "I want you to kiss me like there's no tomorrow."

He softly chuckled. "I will." Every cell yearned to make Beth his.

Her face softened as he cupped her cheek and leaned in, brushing his lips against her mouth. His fingers weaved into her loose curls as he deepened the kiss. A sigh of pleasure escaped her lips, causing his pulse to race. She clutched his shirt collar and kissed him hungrily. The two years of waiting made this moment a climax of ecstasy. Man, what a great kisser. For minutes, he'd forgotten where they were.

Their lips broke free for three beats so he could catch his breath. "Beth. You're amazing." He kissed her once more, and sat back in his chair, drained of all his strength. "That was intense."

She angled into him, snuggly like a teddy bear. "So intense. Why is that? I've never experienced anything like this with anyone before."

His hand brushed her arm and tucked her into his side. "We're a good match."

"Equally yoked—spiritually, emotionally, and physically."

His heart sang at her words, and he smiled when she gazed up at him. He touched the end of her nose. "Does this mean we're officially dating?"

She playfully smacked his chest. "It better."

He chuckled. "Good. We have an understanding." He kissed her forehead. "Shall we look at these menus?"

"No." Beth wrinkled her cute, freckled nose. "Let's skip to dessert." She slid her hand behind his neck, pulled him in, claimed his lips along with his heart that would never be anyone else's but Beth's.

EPILOGUE

Two years later

BETH GRIPPED LACHLAN'S hand tighter as she squinted toward the sea of faces among the congregation. Dad's deep voice broadcast over the people explaining the recent changes. She smoothed her other hand over the tiny baby bump, then quickly dropped it. That announcement could come later—after the first trimester. Not today.

"The number of members has doubled in the two years since Lachlan has been on staff, and Beth increased her days. Most of all, I'm pleased about the character and spiritual growth we've seen." He pointed in their direction. "Beth has also brought us up to speed with the latest technology. Her media skills have helped us reach remote country towns without churches. Seven connect groups joining us in our weekly bible studies are from the South West." He raised a brow. "Is it YouTube live or Facebook?"

"Zoom for the connect groups and YouTube for Sundays," she whispered.

"Okay, so she has all bases covered." He chuckled. "We have followers from all over the world, watching our sermons."

"Lachlan and Beth have settled into marriage nicely over the last six months and feel they are ready to take on more responsibility. I agree the time has come for the next generation to lead the way." His voice nearly cracked on the last word. "Which they are doing already."

She looked up at Lachlan. He smiled and mouthed the words, "Love you."

Beth squeezed his hand. She loved this man so much and trusted him completely.

Dad continued. "I don't plan to retire from ministry, but I am getting older and want to cut my days at the church." He swung his arm, flashing a huge smile. "The elders have agreed that this amazing couple beside me . . . should become . . . The. Next. Lead. Ministers!"

A few gasps and squeals flew from the crowd.

Dad laughed. "Today, I present to you . . ." He stepped closer and gripped Lachlan's shoulder. "Pastor Lachlan and Bethany Peters, the new senior ministers of New Life Church!"

The congregation roared in cheers and created a Mexican wave from the front to the back as they stood. Trudy and Amy's wild jumping caught her attention. Their arms flew in all directions as they hooted and hollered. A wide smile spread across Beth's face.

On the other side, Melissa's peroxide blonde hair gained her attention. She stood behind her daughter and they both waved excitedly. Chris and Cassie where on the same row. They'd decided to join New Life to support Lachlan as the new pastor.

What a dynamic couple to have on the team. The youth group would flourish too.

Dad stood in front of Lachlan and shook his hand. "Congratulations, son." They embraced, then Dad approached her, holding her hands in his. "I'm proud of you, Bethany. If it weren't for you, this church wouldn't be where it is today. God's grace, of course." He winked. "But you gave up your twenties to look after your younger siblings, so I could keep working. And thank you for the years that you filled the role as Assistant Pastor." He placed his arms around her, and she soaked in the moment of passing on the baton.

The three elders gathered about them and joined Dad in praying a blessing. "Lord, God. We give you the glory for this day and what you are about to do through this dedicated couple, your servants, Lachlan and Beth. Thank you for bringing Lachlan to the Great South Land of the Holy Spirit. Continue to bless their marriage and the ministry. Expand their vision to see your plans for Fremantle, Western Australia, and beyond. May they be instruments in your hand to see your kingdom come and your will be done. In your name, Jesus. Amen."

Applause and whistles filled the auditorium. The receptionist, Marnie, approached with a massive native bouquet of Grevilleas, red Iron Bark Eucalyptus, and Bottlebrush. She kissed Beth on the cheek and handed the flowers to her.

From the black curtains at the edge of the stage, her brothers hoisted a glossy wooden pulpit. They placed it next to the old plexiglass one. Simon and Jacob smiled at Lachlan and patted the jarrah surface, then left with the plastic pulpit.

Her husband's eyes lit up. "What's this?" Lachlan walked over and inspected the woodgrain one-yard stump. He stood behind and smoothed his hands over the surface where his Bible would soon go.

Dad's voice came from his wireless earpiece into the sound system, "Time to preach your first sermon as Lead Pastor."

A steward passed a hand mic to Lachlan. Another usher behind delivered his iPad and Bible. The first PowerPoint image lit the screen. He waved her over to join him as everyone else left the stage.

He tapped the microphone and static echoed throughout the room. "Good morning, Church."

Several people called out, "Good morning, Pastor."

Lachlan slipped his hand around Beth's waist as she stood beside him.

"Wow." He swallowed and touched the new pulpit. "Thank you." Lachlan took another breath. "I hadn't imagined I'd be a pastor, serving in Australia." He glanced at Beth, then looked to the congregation. "It's the least I could do to thank you for raising this beautiful daughter of the house. Bethany is a gift from God to me. My soul mate." He kissed her cheek. "Thanks for choosing to do life with me, baby." He grinned. "Or Pastor Beth, I should say."

She gently nudged his shoulder. He chuckled.

"First, my wife and I would like to honor her father and my spiritual mentor, Pastor Winston Michaels. The elders have something special to give him." He nodded to the back of the auditorium.

Heads turned as Stephen, one of the elders, walked down the center aisle with a large core flute rectangle. An enlarged bank cheque. In his other hand, a glass trophy shaped like a pulpit.

"Pastor Winston, please return to the stage. Can everyone stand?"

Applause erupted as Dad climbed the stage steps and stood beside them. Stephen handed him an engraved mini-pulpit memento, then collected a microphone.

"On behalf of the elders and all members of New Life Church . . ." Stephen held the cheque under his chin. "We present to you this honorarium for the long service of forty-one years, laying a strong foundation for others to build upon. Your full reward is in heaven, and although you aren't retiring completely yet, this will pay for a fishing boat or something to enjoy on your extended days off."

Dad smiled, and his eyes glistened. "Thank you." His voice crackled.

His words could barely be heard over the roaring crowd. After more hugs and prayers, people took their seats, and Lachlan opened his Bible.

He touched Beth's lower back and whispered in her ear. "Are you okay to keep standing?"

She tilted her head. "Yes, the ginger tablets worked. I feel good."

"You should've discovered those years ago for seasickness." He shook his head. "But maybe we wouldn't have met." He winked.

Lachlan cleared his throat and faced the church. "Today, my lovely wife, Pastor Bethany Peters, will tag team preach with me." His loving gaze warmed her heart. "Beth, would you open in prayer?"

Everyone bowed their heads and closed their eyes.

"Father God, thank you for the privilege of sharing your Word today. Thank you for bringing Lachlan into this church family. Open hearts to receive your refreshing truth that has the power to set people free—as you've graciously done for us. To you be the glory, forever and ever, amen."

ABOUT THE AUTHOR

Lisa Ren'ee is a member of American Christian Fiction Writers and Omega Writers, Australia.

Lisa adores babies enough to have seven of her own. Recently, Lisa has taken up breeding Ragdoll cats instead of breeding humans.

The tribe lives in Australia, where Lisa and her husband enjoy their writing projects, publishing, and public speaking.

Visit http://lisarenee.com.au
to keep in touch with her new releases.
Or like her page: https://www.facebook.com/lisareneeauthorwriter

ACKNOWLEDGMENTS

Polarized Love was lots of fun to write. It also wasn't an easy one with the sensitive issues surrounding mental health. I thank those beta readers who have Biploar or training in therapy to check over sections of my manuscript to make sure it was sound but also compassionate.

Thank you to my critique partners, Tabitha, Donna, Naomi, and Sara who read my first draft and encouraged me to expand on certain character developments. My story is so much better with your insight.

A huge thanks to Gwen Gage, my manuscript editor. She has faithfully helped me with each story from the *Single Again* series. Gwen's suggestions and nudges stretched my writing abilities, and it was just what I needed.

And finally, but mostly, thank you to my Lord who receives all the glory, for without Him I can do nothing of true worth and eternal value.

Have you read *More Than a Second Chance* featuring Cassie and Chris's story? Here's two chapters for you to read.

MORE THAN A SECOND CHANCE

CHAPTER ONE

CASSIE CHAMBERS SHOOK out her hands, but her fingertips still tingled. Annette could overdose if she didn't hurry. She sprinted down her brother's dim driveway and stumbled in her platform shoes, nearly twisting her ankle. Hadn't he changed that garage light?

With a dry mouth and racing heart, she pounded on Jackson's screen door. His kelpie yapped in the distance, followed by heavy footsteps.

The porch light flicked on and the door swung wide.

Jackson squinted like he'd fallen asleep on the sofa again. His black hair stuck up in all directions. "What are you doing here so late?"

"I need help." Cassie panted. "Annette's taken off. Her house mate went to her room to say goodnight, and all her things are gone."

Jackson groaned and ran a jerky hand through his two-inch beard. "So, you think she'll quit the program, too?"

"She's been struggling with withdrawals. I should've booked her into a clinic."

An offensive muffler rumbled down the street, growing louder. Cassie's heart accelerated. She turned and shielded her eyes from the vehicle's high beams. The Holden Commodore skidded as it rounded the corner and headed down another road.

"I hate it when this happens." Cassie smoothed out the lines of her forehead. "You give these girls your everything, only to watch them go back to the habit." She clenched her jaw. "But I'm not giving up on her. She may not have found a fix yet. There's still time to stop her."

Jackson straightened, his large brown eyes becoming wider. "You want me to come with you? That's why you're here?"

Cassie gave him a sheepish smile. "Yes. I may need protection." She whipped out her phone from her back pocket and zoomed in on the satellite map. "Annette had asked me to keep her accountable. I checked the Find Your iPhone app and her last location was an apartment in South Perth. Either she's got rich friends, or it's a dealer."

Jackson shoved his hands under his armpits. "You can only work with those willing to stay clean. If someone wants to give up, that's on them."

"I can't let her go back to that lifestyle—anything could happen."

"How long has she been missing?"

Cassie glanced at her phone. Ten o'clock. "Tamara said she went straight to her room after dinner. So, a few hours? I've called and left messages."

Jackson pulled on his creased shirt. "Maybe she's staying at that Perth apartment tonight." He glanced over his shoulder toward the sound of the television ranting about some sale. He turned back to Cassie. "I agree you should search for Annette. She looks up to you. Trusts you. Go find her and talk some sense into that girl. But, take Chris with you. He's better at mentoring than me."

"Chris is working at his restaurant job." She held her hands in a prayer. "Jackson, you come with me."

He hesitated then nodded. "All right. Let me tell Laura, and I'll meet you in the car."

She nearly melted into a puddle. "Thank you."

Cassie and Annette had shared a real connection. If Cassie went after her, it would speak volumes. Someone cared. Annette didn't know her true worth.

* * *

Deep calming breaths came easier with Jackson in the passenger seat of her trusty Toyota. When they arrived at the mystery apartment, she would let him do the talking.

The smell of stale coffee milk drifted between the seats from a used takeaway cup.

Jackson's jaw hardened, and he leaned his bony frame against the passenger window.

Thank God for Jackson's help, even if he wasn't happy about this mess. Her duties as a youth mentor didn't include rescue missions.

"Mate, I wouldn't appreciate my wife putting herself in danger like this. What if something bad happens?" Disapproval gleamed in his eyes.

She smoothed her hands over the wool-covered steering wheel, but the softness didn't bring comfort. "I've participated in plenty of street ministries over the years, and sometimes you need to go the extra mile with these kids."

Jackson kept quiet, just the low hum of radio static filled the silence.

Her brother didn't get the vision of her cause. "Annette needs direction. A purpose. Once she discovers her raw talents, I can find the right mentor to come alongside her and polish off the rough edges." Her voice sped up. "Many youths don't fit into the school system. When they drop out, they're bored, do drugs, and mess up their future. I can change that."

"You're one determined woman." He smiled when she glanced over.

His affirmation encouraged her.

"If Annette focused on the end goal, she'd have the motivation to stay clean. I need to help her see that, so she doesn't give up so easily."

She tapped her fingers on the steering wheel. "And, I need more ways to raise money to keep Youth Connect going."

A quizzical look crossed Jackson's bronze features. "Is the ministry struggling?"

"Sort of. Last month, I had to use all my savings to keep it afloat."

"That's not good. Sorry I can't help more. With Laura being a stay-at-home mom, money is tight."

She crunched the gears into second and maneuvered through a roundabout.

"I once wanted to be a stay-at-home mom." Her tone came out wistful. "But it looks like God has other plans for my life." She fixated on the road ahead and refused to wallow in disappointment.

"Cass." Jackson placed his hand on her shoulder. "Your time's not up yet. Plenty of women have babies in their forties."

"Hugo and I were married five years—no baby." She flexed her shoulders to release his hold. Jackson removed his hand.

"I'm sure it still hurts that he left you for that." Jackson's voice became angry. "He's probably the one with the fertility issues. Did you both get tests?"

She squirmed in her seat. The humidity and the conversation made her sweat. "It's all in the past. Can we not talk about this?"

The LED streetlamps flickered through the car window at the pace of a slow disco ball. Time ticked away. How long did they have left to find Annette?

"We need to pray, Jax. We're nearly there."

Jackson led the prayer through the final minutes.

As they drove around the bend, flashing red and blue lights pierced Cassie's vision. She pulled over to the curb, near a huddled group of people, and bolted out of the car. The stench of body odor hit her first, followed by bourbon and cigarettes as she struggled to press through the onlookers.

Police radio announcements blared through the airwaves. A young woman with messed up mascara covered her sobs with a hand.

With stomach coiled, the adrenaline pushed Cassie forward. What was going on? Was that Annette's auburn hair? Cassie came to an abrupt stop. A chill ran through her. She needed to move closer to be sure.

A heavy hand clamped her shoulder. "No closer, ma'am."

"You don't understand. Let me see her." She wriggled to get free.

The authoritative voice bellowed down, allowing no discussion. "No farther."

Jackson stood beside Cassie and brought her into a side hug, rubbing her shoulder.

Two ambulance officers hoisted Annette's limp body onto a stretcher, secured the straps, and placed her into the van.

Cassie's heart pounded in her ears. Her stomach threatened to empty its contents. Instead, painful reflux rose in her throat.

As the ambulance's back doors clicked shut, Cassie snapped out of a daze and moved from Jackson's hold. A policeman stood near her, so she touched his arm. "That's Annette Marshall. She's only sixteen. I'm her support worker. Please, can you ask the driver which hospital they're taking her to?" She fumbled to retrieve her photo ID from her phone case.

The man scowled down his long nose at the Youth Connect access card and opened his mouth, but hesitated. His expression softened. "All right. I'll ask." With little time to waste, he jogged to the Ambulance driver.

* * *

The scent of bleach and lemon permeated the white hallways of the Royal Perth Hospital. Cassie had driven Jackson home and returned alone. Finally, a plump nurse with a whipped-up ponytail approached with an update.

"She's doing much better. A little groggy. The medicine we've given her has helped counteract the drugs she took. You can go in and see her now."

Cassie whispered her thanks to God as she followed the nurse's squeaky footsteps down the corridors.

The nurse drew the blue curtain with a rattle of its mini wheels along the track. Annette slowly blinked at Cassie, then a small smile appeared.

"You came." Annette croaked out the words, coughed, cringed, then rubbed her stomach.

Cassie slipped into a cushioned chair beside the bed as tears welled in her eyes.

She took Annette's hand in hers. "Yes, I was there when the ambulance took you away. I didn't know if you were dead or not. You scared me, Annette."

"I scared myself." Annette turned her head toward the window which had no view with the blinds down. "I'm sorry. You must think I've got no backbone." Her chin trembled.

Cassie stroked her hand. "Please, look at me."

Annette turned her pale face. Gray shadows lurked beneath her blue eyes.

Cassie's heart broke for this girl. How could she get through to her? "You can make it. Listen, I want to book you into a detox program. That'll give you the support you need to stay clean for the next twelve months and beyond—for the rest of your life. But it takes your determination." She squeezed her hand, careful not to touch the IV drip. "I'll be there for the journey. God is committed to you. What about Annette?"

Annette placed her free hand over Cassie's and met her gaze full on. "I'll do it. I need to."

Cassie's shoulders dropped and the tension in her neck eased. "You can do this. Then make sure you to come back to Youth Connect. Next year."

Annette's eyes lit up. "You'll let me join again? What about the quit policy?"

"I believe in you, Annette. You have great potential."

"Me?" A weak voice emerged from Annette's chapped lips. "I'm just a low-life nothing." Her mouth pulled downwards into a pout.

What a terrible thing to say. Did she have any self-confidence? "Not in my eyes. You're gifted. I've seen your sketches and the artwork on Instagram. I believe you could make a career using your creative flare."

A glimmer of hope flashed in Annette's blue eyes. Their sparkle was back. "You reckon?"

Cassie nodded. "I know so. You finish the recovery program first, then become an intern at Youth Connect. That'll offer everything you need to be self-sufficient and get your life back on track." A buzz flowed through Cassie's veins. The natural high from serving her Maker always got her blood pumping.

Annette gripped her hand tighter. "Thank you. Thank you. You've given me hope, something to live for."

CHAPTER TWO

A S CASSIE THUMBED through a file, her glass door echoed with a rap-a-tap-tap. On the other side, stood her best friend. She waved a welcome.

As Chris entered her office, a gust of air conditioning washed over her along with the scent of cinnamon and vanilla. He must've prepared the desserts for the Christmas breakfast tomorrow. His hair remained ruffled and rolled-up sleeves suggested he wasn't going to work today. The white cotton highlighted his summer tan.

"I was just thinking about you."

His smile stretched and an amused look crinkled the corners of his eyes. "Good things, I hope."

"Always." She stood and weaved her fingers together. "I'm curious to find out what you're cooking for the Youth Connect breakfast. Still not dropping hints?"

He slipped his hands into his jean pockets. "Nope."

"Well, I won't give any clues about what your present is then."

"I hope not. I love surprises." He winked.

She feigned a pout.

His eyes sparkled. "Listen, I've got some exciting news." He bounced on his runners. "I signed a lease yesterday. I'll be setting up my new restaurant over the next few weeks."

Cassie straightened with her hands to her side. "You didn't tell me you were about to sign a contract. I could've checked it over and made sure the conditions were fair."

"Cassie, Cassie, Cassie." He lifted his hand in a signal to stop. A smile danced across his strong jaw. "I asked your advice on starting a business, and now you're my CEO?"

Cassie rolled her eyes, and gave him a *your-a-cheeky-monkey* glare. If she answered his challenge, it'd give him the satisfaction of riling her. He'd love that way too much. "Congratulations. That's really great. How's your boss taking it?"

"He's known for a while. Anyhow, I can officially offer apprenticeships to the youth."

She tilted her head to one side. "You have someone in mind?"

"I've arranged for Kyle to meet me here at two. He's interested in a trainee position."

She pitter-pattered her hands in applause. "That's wonderful. Kyle's worked diligently through the program. I think he'd be a reliable worker."

"And the kid needs a break." He shook his head. "Without a dad around, he needs someone to step up and teach him life skills."

Cassie fiddled with her necklace. "I can sit with you in the foyer while you wait for him."

He nodded and made his way to the small waiting area.

Cassie followed, passing the colorful artwork on the walls. Throughout the building, murmurs echoed off the walls, from the students working on projects together. Cassie gave a satisfied grin.

Before she sat down, she asked, "Can I get you a drink?"

Chris, already seated on the vivid blue sofa, squared a leg across one knee. "I'll help myself when Kyle gets here."

She folded her arms and stared down her nose. "Yes, you're good at making yourself at home. I should be asking *you* to get me a drink."

Chris stood, commanding attention when his six-foot frame became rigid and bowed from the waist. "Would you like tea or coffee, my dear lady?" he asked in a feeble attempt at a posh British accent.

Cassie's insides bubbled with mischief. "I'll have tea, sir. White with one sugar. I like it stirred two times to the left and once to the right. Can you manage that?"

"I have the culinary skills to prepare the finest tea. I'll endeavor to brew it to perfection. At your service, mademoiselle." He swaggered toward the kitchen.

Cassie sunk into the sofa as Hillsong United lyrics belted out from the sound system.

Might as well enjoy a moment's rest before her next meeting. And Chris was fun. Cassie rested her head on the soft leather. If she took more breaks during work, she might sleep better at night. It was difficult to drift off after a fast-paced schedule.

Working with youth brought satisfaction, but spending time with friends her age refreshed her soul. Since most of her acquaintances were married, Cassie had focused the last two years establishing Youth Connect. No regrets. It was finally paying off.

But perhaps it was time to slow down and enjoy a social life again.

Chris re-entered the room with a round tray held above his right shoulder. He stepped up to Cassie and lowered the tray. On it sat a cup of light tea and a plate of Scotch Fingers. With a flourish, he set both on the side table next to the sofa. "Your refreshments, milady. May I be of further service?"

When she snickered, he broke out of character and spoke with his American voice. "I helped myself to the cookies. Hope you don't mind." He popped one in his mouth.

"Sure. I don't pay you to help out here, so I guess I could pay you in biscuits."

A serious expression swept over his olive-skinned face. "I'm sorry to say, I won't come here as much in the future." He slipped his hands into his pockets and rocked back and forth. "But you're welcome to visit my restaurant as much as you like. A free meal on me, anytime." Chris gave a small grin.

She broke eye contact as her stomach clenched. Would he be too busy for her with the new restaurant? No, it would be fine. They could catch up as usual over coffee or lunch.

"I'll take you up on that offer. I devoured your chicken and roast pumpkin risotto last week. You should put that on your menu." Her mouth watered. "And I can't wait to enjoy the cooked breakfast tomorrow." She tilted her head. "Thank you for donating the food supplies. You've saved us hundreds of dollars. I appreciate all you do for us."

He sat across from her. "It's all I could do to repay you for how you've worked with my nephew. You should see Max at church now, singing his heart out. It's hard to believe what a respectable young man he's become. But you believed in him, and Max has lived up to the words you've spoken over his life."

Warmth filled her insides. "Thanks, Chris." She needed to focus on stories like this when things got tough financially. "You've been a great support to the other boys too."

"I'm glad I've shared a part of it over the last eight months. Shortly, I can take on those who want kitchen experience. If they do well, I'm happy to have them as apprentices."

"Wonderful." Cassie's mobile alarm buzzed, and she stood. "My next appointment is due in five minutes. I'd best get back to my office." She picked up her cup of tea to take with her. "When you see Kyle, remind him that he's sharing his testimony tomorrow. I'll be there early to help set up."

"No need." Chris's smile revealed straight, white teeth. He must've worn braces as a teen. "Arrive when the guests come. I'll be there before the sun rises, and have the boys assist me with the tables and chairs."

Cassie's heart flooded with gratitude. "Well, then, I have nothing left to do."

"Nothing but enjoy." There was that contagious smile again.

She touched the base of her neck, and hugged her waist with her other arm. "It's hard to believe it's Christmas Eve. Can't wait for the big day."

* * *

Chris browsed the trail of tables, each covered with a delectable array of tropical fruits, croissants, bacon, cooked mushrooms, scrambled eggs, mini quiches, and blueberry muffins. The aroma of the crispy bacon was what made him hungry the most.

Chatter filled the air as everyone found their seats. Satisfied when everything and everyone was in their place, he nodded the go-ahead to Cassie.

She stood, picked up her glass and spoon and lifted them high. *Ting—ting—ting.*

"May I have your attention, please?" The noise continued as people scraped chairs and called across the table to each other. Chris gave a loud whistle that echoed throughout the open marquee. Instant silence.

"Thank you." Cassie giggled in that cute way she always did. "Now you can hear me—I'd like to welcome you all to our first Youth Connect Christmas Breakfast!"

The crowd cheered, the male voices drowning out the females.

Cassie paused. When the youth settled, she continued. "Before we dig into this delicious food, I'd like to say a few words of thanks to the team who has made this possible. Thank you, Vicky, Emma, and Tina, for organizing this event. These ladies work tirelessly in the office, week in and week out." Cassie pulled three bouquets of native Australian flowers from under the table. She walked over, handed each lady an arrangement with burgundy Kangaroo Paw, dusky pink Protea, red-wine Banksia, and silver gumnuts.

"A special thanks to Chef Chris and his team. Doesn't this food look superb? Well done, Chris!"

His face warmed as he waved down the loud applause that vibrated in his eardrums.

"And now, let's thank our Lord, as we all wouldn't be here if it weren't for Him." Cassie glanced to her right. "Max, would you do the honors?"

His nephew paled but stood with a smile. "Sure. Can everyone bow their heads as we pray?" Max cleared his throat. "Happy Birthday, Jesus." A few chuckles sounded throughout the room.

Chris cracked one eye open. Max had his charming grin in place with his eyes shut.

"Thank you, Lord, for today and for bringing each of us through our challenges this year. Bless Cassie and the Youth Connect team for being there for us. And please bless this food. In Your name. Two, four, six, eight, dig in, and don't wait!"

"Amen!"

Like seagulls at a beach picnic, the youth dived into the abundance of food, piling their plates high. Chris and his helpers offered juice, tea, and coffee. Laughter and conversation buzzed around the room. Cassie must be proud of such a great turnout.

He surveyed the sincere smiles on familiar faces. Energy teemed throughout the room. Youth Connect had become one large family.

Metal scraped against the floor. Chris flinched as Marcus exploded out of his chair, grabbed Jordan by the front of his shirt, and dragged him across the table. A glass of juice splashed across the plastic surface.

"You want to say that to my face?" Marcus pulled Jordan closer, his eyes glaring. "I heard what you said to Mike. Now say it to my face. I dare ya!" Marcus's nostrils flared.

Cassie rose, but Chris held up his hand. "Let me handle it."

He rushed over to the boys. One at a time, he unwound Marcus's fingers from Jordan's shirt. Like a deflating balloon, Jordan exhaled and slumped into his chair. After a moment, color returned to his freckled face. The room fell silent.

"Continue mingling," Cassie called out with a wobble in her voice. "Dessert will be ready soon."

Chris gripped Marcus's shoulder. "Come and help me in the kitchen." As he led the way, Marcus stomped behind him.

Once in the kitchen, Chris leveled his gaze. "Come on, man. You know how much this means to Cassie. And me. We've put our heart and soul into this day—show some respect."

Marcus hung his head and mumbled something. A sorry?

"Bro, look at me."

When Marcus looked up with seal pup eyes, Chris's heart softened to the giant of a boy. Sixteen-years-old left a long way to go in learning how to harness all that wild testosterone. But Chris saw potential.

"I want you to join Kyle and me at my new restaurant. How does an apprenticeship sound?"

Marcus's eyes bulged and his jaw dropped. "Serious? You ain't messin' with me?"

Chris chuckled, then feigned a straight face. "Very serious, bro."

"That would be awesome. I won't let you down." He grabbed Chris's hand and pumped it like a blood pressure gauge.

Oh, how he loved these boys, even with their rough edges. "Now, we'll have to work on your temper. I'll send Jordan in. You guys need to apologize. Then you both can help serve the next course."

"Deal."

Chris gave Marcus instructions on how to dish the dessert, then left him to it.

As Chris approached the guests in the next room, he spotted Cassie sitting in Marcus's place. She leaned forward, having words with Jordan by the looks of it. Chris clasped his hands behind his back and admired her determined spirit from a distance. Jordan wasn't getting away with anything. Teaching them to work out disputes was an essential part of the mentoring process.

Jordan nodded at Cassie, his eyes sorrowful, and whatever he said yoked a tender expression upon Cassie's face. As he rose and headed Chris's way, Chris scanned Jordan's scrawny arms and thin face. Marcus could've pulverized him in seconds.

Chris offered a smile and tilted his head toward the kitchen. "Marcus has calmed down and is waiting to talk things over with you."

His cheeks flushed a dark red hue. "He overheard me. I didn't know he was listening."

"What can't be said to a person's face shouldn't be said behind their back. Marcus is reasonable. I'm sure he'll forgive you."

He pulled at his black T-shirt. "I hope so."

"After you've resolved your issues, ask him if he needs help with dessert."

Chris laughed inside as he watched Jordan leave. These kids. He turned back to find Cassie's gaze on him. He gave her a thumbs up and went to collect the empty carafes before heading back to the kitchen.

Ten minutes later, Chris, Marcus, Jordan, and Kyle exited. Each held a tray filled with dessert bowls of pavlova. They made their way to each guest and presented the creamy meringue.

Chris delivered one to Cassie. "An extra-large portion for you, Madam." As he bent to serve her, a floral perfume filled his senses. She sure smelled incredible.

"My favorite. So thick and fluffy. Thank you." She gazed at him through thick eyelashes. Cassie called across the table to Vicky, her assistant. "This looks amazing, doesn't it?"

"Chris has outdone himself again." Vicky's red bob bounced as she nodded. "I spied Christmas puddings in the kitchen."

He cringed inside as he wanted to surprise Cassie with those.

As Chris continued to serve the desserts, his skin prickled. Out the corner of his eye, he spied Cassie watching him, but she diverted her gaze. His heart kicked into overdrive. Why did he react like that? Admiration, no more. Cassie was a fine woman and a dependable friend.

Chris shook his head. Focus now. On his tray, small bowls of pavlova awaited the guests. Sliced mango, strawberries, kiwifruit, and passion fruit pulp topped the swirls of cream. Chris's mouth watered at the possibility of leftovers. The dessert compartment within his stomach always had room for more.

After sweets, Cassie invited Kyle to give his testimony. Chris had looked forward to this speech. Kyle waltzed across the open floor and turned to face his peers.

No need for a microphone with everyone positioned close enough to hear once the activity stilled.

Kyle flicked long hair from his eyes as he pulled out a folded paper from the back pocket of his tight jeans. "I scribbled down a few notes to keep me on track." He smirked, and some friends gave him a friendly grunt.

"My name is Kyle Lewis." One hand shook a little, but his grin conveyed excitement. Kyle loved attention.

"I left home at fourteen. Went from house to house, to whoever would give me a piece of carpet to lay my head on. All my friends smoked marijuana, so I soon became addicted as well."

He shifted his weight from one leg to the other and scanned his notes. "We broke into schools and houses. Stole whatever we could find to sell for drug money. I was in and out of court until no one would bail me out. My mum was finished with me, and my dad had faded out of the picture years before." Kyle rubbed the back of his neck. The audience hung onto his every word.

"They chucked me in juvenile detention while my caseworker tried to find me somewhere to live, and there I agreed to participate in a Christian recovery program. The best decision, but tough. I had to face the root issues, like my dad's rejection."

Kyle clasped an imaginary ball in front of him. "Before, I'd gravitated to boys who held the same hurt. The common factor—no dad around. So, we acted tough, like we didn't care, and did whatever we wanted. But that didn't work out great. Obviously." He smirked.

"While in the program, I gave my heart to Christ. That's when I started to heal and discover my true self. After twelve months of recovery, my mum took me back, totally shocked by my transformation, and now comes to church with me." A few hoots rose from the crowd, including Chris's supportive whistle.

"In July, I joined Youth Connect with Cassie." He glanced her way. "She has been my rock. Cassie didn't do everything *for* me. Instead, she showed me the way. Helped me get my certificate in general education and put up with my frustration as I worked through the assignments. Then she linked me up with work experience."

With a huge grin on his face, Kyle gestured toward Chris. "Now I get to work with the awesome Chef Chris, who's taken me on as an apprentice. Watch out world. I'm gonna open my own restaurant one of these days!"

Chris called out. "As long as it's on the other side of town!" Laughter erupted throughout the audience, followed by applause. One by one, friends stood for an ovation. Kyle gave Cassie a side-hug, then high fived Chris. Chris pulled him in for a manly embrace with a pat on the back, a ruffle of the hair, then let Kyle go. As Chris turned to Cassie with raised brows, they exchanged a 'Kyle's-a-character-all-right' look, and both laughed. Chris stepped closer and whispered in Cassie's ear. "We make a good team, you and me."

Her face seemed flushed, and she laughed nervously. Perhaps she read into his words more than he'd meant. At another time, he should clarify any misunderstanding. The invisible friendship boundary wasn't meant to be crossed. Or could those rules change since he'd extended his working visa and aimed to gain permanent residency?

* * *

Search for *More Than A Second Chance* on Amazon. Or follow the links from www.lisarenee.com.au

* * *

Dear Reader,

Thank you for reading *Polarized Love*. I'd love to hear from you! Please visit my website or say "hi" on Facebook. I'd love for you to leave a quick review on Amazon and Goodreads too.

Keep in touch,

Lisa Renee

CPSIA information can be obtained
at www.ICGtesting.com
Printed in the USA
LVHW091939050920
665076LV00025B/217

9 780648 664994